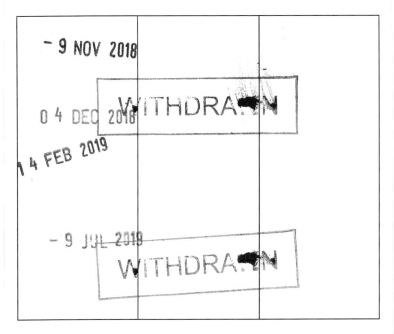

TRUTH STONE

TRUTH STONE

Michael O'Byrne

ROBERT HALE

First published in 2018 by
Robert Hale, an imprint of
The Crowood Press Ltd,
Ramsbury, Marlborough
Wiltshire SN8 2HR

www.crowood.com

British Library Cataloguing-in-Publication Data
A catalogue record for this book is available from the British
Library.

ISBN 978 0 7198 2657 3

Typeset by Chapter One Book Production, Knebworth

Printed and bound in India by Replika Press Ltd

Lapis Lazuli stones (truth stones) are powerful intense blue stones for opening the third eye and stimulating the pineal gland. Lapis is a prominent third eye chakra stone, that will develop intuition as well as amplifying and expanding psychic visions and clairvoyant abilities.

Truth is a pathless land, and you cannot approach it by any path whatsoever, by any religion, by any sect.

Jiddu Krishnamurti

For my heroes, Carole and Kathryn

Acknowledgements

The facts (but not the characters) of the opening chapters are based on a true case where the SIO, Steve Fulcher, made a decision admired by cops and condemned by lawyers. He paid too heavy a price for doing so.

I would like to thank all my friends at the Village Writers for their encouragement and support. In particular I would like to thank Judy Hall for editing my script, Denis O'Connor for all the 'tough love', Margaret Graham for keeping me in the moment and Mike Sharland for keeping the faith.

Chapter 1

'TELL ME WHERE SHE IS.'

The trio, two women bracketing the man between, stood at the edge of the nature reserve's car park, looking out over the dense woodland that stretched away below them into the distance under the louring clouds. The figures formed a diorama against the black horizon, the women appearing to tower over the bowed figure of the man, their hair being blown back from their faces by the chill blast blowing off the moor. DCI Rachel Stone reached out and touched Mickey Fleming's sleeve, trying to get him to look at her, willing him to make her gamble bringing him here work. But his head remained bowed, his thinning black hair blowing in the wind. The other woman, DS Tricia Downing, started to speak.

'Ma'am, don't you think ...'

But Stone stopped her with a look. She was only going to get one chance at this before the lawyers shut him up and her out. She had told the arrest team to say nothing when they lifted him. One minute he'd been walking down the street on his way to work, the next he was in the back of a police car arrested for abduction, and on his way to Franklin Park. She had told them to park away from her and walk him the last fifty yards across the car park towards her. The look of resignation and not puzzlement on his face as he was taken from the car told her that she was in the right place. Now she needed to maximize the shock of the arrest, putting away any thought that if he bluffed her well enough he might walk away. Everyone called him Mickey but his mother. Maybe invoking her would work.

'Michael,' she said, squeezing his arm gently. He looked up at her, a gain in itself.

'Michael, we know you took her. We've got the CCTV. You did it less than forty-eight hours ago so we will find the forensics.'

'A lawyer ...' his first words.

'A lawyer can't help you now, Michael. He'll only make it worse for you when we do find her. When people find out just how heartless you've been.' Pressure on his arm again. 'We need to find her, for her sake, for her family's sake, for your sake.' A pause. 'For your mother's sake, Michael. If you don't, they'll pillory you, your family, your mother.'

His head was bowed again, studying his shoes, but through the sleeve she could feel his shoulders sag as the resistance drained out of him. Downing tried to speak again but she stopped her with a small hand gesture and a barely perceptible shake of her head. She needed to let the silence work on him. Just when she was about to give up, she heard him mutter something. She couldn't believe what she thought she'd just heard and asked him to repeat it.

'I said, I'll show you.'

After the gloom of the day, the glare of the lights under the tent was blindingly unnatural. The trio of Stone, Fleming and Downing stood in one corner. In the middle, two SOCOs were slowly uncovering an area about four feet square which Fleming had pointed out to them. They were all in white maggot suits and shoe covers. Fleming may have brought them here but she wasn't going to lose any DNA matches on a technicality. Two DCs from the squad were standing by the entrance to the tent in case Fleming acted up. Autumn had come early and the ground was deep in fallen leaves. The air was thick with their musty smell. Any conversation had to overcome the noise of the generators and the periodic machine-gun patter of water falling from the trees onto the roof of the tent. The topsoil under the leaves was loose and the SOCOs were making quick progress. They began to uncover a white, painted surface.

'It's just some chipboard I got from a skip,' Fleming volunteered. 'I didn't want some dog digging her up.'

His belated concern elicited neither sympathy nor agreement.

The SOCOs cleared all of the ground around the board, leaving it in place. Its size told them what they would find. When the photographer had finished, the SOCOs looked at Stone for permission to carry on. She nodded and they got their spades under one edge and lifted it, like opening a trapdoor. As it cleared, they could hear Bernie Cox, the senior SOCO, mutter 'God save us' not quite under his breath. When the board was lifted clear, it exposed the naked body of eight-year-old Emma Bolton lying fully exposed, arms by her side, just fitting into the little trench. There were no obvious marks or injuries so Fleming had probably smothered her. He was the only person in the tent who did not register any reaction – but then again he knew exactly what they would find.

Bodies were one thing, a routine part of every cop's life. Children's bodies were something else. In death their vulnerability was magnified, the wasted beauty of the life now never to be, took the power of speech away, displacing it with a crude desire for simple revenge. Everyone in the tent stared at Fleming while he stayed in the refuge of his stance, head bowed, looking only at the ground at his feet. Stone was still taking it all in, thinking about how she would tell Emma's family, sizing up where she stood now that they had recovered a body and not a living hostage when she felt her own arm being touched by Fleming. She started involuntarily. She had touched him thinking he was the killer, but now that she knew, now that she was looking at what he could do, his very presence was repulsive. When he was sure that he had her eyes and her attention, he spoke.

'I killed another one. Three years ago. I can take you to her too.'

'Where is she?'

'I can describe it but it'll be easier if I show you. It's not far, just a couple of miles away.'

She could see over Fleming's shoulder that Downing was almost exploding with frustration.

'Ma'am, we can't—'

'Wait over there, Sergeant. By the entrance.'

'But you can't—'

'Not now, Sergeant. I know what you want to say. And we'll talk about it – but later. Now wait over there.'

Downing stalked over to join the two DCs and Stone turned back to Fleming.

'You're not messing with my head here are you, Mickey? I'm not someone you want to piss off.'

'No. I brought you here. I'll take you there. I want it done with.'

Stone signalled to the two DCs by the entrance.

'Take Mickey here to the car. We're going on a little trip. We'll need a couple of patrol cars for an escort. And some vehicles to block off any press following us.'

Then she turned to the older of the two SOCOs.

'Bernie, it looks like we're going to get another scene. Can you leave this one to Maggie and supervise the changeover from here to the next one? I don't want any problems with cross contamination.'

'OK, I'll get on with that.'

He climbed out of the grave and made his way out of the tent.

Stone followed Fleming and the two DCs out of the tent, signalling for Downing to follow her. Outside, the looming clouds were now weeping a fine drizzle. In the time that they had been in the tent, the media had gathered in force at the police tape demarcating the scene. Stone thought that she had placed it far enough away that the cameras would not be able to intrude but she could now see that the cameramen on their hydraulic platforms were able to look over the police cars. The pair reached the edge of the car park, well away from the lights and the cars. Even so, Stone made sure that they kept their backs to the cameras. She had retrieved her e-cigarette from her pocket as they walked and was now vaping it, waiting for Downing to have her say. She didn't have to wait long.

'We can't do this.'

'Do what, Tricia?'

'You know what. You're endangering the whole case.'

Stone took a long drag on the e-cigarette, wishing it were real.

'I'll tell you what I know, Tricia. I know I've got that bastard bang to rights. And I've found Emma's body. That's what I know.'

Downing paused, marshalling her thoughts. 'We had this out when you told me you were going to bring him directly here. He should have been taken to the nick, formally cautioned again, given access to a lawyer – all of that.'

'I needed to act quickly if I was to have any chance of getting Emma back alive.'

'Come on, boss,' she threw her hands up in exasperation, 'I'm not his bloody lawyer. We knew after two days that if he'd brought her here,' she waved an arm to take in the wilderness of the reserve, 'then she'd be dead.'

'No, we thought that she might be. We only knew when we dug her up.'

'But if we'd taken him to the station, with all the evidence we've got, he would probably have told us anyway.'

'You may be right. He might have. But I don't need to worry about what he might have done now, do I?'

'But some of this evidence may be excluded now. You've ridden a bloody coach and horses through the PACE codes, trampled all over his rights.' The tension in Downing's voice showed how close she had come to shouting.

'His rights. Actually, Tricia, do you know what's at the front of my mind right now? Not his bloody rights but Emma's rights, her mother's rights, her family's rights.'

She pulled furiously at the plastic tube, desperate for that never to be achieved proper nicotine hit.

'We both know that the most important person in a murder inquiry is the victim. Right? Up until we make an arrest that is. Then it's the suspect. The victim suddenly becomes invisible. I know. I've learned that hard lesson. And I won't let it happen again. If I'd taken him to the nick and he had "no commented" me to death, then I would have needed to go to Mrs Bolton; told her I was sure I'd got the right man; but that I didn't know where Emma was; what had really happened to her; left her in limbo for the rest of her life.' Another furious drag. 'I don't need to do that now. I can tell her – "I've got the bastard who killed your baby. I've found her. She didn't suffer. You can bury her and maybe, just maybe, get on with the rest of your life. Be a mother to the rest of your family."'

She walked a few paces away and then turned back, needing movement to contain her anger.

'And you know what else I know, lady. That in ten years' time, after Mickey boy here has been a model prisoner, got some soft-minded prat to think he is really quite a good guy, not capable of something like this. He won't be able to say then that all the evidence was circumstantial, that there were some other freaks in the town who were never properly eliminated, that there's a reasonable doubt.' She grasped at the air. 'I've got him by the balls. He's got nowhere to go. I can show that that bastard has got her blood on his hands.'

Downing put her hands up.

'OK, OK, I get that. That's Emma, but not this second one. He says she's been dead three years. We must follow the PACE codes on this one.'

Stone slowly shook her head.

'I think – no, I know that this is a once-only chance and I'm not letting it go. We don't get little girls abducted every other day. We both know this one's going to be Tracey Gibbons. I've had to do some of the follow-ups with her family. Three years and they're still in a state of shock. It caused the marriage to break up. Come on, Tricia, if I can tell them that I've found her, that they can bury her, then I'll take the consequences for that. Right now, this minute, the only rights that I'm concerned about are theirs – not that murdering bastard's. His come later, much later.'

They started to walk back towards the cars. Stone touched Downing's shoulder.

'I know you're saying this for all the right reasons, Tricia. And you've got to put your reservations and advice on the record. These decisions have been mine and mine alone. I'll live with the consequences. And we both know there's going to be a shit load of those.'

Chapter 2

MEGAN FREELAND WAS STANDING OUTSIDE the conference room with the prepared statement on the murders in hand. Her assistant had told her that all was ready. She wasn't normally nervous but these were the most dramatic murders that she had ever dealt with. The murder of one child was unusual, uncovering two was unique. Like everyone else involved in the investigation, she was on a high from the discoveries and a low from the grief she had had to witness. She could hear the buzz in the conference room and knew they were going to be hard to handle. And the contempt of court rules meant that she would need to stonewall them. She would not be popular. But they couldn't sack her or lock her up for it. As she checked her watch for the last time before going into the room, a flurry of colour caught her eye. Akila Naeem, the Police and Crime Commissioner, was striding towards her with her press advisor, Ryan Peterson, following half a step behind. Naeem usually wore a dark business suit with a white blouse but now she was in a blue Anarkali suit with a matching dupatta. Today was obviously show day. All Freeland's twenty years' experience told her that this would not end well.

'Megan,' said Naeem, 'are the press all here?'

'Yes, Commissioner. I was just about to go in and deliver our prepared statement.'

'There's been a change of plan. I will take the conference.'

'Does the Chief Constable—'

'As far as I'm aware, Megan, I'm the Police and Crime Commissioner and this is my force. I do not answer to the Chief Constable.'

'It's just that our judgement is that—'

'Ryan has explained all that to me. It's my judgement that I should take the conference. And that's what counts, isn't it?' She waved a sheet of paper in her hand. 'I've read through the statement. It'll do. A bit drab and lifeless but adequate.'

Freeland tried to recover some ground. 'They've been told that there'll be no Q&A.'

'I know, but Ryan here has arranged with Swanson from the *Gazette* to ask me what we are doing in my war against paedophiles.'

'I'm not sure that's a good idea, Commissioner.'

Naeem laid a reassuring hand on Freeland's forearm.

'And I am sure that it is.' She checked her watch. 'Let's not keep them waiting any longer.'

With that, she drew the dupatta up to drape over the back of her head, waited till Peterson had pulled the door open for her, then processed into the conference room. Freeland sighed, took out her mobile and speed dialled the number of the detective chief superintendent.

'John, Megan here. The bloody Commissioner has decided to take the press conference. You'd better get down here ASAP.'

Simpson's 'shit' was still resonating in her ear as she pocketed the phone and followed Naeem into the conference room.

'So, ladies and gentlemen, that is the Force's prepared statement on the arrest. I cannot say anything more on the case itself, but I am willing to take some general questions. Mr Swanson?' she said, pointing to a small bespectacled man in the front row.

'What is the Granbyshire force doing to protect the young people of the county, Commissioner?'

A muted groan went up from the more seasoned hacks to this obviously planted question.

Undeterred, Naeem replied, 'As you know, when I was a local councillor, I was head of the council's child care programme. I have used my experience there to help the force to develop a more holistic approach to children who are in care, or in need of protection. I have doubled the size of the family protection team and it now works much more closely with the council's social care agencies.'

'How have you managed this with all the cuts the police are being forced to make?' Again from Swanson.

'It wasn't easy, John. The Chief Constable and I had long discussions on it and I think it's fair to say that I had to be quite forceful to ensure that I got my way. But we both recognize the need for the service to do better by our young people, to provide them with as much protection and safeguarding as we can.'

She was getting into her stride now, enjoying the national platform. She knew that it was unlikely that the TV people or the nationals would carry anything other than the prepared statement, but it might be a quiet news day. At least now they knew her face, her voice. She knew that she looked and sounded good. If all she got out of it was an invitation to one of the morning TV shows or the *Today* programme, it would be worthwhile.

Knowing that the press had been told by Freeland that there would be no Q&A, she thought that all she had to do now was step away from the lectern and let Freeland close the conference. Before she could, one of the reporters in the middle of the second row stood up and spoke, without waiting for her to invite a question.

'Martin Johnson, the *Guardian*. Commissioner Naeem, as well as the commitment to young people, in your manifesto you said,' he looked down at a leaflet in his hand, '*that the police had been unaccountable for far too long and that it is my intention to change this, to make them transparently accountable to the public, get rid of officers who did not live up to my standards.*'

She smiled, pleased that he had read her material. Megan Freeland was standing behind her so Naeem could not see the look of concern that suddenly appeared on Freeland's face. Before she had an opportunity to say anything, Johnson went on.

'So I can take it as read then that you intend to sack the arresting officer in this case.' He looked down at his notes. 'This Detective Chief Inspector Stone.' The background mutter ceased and the room became silent. Johnson continued, enjoying the drama. 'According to my sources, she completely ignored the requirements of the PACE codes of practice. She refused to give him access to a lawyer and intimidated and bullied him into making the admissions that led to the discovery of the bodies of the two girls.'

The room erupted around him but Johnson stood impassively, knowing that in time the effects of the grenade he had just thrown would die down and his fellow professionals would let him get on, happy to feed off his exclusive.

When it had, he asked again, 'Well, Commissioner, are you going to sack her?'

There was a chorus of 'what are you going to do? Will she be sacked? Are you going to refer the case to the Independent Police Complaints Commission?' from the press pack, hackles up now, scenting blood. Naeem grasped the lectern, glad of its support and protection. She knew she had to say something but could not think what it could be. All she could think was how could triumph turn to tragedy so quickly? She dare not say anything about the case because of the contempt rules. Or about the officer. It was clear that Johnson's knowledge of the case was better than hers. But she had made that commitment, and she felt bound to follow through on it. Before she could speak she felt Freeland by her side, speaking across her into the mike.

'The Commissioner did say that she would not be taking any questions on the arrest but Detective Chief Superintendent Simpson will reply to the issue you have raised, won't he, Commissioner?'

As she was speaking, Freeland was gradually edging Naeem to one side and, having cleared a space in front of the mike, she stepped back and Simpson pushed forward to claim the lectern.

'Mr Johnson, I'm sure you appreciate that it's not possible to make any reply to that. All of the facts surrounding the arrest are now sub judice. The investigating team are currently liaising with the CPS on the next steps, and the arrest process will form part of those discussions.'

'But will DCI Stone be suspended? These are very serious allegations.'

'I can't comment on that.'

'Will she at least be removed from the investigation?'

'I've already said I can't comment on that or anything else connected with the case so this conference is now at an end.'

As he was speaking, Freeland was moving Naeem towards the door. Naeem began to turn to speak to the clamour of questions that the pack were now shouting at her back but Freeman kept a hand in the small of her back, propelling her forward. When Simpson brought his weight and mass to bear, she found herself outside in the corridor, being hustled back to the safety of the press office.

As soon as the door of the office closed, Naeem exploded.

'How dare you do that to me! How dare you embarrass me like that! Rushing me out. Making it look as if I was running away.'

Simpson knew that Freeland was good at her job. She had shown how good by the way that she had ended the conference and got Naeem out of it. He knew she was used to people in the job taking their frustrations with the media out on her, but could see the physical effect of Naeem's rant on her as a pink colouring slowly spread from her bust to her neck, a living graph of her stress levels. She was obviously waiting for the Naeem storm to blow itself out before replying. But he decided that it was his job to manage the Commissioner. She couldn't sack him – not yet anyway.

'Commissioner, you should be thanking Megan here, not criticizing her. She just saved you from talking yourself into a very deep hole.'

'I was in complete control,' Nadine bridled, 'I just needed a few moments to think, that was all. But before I could, you both intervened, made me look a fool.'

Simpson bit back a 'couldn't improve on what you were already doing' and all the other easy responses that line invited and went calmly on.

'Think about it, Commissioner. Why do you think the Chief Constable, the ACC and even I didn't take the conference? We knew there were problems with the arrest. If it had been the press officer doing the briefing, they wouldn't have asked any questions. There's no gain in showing her dodging the issue. It's what she's paid to do. Johnson would have kept his powder dry. A chief officer, however …'

He let her imagination do the rest.

'But the DCI found the bodies. We can tell the families what happened to their children.'

'She did. But she also did exactly what that reporter said. She didn't follow the PACE codes of practice. She denied him access to a lawyer.'

'But what difference can that make now? He took her to the graves. He couldn't be guiltier.'

Christ, Simpson thought, the fact that you can ask that question shows that you should never have gone near the bloody press. But he said, 'It's a bit complex, technical, Commissioner. The admissibility of the evidence is the key. By not following the PACE codes of practice, the DCI took a chance that any evidence obtained may not be admitted at his trial.'

'But he took her to the graves. Everybody knows that now. How can he deny it?'

'He doesn't need to deny it. Just plead not guilty and get his brief to argue that the evidence of finding the graves shouldn't be admitted. If he succeeds in that, as far as the jury is concerned, he didn't take us to the graves. And he is currently, on the advice of his brief, saying nothing.'

Naeem paced the confines of the little press office, taking time to rationalize her position, work out what to do next.

'So he could get away with it because of what she did? Because she denied him his rights?' Her voice was soft now.

Simpson shrugged. 'Theoretically, yes.'

'How could she be so unprofessional?'

The breath-taking speed of her U-turn was only matched by her immediate crucifixion of the woman who, seconds ago, had been a folk hero.

'She thought it was the best way to get Fleming to tell her what he had done to Emma. And it worked. In Emma's case, we've got a lot of other incriminating evidence. He will go down for that one for sure. Fleming telling her about the second body came completely out of the blue. I've never known anything like that in thirty years as a police officer.'

'And what is she doing at the minute? Presumably if she has done all this, she's been suspended and she'll be sacked.'

'At the minute she's still the SIO. She did get the evidence on him and recover the bodies. There's a lot of support for her in the force – and the families are very grateful for what she did. Any decision on what happens to her will only be made by the ACC and the chief.'

Naeem was now beyond taking any interest in the merit of Stone's approach. Like the media, her hackles were up, a blood sacrifice was required.

'But we can't be seen to be endorsing what she did!'

He stonewalled her. 'With all due respect, that's a matter for the Chief Constable, Commissioner.'

'We'll see about that,' she said as she made her way to the door, signalling Peterson to follow her.

Chapter 3

'So you don't think there's any chance of getting any more out of him?'

The three of them, Stone, Simpson and Roger Cartwright, the senior prosecutor from the CPS, were sitting around the end of the table in the major incident conference room.

'No,' Stone replied to Cartwright's question. 'Not a thing since I rearrested him for Tracey. And now he's lawyered up, he won't even talk about Emma, and we've got him bang to rights with CCTV and forensics on that, without any admissions. He's not even saying "no comment". Every question is answered by his lawyer with a statement that his rights have been so fundamentally breached that he will now say nothing. So we can't even get the questions in without getting that answer every time.'

'Frank Baxter may only be a local lad but he is an astute lawyer,' said Simpson. 'I've been up against him quite a few times and it was always hard work.'

'And I'm told that they're briefing John Maxwell,' said Cartwright. 'He only takes cases that will bring him loads of publicity so they're obviously going to make a fight of it. It doesn't look good, Rachel. We need to charge Fleming today. The key question is do we just charge him with Emma's murder or do we charge him for both?'

Stone sat back, blowing her breath with exasperation. 'I can't believe we're having this conversation, Roger. He volunteered the information on where we would find both girls. He volunteered to take us to them. We found them where he said we would. Surely to God no judge is going to rule all that inadmissible just because I didn't follow the technicalities of the PACE codes.'

Cartwright smiled ruefully. 'Hardly technicalities, Rachel. You ground his rights into the dust. Treated him as if we were back in the seventies. Made *Life on Mars* look ethical.'

She tutted. 'It wasn't that bad, for God's sake. He wanted to talk. Wanted to tell me where they were.'

Cartwright shrugged. 'I'm only describing it the way I know that Maxwell will play it. He'll be comparing you to the Gestapo, the KGB, the bloody Spanish Inquisition, all rolled into one. Trust me. It's his only possible line.'

Simpson intervened. 'But we are rock solid on Emma, aren't we?'

'Yes. The forensics and CCTV are easily enough. It may even be that he'll plead to that one on the day, hope that by not putting the parents through a trial that he'll only get a life sentence, not a whole life one.'

'What!' Stone shouted. 'Are you telling me that there is even a slight possibility that that monster will get parole?'

'I think he'll have to do twenty to twenty-five years, but yes, if he only goes down for Emma's murder, that's a possibility we've got to face.'

'Then we've got to go on with Tracey. It's the only way of ensuring that he never gets out of jail.'

'The trouble is, Rachel,' said Cartwright, 'all we've got on him is the fact that he took us to the grave. The defence will argue that as soon as he told you "there was another one", you should have rearrested him, cautioned him, taken him to the police station and given him access to a lawyer. The judge may rule that his rights had been so prejudiced that the evidence of his taking you to the graves can't be admitted. If he does that we've got nothing else, have we?' He paused and then began counting the issues off on his fingers. 'We've got no forensics. We've got no witnesses. We've got no CCTV. We've got nothing. Nix. Zilch.'

'OK, Roger, I get the picture. So how do we explain finding Tracey's body to the jury?'

'If the judge doesn't admit the evidence, we don't. We begin with the body. We begin from the point where you rearrested him and cautioned him for Tracey's murder. But he said nothing then so that's not enough to get past half-time. Maxwell will submit a 'no case to answer' motion and the judge will have to agree. It won't even go to the jury.'

'Surely we can at least argue similar fact evidence. He used a board to cover both graves.'

'That's not enough in itself.'

'M.O.?'

'We don't know his M.O. for Tracey. All we've got is most of her skeleton.'

'Cause of death?'

'Come on, Rachel, all we've got is a skeleton. The pathologist thinks that he probably smothered her too but that doesn't leave any skeletal trail. He needed to have strangled her for that. It can be hard enough to establish the cause of death in asphyxiation, even with a relatively fresh body. There's no chance with only a skeleton.'

As he was speaking, Stone was clicking her ball-pen, the pace of the clicks speeding up as he covered the lack of evidence. When he finished, she threw it down on top of her papers. Before she could say anything, Simpson intervened.

'Are you telling me that we're not even going to give it a run?'

'No, of course not, John. I'm just pointing out the difficulties. We'll charge him with both and see how it plays. If the admission goes in, the case is good. And I'll do my best to get it in.'

There was a knock at the door and DS Downing came in. She addressed Stone.

'The ACC would like to see you, ma'am.'

'Does he know that I'm in conference with the CPS on the case?'

'I did tell him that. He said he doesn't care if you're in conference with God Almighty, he wants to see you straightaway.'

Stone collected her papers and got up from the table. As she did, she could feel Simpson's discomfort and looked across at him.

'Do you know what this is about, sir?'

'No, but I can guess. So don't overreact, Rachel. Think about the longer term.'

She looked hard at him, steady eye contact, the beginnings of a cold smile showing.

'He's going to give me the bloody bum's rush, isn't he?'

'I don't know. But listen to what he says, take advice, then act. Not the other way round – that's what got you here.'

She left the room and as she turned to walk away along the corridor, she met Detective Superintendent Tony Bradshaw walking towards her. She stopped in front of him, blocking his way.

'Not you. Tell me it's not you, Tony. How could they do this to me?'

He held up his hands in surrender. 'I don't want the job, Rachel. I'm just doing what I'm told.'

She brushed past him, muttering, 'Fuck you, Tony, fuck you very much.'

'She's got to go, David. Today. You've got to sack her.'

Naeem and Chief Constable David Hill were sitting in the lounge area of her office which she had based on the one in the Oval Office. She was in a wing-chair at the top of the inverted U, he was in the sofa which made up one of its legs. His height cancelled the edge that her more upright chair usually gave her. It had been a committee room when the force was answerable to a committee, but as soon as she saw the modest office of the chair of the committee, she rejected it and took over the committee room itself. She now had a much bigger office which of course meant that she could have a bigger desk, a bigger conference table and this comfortable lounge area. It was only cost that had stopped her from having a giant copy of the force's badge made for the wall behind her desk.

'She's made a few mistakes, Akila, but with the best of intentions. And she did find the bodies.'

'A few mistakes! I've had a chance to look at what she should have done under PACE and the force's own policies. She ignored them all.'

He forced a chuckle. 'It's not the first time a police officer has done that. And the families are definitely on her side. I think we need to wait to see what the CPS decides to do.'

'But look at this.' She waved a copy of the *Daily Mail* in his face. 'This isn't exactly a left wing rag. Look at the headline.' She read it out. '*Detective Railroads Murder Suspect.* It goes on to say, *PCC Naeem made making the police more accountable a major plank in her election manifesto but has shown no sign of doing anything about this maverick officer.*' She threw the paper down on the coffee table that separated them. 'And I did. And what's more, I meant what I said. She's got to go. Now. Today.'

He raised his hands in a gesture of appeasement.

'Usually we have the trial, make a judgement, then have the execution, Akila, not the other way around. Police discipline is very formal. I can't just sack her summarily. It would be illegal and, trust me, very expensive.' She harrumphed but he continued. 'And I think you'll find that the public's view isn't quite what the *Daily Mail* or the *Guardian* say it is. There's a hell of a lot of support for her from the families and the local public. She's a bloody hero inside the force. So even if I could sack her, I wouldn't. Not at the minute. We need to wait to see what the CPS say in the first instance. She's in conference with them as we speak.'

'You mean she's still on the case! How could you do this to me, David? You know how I feel about police who don't obey the rules, act as if they're above the law. I was elected to sort this force out. I selected you as my chief constable to get that done.'

He visibly stiffened as she said this and no longer forced the humouring smile to stay in place. The thought of how much better the job was when the chief ruled the roost rather than held office at the whim of a politician flashed through his head.

'And now you refuse to support me in my decision to get rid of her.'

'I've supported you in everything you wanted despite my reservations—'

'What reservations?'

'An easy one was the decision to double the size of the Family Protection Unit just when I had to find an eight per cent cut in the budget. That caused real operational difficulties and stretched the CID. God knows how we would have managed if Stone hadn't cleared up the Emma Bolton murder so quickly, or if we'd gotten another difficult one at the same time. I wouldn't have had the detectives to cope. Make no mistake, Akila, that was a political and not operational decision and I went along with it.'

'It was what I was elected to do.'

He raised a hand, palm upwards again. 'Look, let's not fall out over this. The decision to discipline Stone is mine. It's my backside that's in the fire if she takes us to an Employment Tribunal. We need to see how the case develops before we can do that. But I'm aware of what you want here, so I have a proposal.'

'And what is this … proposal?'

'I'm going to take her off the Bolton case.'

'But you said—'

He cut across her. 'I said I couldn't fire her. I can justify taking her off the case on the grounds that she can no longer deal effectively with the suspect or his counsel. It's weak, but it'll do. I've already spoken to the ACC and he'll be seeing her later today. Fortunately, today's Friday, so we have a break over the weekend; she takes a week's gardening leave, then she comes back to take charge of a new cold case squad. The Home Office has been on to me for over a year to do this so I can kill two birds with one stone. I'll give her some dead wood for staff. With a bit of luck, that'll keep her busy and out of the public eye until she goes back to the Met, where she came from.'

'From the Met? That's not usual, is it?'

'No. She transferred up with her husband, Tony Bradshaw, they'd both been DCIs in the Met. He came on promotion to superintendent and she took a drop in rank to DI to come with him.'

'So why is she going back?'

'They're not together anymore. The usual. Tony found someone else. Someone younger. The cold case squad may be the best place for her to wait until all this blows over.'

'All right, David. I don't like it but I'll live with it – if it doesn't work out, I'll make sure everyone knows it was your decision.'

Stone was still muttering to herself as she entered the command suite on the top floor of police headquarters. The three PAs who serviced the ACPO team were grouped in a triangle of desks in the centre of the room. As soon as Rachel entered, one of them got up and went to the door marked Robert Jackson, ACC OPERATIONS. She knocked and opened it, waving Rachel through. She had been around long enough to recognize when, and when not, to stand her ground controlling access.

Jackson looked up from the paperwork on his desk as soon as Stone entered. He smiled and waved her to sit in the chair on the other side of his desk. He was near retirement and was old-style, not a believer in the need to remove barriers when having a conversation. The desk was there to remind you, should it be needed, just who he was and who was in charge.

'Sit down, Rachel. Would you like a coffee or a tea?'

'No, thank you, sir.'

'That's all, Mary,' he said over Stone's shoulder. 'Make sure we're not disturbed, please.'

The PA who had been waiting at the door left, closing it quietly behind her.

'I …' Stone began but he raised a hand to silence her.

'In the old days, Rachel, I would have got a bottle out and helped you drown your sorrows. But all I can offer these days is coffee. So,' he paused, 'you know we're taking you off the Emma Bolton murder?'

'It wasn't hard to guess. I met Tony, Superintendent Bradshaw, in the corridor on my way here.'

'I'm sorry about that. He wasn't supposed to go down until I'd spoken to you. But I was delayed. Still, he should have waited.'

She sat, silent. Inside she was still seething from the double humiliation of being taken off the case, her case – and that it was being handed to Tony on a plate. There was no way that she was going to make this easy for him.

'I'm only too aware of your history with Tony.'

'Oh, by history, you mean that I took a demotion to come up here with him only to be dumped a year later for my ten years younger clone?'

He shrugged. 'He's the only SIO I have available. And even that was only because the trial he was in collapsed when the defendant decided to plead.'

She sat in grim silence, not to be mollified.

'And it's not all bad. He is a superintendent. We can put it out that the complexities of the case are such that we think it is better handled by a more senior and experienced officer.'

'More experienced! We were both DCIs in the Met. He is not more experienced. I'd laugh if I didn't feel so much like crying.'

'Rachel.' His tone told her that he was moving from avuncular to get real. 'Rachel, there isn't an officer in the force who doesn't agree with what you did. Most of us admire the guts that it took to do it. But you knew what you were doing when you did it, didn't you?' He took her nuance of a nod as agreement. 'You knew that there would be consequences. That you'd have to live with them, didn't you?'

She gave another nod then looked up. 'But I found the girls. If I had gone by the book like he would have, they would still be in the bloody ground. It's not bloody fair.'

It was what she believed even though she knew it sounded like a whine.

'Fairness doesn't come into it. You knew you were taking a chance. Live with it.'

There was a silence that neither felt inclined to fill, then she said, 'OK, sir, what's to happen to me now?'

'The Commissioner wants you suspended, then sacked.'

'That bitch was trying to grandstand on my work until it went belly up on her.'

'She thinks you've embarrassed her.'

'I embarrassed her! She ...'

He put a hand up to quiet her. 'The chief is on your side. He's moved her away from that. You're not suspended and we are not starting a disciplinary investigation. And we know he could do both.'

'So, what then?'

'First, you're going to take a week's gardening leave.'

'I live in a flat.'

This did not raise even the vestige of a smile. 'You're going on gardening leave for a week. That'll give the media a chance to move on and the Commissioner a chance to find some other way to tell the public what a great job she's doing. Then you come back and head up a new unit.'

'A new unit? Doing what?'

'We've been under pressure from the Home Office for the last year to set up a cold case unit, to review all of our undetected serious crimes. You'll head it.'

She knew very little about cold case work. Budgetary pressures meant that the one constant seemed to be that it was done by retired officers – so much cheaper than using real police officers doing real police work. She knew that the force was short of detectives. Was this what was on offer? She had to test the premise.

'Do I get a chance to select personnel? I'd like DS Downing at least.'

'You'll get what you get, Rachel.'

The reality of the outcome hit her hard. She could feel her career slowly disappearing into the quicksand of police politics.

'That'll be all the bloody dregs that everyone wants to get rid of. I can hear it already; it won't be the cold case squad – it'll be the dead but not buried yet squad.'

The humour didn't work this time, either.

'It'll be who we can afford to allocate.' He leaned across the desk. 'Like I said, Rachel. Every cop knows why you did what you did. The Chief's gone out on a limb for you. Make it work.'

'Thank you, sir, thank you very much,' she said as she rose and left the office.

Back in her office, she sat with her door locked and the window open to the chill of the late autumn air, vaping furiously through the open window. She knew that she had taken a risk with Fleming, ignoring his rights in preference to that of the victims. But it was one that she felt she had to take. And it had worked – in spades! But rather than glory, it had led to the double humiliation of being taken off her case, her bloody case, and it being handed to Tony of all bloody people.

She took another long drag of the e-cigarette, looked at it and thought, I can take control of one thing in my life at least. With that, she jammed it in the edge of the drawer, broke it in two and threw it in the waste-bin.

Chapter 4

'YOU WANTED TO SEE ME?' asked Ryan Peterson, peering around Naeem's door, ready to retreat.

'Come in, Ryan. We need to talk through last Friday's debacle and plan for the election.'

'So, you're definitely going for it?'

'The mayor's job? Of course. Did you ever doubt it?'

'You seem to be well settled here and you've got a good working relationship with the Chief Constable.'

Naeem got up from behind her desk and indicated they should move to the more comfortable conference area. There was already a pot of coffee and cups on the table between the sofas. He sat on the right-hand sofa and she in the slightly higher chair that bottomed the horseshoe.

'This job,' she waved her arm to bring in the whole of the office, 'is just a step on the way for me. It's got no real political clout. All the operational decisions are made by the chief. And you know by now that the press and media much prefer to talk to the top cop – not the top cop's boss.'

While she spoke, he was nodding his agreement. 'It's certainly harder for me to get you airtime or column inches than it is for Freeland. She can open or close access to ongoing cases in a way that I can't.'

'Exactly.' She nodded towards the coffee and he began to pour for both of them. 'And that bitch has never forgiven me for developing my own press office. My own approach. Just look at what she let me in for on Friday.'

Peterson preferred to take a drink of coffee than address that point. She picked up her own coffee cup and took a sip. He used the break to change the direction of the conversation.

'That seems to be a bit of a spent force now,' he said. 'Fleming's been charged with both murders so it's all sub judice. There's not much that the media can get its teeth into. And you did take immediate action, taking her off the murder inquiry.'

'I wanted her sacked for humiliating me like that – but it would have taken too long and Hill didn't think it was a good idea. He was right that it would fade away as soon as Fleming was charged.'

She stood up and began to pace the room. 'I can't get used to all the constraints that there are in this job. Look at Friday. Great news one minute becomes a disaster in the course of one question.'

'That's behind us now, Akila. You've done as much as you can. It's time to move on.'

'You're right. The selection committee for the party's candidate for mayor meets next week to finalize the choice. But I'm quietly confident. There's only two of us and Miller is an old, fat, white, middle-class male. I'm a young, feisty Asian, wife and mother of two delightful children. I know I can get my own people out – having an uncle who's a peer of the realm helps with that - and I appeal to all those working mothers. The profile this job has given me – up until Friday at least – means that I'm better known. Being the only Asian PCC has definitely been an advantage there.'

'Is there anything in particular you need from me,' Peterson asked, 'other than working on your campaign,' he paused to smile, 'once selected of course?'

'No, nothing at the minute, Ryan.'

He recognized the dismissal, got up and walked to the door. As he opened it she added, 'But keep an eye on that murder inquiry and what both Freeland and Stone are doing. I won't have them get in my way again.'

The chief officer team was breaking up from its usual Monday morning meeting when David Hill asked Bob Jackson to wait behind.

'I'd like a quick word about Rachel Stone and this Cold Case Unit. Have you selected all the people yet?'

Jackson puffed his cheeks. 'Not yet, with two murders running it's not easy to find the extra bodies. I suppose there's no chance of delaying it – even a couple of weeks might make a difference.'

'No chance,' said Hill, 'and anyway, the way this year has gone, it's just as likely to get worse as better.'

'True enough. The trouble is my first trawl around the divisions has got me no decent offers, just dead wood.'

'The good thing about dead wood, Bob, is that it's easy to burn. This unit is just an expediency for me. I get to kill three birds with one stone. I keep that bloody woman happy, I keep the HMI happy and I take Stone out of the limelight, at least until she goes back to the Met.'

'Personally, I'll be sorry to see her go. She's a good detective and God knows we haven't got enough of those these days. She only did a year as DI before she was promoted to DCI. She's in the running for the next detective superintendent vacancy, would probably be one by now if there had been one.'

'Well, she can forget that now, at least as long as we have this PCC.'

'She's still a bloody good detective and they don't grow on trees.'

'The cemeteries are full of indispensable men, and women, Bob. No one is irreplaceable. I want it in place when she comes back – a *fait accompli*. Get it done by the end of the week.'

Chapter 5

She was awakened by the light streaming in through the break between the curtains where she had not drawn them together properly. She loved the big windows in the loft flat and the view they gave over the River Dean, but they did let in a lot of light. Realizing that it must be late, she started then relaxed, remembering she didn't have a job to go to today. The flat, three bedrooms, two bathrooms and an enormous living area, was bigger than she needed but when she and Tony had split up, she had bought as big as she could afford so as to make the move back to London easier. The difference in price growth between the Midlands and London was already making a mockery of that clever plan.

She pulled on the dressing gown that lay in a heap at the bottom of the bed and crossed the room to open the curtains properly. That was when she became aware of the hubbub in the narrow service road which separated the old warehouse from the river. She peered out between the curtains and saw a huddle of cameramen and reporters in the street below. If the bloody newspapers were going bust, she thought, how can they afford all these reporters and cameramen? There were two PCSOs trying vainly to keep them on the narrow pavement opposite the entrance to the flats. She remembered now that she had cut off the doorbell and unplugged her landline the night before to ensure a night's peace. The media huddle had made it almost impossible for her to get to her door and she had asked the local station to provide a police presence, knowing that it would get worse once it became public that she had been taken off the case.

When she switched her mobile on, it zapped into life, telling her that her voicemail was full and that she had thirty unanswered calls. She debated clearing the voicemail but decided it would be a waste of time as it would only fill again with messages she had no intention of replying to. It was clear that she could only stay in Granby if she was willing to hole up in the flat. She knew that this was impossible. She would go stir crazy before the day was out. She reconnected her landline and dialled.

'Hi, Mum, it's me.'

'Rachel, I've been calling since yesterday afternoon but couldn't get through – or even leave a message on your mobile.'

'I know, Mum. Sorry, but I've had to cut everything off just to get some peace from the press.'

'But you're the police. Surely you can tell them to stop …'

'Not without taking a couple of them out and shooting them, and I don't think the Chief would want me to do that.'

'Well, I …'

'Look, Mum, that's a reason I called. I need to get away. I've got a week's leave. Can I use the cottage?'

'Of course, you know you can, whenever you want.'

'I needed to check that you and Dad aren't using it.'

'No, but if the weather's good, we may come down at the weekend.'

'Good, I might see you both. I'm not sure of my plans beyond the next couple of days.' She was now sure she was not going to be there at the weekend. 'I'll be leaving shortly. Call you when I get there, get the chance to speak properly then. OK?'

'All right, Rachel. I'll call Mrs Little and tell her you're coming. She'll get the place ready and turn up the heating.'

'Thanks. I'll call you when I get there. Bye.'

She had no sooner hung up when the phone rang. A check on the caller ID said it was the local station.

'Stone.'

'Morning, ma'am. It's Sergeant Collins—'

'Yes, skip, what's the problem?'

'One of the PCSOs outside your place says that there's a man who wants to deliver some flowers. Will she let him come up?'

'Hang on a minute while I check.'

She walked to the window and looked through the narrow parting. Sure enough, there was a man in a brown work coat holding a large bunch of flowers talking to the PCSOs. Further down the street, she could see a white florist's van parked.

'Who are they from?'

'She doesn't know and he says he doesn't, either.' A pause. 'What do you want her to do?'

'OK. Send him up. I'll open the door. Tell her to listen for the buzz.'

She released the front door, pulled the belt on her robe tight and waited by her open flat door for the deliveryman to appear. She heard him come up the stairs two at a time and then he presented himself at her door. A quick look confirmed that he was all wrong. No working man with a day of deliveries before him took stairs two at a time. The work coat was just too small for his six foot frame. The clothes under it were too smart for a deliveryman. Oh, to have had a suspicious cop and not a naïve uniform carrier on the door. He smiled and held out the flowers towards her. It was a very expensive bouquet and had its own water supply in a large plastic bag at its base. She did not reach out to take the flowers.

'Who the hell are you really?' she said. 'Don't bullshit me or you'll be wearing those bloody flowers.'

The smile left his face.

'No, really I'm …'

She stepped back inside the door and began to close it.

'OK, OK.' He took the card from his pocket and handed it to her. 'Dave Bates, you're right, I'm a journalist.' He quickly carried on making the most of what he knew was the one chance. 'Look, I only want to give you a chance to get your side of the story across. The force is treating you abominably. The public and the families are on your side and I can help you get your story out. Keep it anonymous. Might even be something else in it for you if I can get any of the nationals interested.'

She opened the door from the crack that he was speaking through into a space that was wide enough for her to step through. He began to smile again.

'Something else,' she said. 'What would that be?'

'We're both men, sorry people of the world. It would be off the books. Could even pay it into a foreign account.'

She stepped onto the landing, her presence pushing him back towards the stairs, still holding the flowers out as a defensive wall. Without a word, she brought both hands together on either side of the plastic reservoir, pulling it back slightly towards her as she did so. The water fountained up through the flowers and cascaded on his head and shoulders – from Jack-the-lad reporter to drowned rat in one easy step.

'What the f… Why did you do that?'

'I could arrest you for that attempted bribe, and I will if I see you again.'

She couldn't help herself laughing. 'Now get the hell out of here while I'm still feeling so generous.'

With that she stepped back, closed the door and made her way back to the slot in the curtains. A few minutes later, Bates emerged and she watched him suffer the indignity of the walk of shame through his colleagues. They showed their sympathy and fellow feeling by photographing him and bombarding him with a stream of mickey takes until he climbed soggily into the florist van and drove off.

After the Bates incident, she decided to take no chances in getting away without any of the press being able to pursue her. Her car was parked a few yards from the front door and she was in it before the pack had much time to react. After that, it was only a matter of getting the end of the road blocked off by a patrol car for ten minutes after she left, penning in her would-be followers until she was safely away. Her plan was to spend five days at the cottage and then come back via a stop off in North London to see her godchildren.

Chapter 6

CHARLTON HERRING IS A VERY pretty village, a couple of miles inland from Dorset's Jurassic Coast. It nestles into the junction of three valleys, each serviced by a narrow road. A network of footpaths blossoms out from the village centre so she didn't need to drive, not even to the pub. Arriving reminded her of her last escape to the village, after the final break with Tony. And here she was again, future uncertain, confidence shaken. She could only hope that the quiet, the grandeur of the cliff walks would work the same magic in getting her life into some sort of perspective.

By day four, she had run out of all the premade meals that she had gathered up in M & S en route. She would eat at the Sailors Return for the last two days of her stay. Experience told her this would be no hardship. She got to the pub early, hungry from the last day-long walk along the coast to Weymouth and back. The pub consisted of a series of small dining areas, each holding a couple of tables and the original long bar area. She did not want to be trapped in the intimacy of one of the dining areas so she opted to eat in the bar. The food was good, as always, and she felt with her walk that she had earned the bottle of crisp Chablis that went beautifully with her fish. A book that kept her attention and the occasional scan and assessment of her fellow drinkers and diners rounded off the day nicely.

It was during one of these assessments that she clocked that she was not the only watcher. For the second time in one of her scans she found herself being watched by a tall, lightly bearded man standing at the bar. His look had 'journalist' written all over him, bringing back unpleasant memories of the siege of her flat the morning after she had arrested Fleming.

As soon as the barman cleared the dishes and condiments from her table, he walked across towards her, smiling what she had to admit was a very charming smile. On her part, she remained po-faced, a look that stopped him about three feet short of her table.

'You're Rachel Stone, aren't you?'

The smile was in full play now. She said nothing. Rude and ill-mannered, she knew, but she was here for peace, not to make friends.

Undeterred he continued, 'I'm Tom Gregson. I'm in the cottage two doors down from your parents' – yours. Your mother may have mentioned me.'

'She didn't.'

When creating an impact on strangers is part of your day-to-day job, it's difficult to give it up. She knew she was making him very uncomfortable and part of her, a large part she had to admit, was enjoying it. All he offered were potential difficulties. She wanted nothing from him but to be left alone. Disappointment filled his face, the smile now a bit lopsided.

'That's a shame,' he said, 'I'd rather hoped she had. It would have made this so much easier.'

'Made what easier, Mr Gregson?'

As soon as she said it, she knew she had made a mistake. She had him completely on the back foot, ready to retreat to the safety of the bar; and then she had stupidly given him a toehold.

The smile came back and with a 'May I?', he reached out, grabbed a chair at an adjoining table, pulled it across to hers and sat down with a brief 'thank you.' He had done that before. To get rid of him now, she would have to be outrageously rude. Not a viable option as her mother would kill her. Silence was her only remaining defence.

Undeterred he continued, 'The thing is, I'm a writer ...'

'I'm not giving interviews, Mr Gregson.'

'No, nothing like that.' He paused, marshalling his thoughts. 'As I said, I'm a writer; so far I've been moderately successful in writing a series of mediaeval whodunits, *The Sister Mary Murder Mysteries*.' He looked at her expectantly but getting no reaction, plodded on. 'The trouble is my publishers think the idea is running out of steam.' He grimaced. 'I must admit there are only so many credible ways of getting my fourteenth century nun out of the convent to run her investigations, and sex is more or less out of the question.'

He looked at her across the table, assessing her reaction so far. She said nothing.

'I'm working on a modern mystery, contemporary. This is quite a jump for me but my agent likes the storyline I've developed and I'm down here trying to put some flesh on its bones. And therein lies the rub. I've done quite a lot of research, you know, on police practice, forensics, and the rest. But at the end of the day, a good story is more about people than it is about plot – and that's where I'm coming up short. I'd like to find out about what the station sounds like, smells like, what happens in the squad room—'

'The CID office,' she interrupted.

The smile came back in full force. 'That's exactly what I mean, getting the bits like that right. TV can be so misleading.'

Against her better judgement, she was beginning to like the guy, his enthusiasm and energy were infectious.

'I mentioned it to your mother when she was down, over the garden fence literally and that's when she told me you were a detective.' He paused, another assessment, the smile faded. 'Look, I've taken up enough of your evening. Here's my card. Check me out.' He raised a finger in emphasis. 'Tell you what. Let me buy you lunch tomorrow. I promise not to be too boring or demanding.' He got to his feet. 'Don't say yay or nay now. Think about it – please. It would really make my time down here worthwhile.' He took a step back. 'I'll be here tomorrow if you decide to come. Till then, I hope.'

After he left, she finished the last of her wine, mulling his offer over. He was good-looking, charming, seemed to have a sense of humour. And anyway, tomorrow was her last day, so whatever happened would start and end with an almost free lunch. She'd think it over on her last morning walk.

Chapter 7

SHE WOKE TO A CLASSIC Dorset November morning. A clear sky, the mist in the hollows dodging what warmth there was left in the sun. She had planned to walk in the morning and pack and clean the cottage in the afternoon. She knew her mother and stepfather would be disappointed not to see her but she wasn't up to their company – her mother's curiosity was insatiable and her questioning relentless. She had missed the life classes in body language and could only be stopped by explicit protest. Rachel wasn't up to that at the minute, mainly because she had, as yet, no answers to the questions. The stop off with her godchildren was a much more attractive alternative.

She packed the flask of coffee and made the long hike uphill up to the coastal path. At this point, she could go either east towards Lulworth or west towards Weymouth. She decided to stay on the Ridgeway and turned west. Her destination was the White Nothe and St Catherine's Church, in her view the prettiest spot in Dorset, sitting above Ringstead Beach and looking over Weymouth Bay towards Portland. As she gained the Ridgeway, pleased that she had to stop only once to catch a breath, the November sun gained enough energy to burn off the remnants of the overnight sea fog. Portland began to emerge from the mist like a giant crocodile, its snout pointing up Chesil Beach, threatening Wyke Regis and beyond.

The little wooden church of St Catherine's was made for meditation. Sitting halfway up the White Nothe, its tiny cemetery giving a view over the sweep of the bay below. By the time she had reached it, the air was crystal clear, the chimneys of the Young Offenders Institute on the eastern cliffs of Portland now etched against a pale blue winter sky. She smiled to herself, comparing the peacefulness of the bay with the turmoil in her head. She didn't regret how she had handled Fleming's arrest and the discovery of the bodies, but she was beginning to get a more realistic appreciation of the consequences. She'd had to do it. She couldn't let another victim down. Her thoughts drifted back to the time that she had. A simple domestic. He was a prison officer, she a nurse. She said he threatened to kill her with his shotgun. He denied it. It was her word against his. He was plausible, she was faltering. They'd seized the shotgun and advised her to move out. She did. He still killed her a week later – used a mate's gun. They should have charged him with threats to kill. But it was just another domestic. After that she vowed never again. The victim would always come first. What was done couldn't be undone, only managed. It was pointless hoping to go back to the Met, or any other force, until the dust from the murder inquiry had settled, until Fleming was safely convicted. So that's what she'd do. Make this bloody deadbeat squad, working on its dead as mutton cases, succeed. There had to be a couple of workable cases in the files. If they were there, she would find them. Then she'd get the hell out of it.

Her resolution and the fact that it was all downhill made the journey back much easier. As she approached the village, the weather began to close down and it was clearly going to be a very wet afternoon. She checked her watch to find that it was a few minutes before one o'clock. She must have subconsciously been timing it to get back for the lunch invitation. Pausing only to drop her backpack at the cottage, she made her way to the pub and the earnest Mr Gregson.

He was standing at the bar and smiled warmly to greet her.

'Ms Stone, I'm glad you decided to come. What can I get you to drink?'

'A glass of the white Chablis.'

'Great. If we're having lunch, shall I get a bottle?'

'A glass will do for the minute, thank you. And it's Rachel.'

A look of uncertainty passed across his face as he tried to work out how to react to this mixed message, but he ordered her wine.

'Rachel, I'm Tom. Shall we sit at the table?'

'Not right away.' A pause. 'Tom. You told me you were a novelist. That you weren't a journalist.'

'That's right.'

'That's not what your website says, it says that you are a journalist, even lists some of the magazines and newspapers you've written for.' He began to speak but she carried on. 'So why did you lie to me?'

'Shit! Are all cops as confrontational as you?'

'Tell me why you lied and I might answer that.'

He paused then spoke. 'Look, Rachel, I know all about the case up in Granbyshire and I thought you may not want to speak to a journalist so ...'

'You're dead right there, Tom.'

'I was a little economical with the truth.' A smile to no effect. 'If you look, you'll see that all of my 'journalism' is about historical fiction and researching. It's really hard to make a living out of just writing books, so I do a lot of free-lance stuff for various magazines – I even teach, run workshops.' He paused again and looked her directly in the eye. 'My publisher won't do any more *Sister Mary Mysteries*. The last one simply didn't sell enough. If they don't like the crime book I'm working on, I'm not sure what I'll do next. I've got used to being a 'writer' now. It's really important for me to get it as right as I can. Your mother's suggestion looked like a God-given opportunity to get all the background stuff right, maybe some unique insights, the chance to describe characters that were that bit different. That's it, M'Lud, my mitigation.' The smile again. 'And, of course, there is always the pleasant prospect of lunch with a very attractive woman,' he said, lifting his glass in a mock toast.

She had left the glass on the counter where the barman had placed it. As he spoke, her right hand was cupping her chin, the index finger beating a slow rhythm with his speech. Decision time. She could cut and run, but to where? The other end of the bar? His explanation made sense. At least she found herself wanting it to. She looked at him long and hard, nodded, picked up her glass and returned his mock toast.

'OK, Tom, but here are the ground rules. Background stuff only.' He nodded agreement. 'No questions about the current case.' Another nod. 'If you start to go there, I get up and walk away. No warnings. No advice not to go there.'

'Agreed.'

'Fine – let's eat.'

As she turned to go to their table in one of the little alcoves he said, 'So, shall I get a bottle?'

She raised her glass. 'This'll get me through my starter – then we'll see.'

The air cleared and the ground rules set, the meal went well. Her scallop starter saw off the first glass and the bottle just about covered their mains of grilled seabass. Tom's main interest was in her experiences in London as that was where he, a Londoner, was setting the book. The combination of the wine, good food, his interest in her and her work meant that she enjoyed the meal for itself. In his turn, he gave her an insight into the difficulties he had in generating enough income from his writing to allow him to do it full-time. It made her realize how lucky she was to be able to do a job that she loved while at the same time having the sort of job security that was almost unique in the current climate. The atmosphere, his interest, the wine also meant that despite her best intentions, she knew that she was becoming more than a bit flirtatious, giving out signals that she, a single woman, would give to any good-looking, apparently available man. This made her reaction to his next question all the more abrupt.

'So,' he said, pouring the last of the wine into their glasses, 'it's obvious from the way you talk about it that you loved working in the Met. Why the move to Granbyshire?'

'I'm not going to talk about that.'

'Sorry,' he said, hands up in a peace gesture, 'I didn't mean ...'

'Don't worry about it. It had nothing to do with the case. I just don't want to talk about it.'

A silence fell on the table. The girl who was waiting on the table must have heard it, no talking, no rattle of cutlery and came in to clear away. As she did so, it stretched a silence to the point that taking up the conversation again was proving to be difficult. He was a guy buying her lunch; not a bloody suspect. An apology was called for. When the girl had gone, Rachel reached across and touched his hand.

'Sorry, Tom. I was way too abrupt. It's a personal issue and I don't want to talk about it.'

He put his other hand across hers, trapping it with the gentlest of pressure. He glanced at his watch.

'Look, they're going to chuck us out of here any minute. Greg, the guy who owns the cottage, told me he had left a bottle of really fine Armagnac in case of emergency.' He pointed to the rain bouncing off the car park tarmac and smiled. 'This feels like a real emergency to me. Why not come back to the cottage and round off this splendid meal with a drink by the fire?'

Why not indeed, she thought. Because the feeling of isolation those last days on the case has left me feeling vulnerable, that's a good reason. Because walking and thinking for four days on my own has made the offer way too attractive, that's another. While her brain was working its way through all the reasons why it was not a good idea, her other hand found itself on top of his and her mouth was saying, 'Why not indeed? I think that a meal as good as this deserves no less than a good ... rounding off.'

Chapter 8

THERE IS ONLY ONE WAY to miss the slow crawl up the M3 to London, that's to use another road and crawl up it even more slowly. Every main route into the capital made the case for driverless vehicles. Still, it did give you time to think and she now had lots to think about. The sex had been very good. As close to a zipless fuck as she was ever likely to get. The best use of a wet afternoon she had had in a long time. Neither had tried to make it more or less than it was. The commitment to a future meeting was left suitably vague. She found herself smiling fondly for the first time in a long time, a fondness more for the moment than any person. The week as a whole had given her self-confidence a kick-start, focused on the future rather than the past.

She ended the week with a stayover at her friend and ex-colleague's house in north London. An afternoon shopping with Anne and a couple of hours playing with her goddaughter had helped her put the whole episode in perspective. Now as she lay on the bed, wrapped in a dressing gown, cooling down from a typically too-hot bath, Rachel listened to the domestic comings and goings in the rest of the house as Anne put Millie and Josh to bed. She had met Anne when she was posted as a new DC to Kensington CID. Anne was already a well-established detective there and took the new girl under her wing, keeping the hounds that populate any CID office at bay, at least until Rachel had decided which of the hounds should be given a run.

Neither could really understand how the friendship had lasted as the only things they seemed to have in common were the job and a sense of fun. Rachel was ambitious, job-focused but with the tendency every now and then to briefly go off the rails, usually in a doomed relationship with another cop, before regaining focus and composure after some counselling, not always sober, from

Anne. Anne was happy just to be a successful detective, good at what she did and content to be rewarded by being sought after as a team member in bigger inquiries where teamwork, and team playing, were the key. Rachel benefited from the fact that Anne would often draw her into this work in her wake. It was a measure of their friendship that both of them recognized this and neither resented it. It had even survived, if only just, the different choices they had made in partners.

Anne had met then married Jim Bates, a CPS lawyer she had worked with in the course of a very difficult rape prosecution. Jim was good-looking, steady, unassuming and he doted on her. They were no sooner married than Anne became joyfully pregnant with Millie. At about the same time, Rachel became involved with Tony Bradshaw. He was very much a Marmite man; to Rachel he was funny, charming and sharp; to Anne he was a slick user. Tony was the epitome of the Jack-the-lad detective. Tall, dark, satiric, always immaculately dressed, usually with a rosebud buttonhole, he exuded excitement and the promise of a good time. By the time he met Rachel, he was already one wife and two kids down. Her career had taken off with selection for promotion to DCI and she was working with him on a major murder inquiry. She had been flattered by his attentions and he was an accomplished and considerate lover. Before she knew it, they were married. A year later he sprung Granbyshire on her. He thought that some experience in a county force would benefit his career so he had applied for the promoted post of detective superintendent in Granbyshire. She had taken the loss of promotion that the transfer cost. A year later he left her for a younger woman. And Anne never even hinted an 'I told you so'.

There was a knock on her door and Anne called out, 'We eat in half an hour. Come on down when you're ready for a drink before dinner.'

'That was delicious, Anne, as always,' said Rachel, 'but I still wish you had let me take you both out for a meal.'

'Not possible.'

'Why?'

'You're sleeping in the babysitter's room. At this sort of notice, the only one I could get to look after the kids would be my mother. And she always stays the night, especially if it's a Friday and she can be with the kids on Saturday.'

'And Sunday,' chimed Jim, but in a good-humoured way. 'Don't get me wrong, Anne's mother has been wonderful – not at all the stereotypical mother-in-law. She's really chipped in and made it easier for Anne to get back in the swing.'

'So you don't regret leaving the job?' asked Rachel.

'No, not really. I tried going back after Millie was born and my mum was very good at filling in. But if you're not there full-time, it's not the same. And of course, if something comes up suddenly, as it does, you either don't get involved or there's this great panic getting everything in place. And that was just with the one. So when Josh came along, I decided to turn my hand to something more predictable.'

'You always were a good teacher – look how well I turned out,' Rachel said with a smile.

'Well, I think I prefer a class of eight-year-olds to a CID office. If only just. When it isn't raining and the noses aren't dripping.' She sipped her wine. 'What about you, when you go back. Is the transfer to this cold case squad the end of it?'

'Don't know to be honest. Fleming hasn't made a complaint even though his lawyer puffed and prattled about the way I had treated him.'

'How about us?' asked Jim. He was now head of the local CPS.

'Roger Cartwright doesn't like it but he's willing to give it a run. See what the trial judge says. What would you have done, Jim, in the same circumstances?'

'I think what Roger is doing. Jump up and down, tell you what an idiot you'd been, tell everyone there was no chance of a conviction on the second body – then try to make it work. He did kill the girl. You've got to at least give it a try. And you say that Fleming said nothing once he was at the station and had access to a lawyer.'

'Not a bloody thing other than "yes" to "did he understand the charges?"'

'So he may not have taken you to the second girl if you had played it by the book?'

'Who knows? Anyway, it's Tony's case now – I just hate it that he'll be getting the credit at the end of the case. But at least I'm pretty sure he'll do his best to watch my back.'

'Only if it doesn't cost him,' said Anne, getting up and beginning to clear away the last of the dishes.

'But he owes me.'

'But he's a snake in the grass and will always look after number one.'

'Come on, he's not as black as you paint him.'

'Only because I can't find paint black enough. You trusted him once, remember.'

Her time in Dorset had given her the chance to review her position, had made her appreciate the degree of her vulnerability. Talking to Anne, and before that to Tom, had made her realize how much she loved, needed the job. If the CPS decided to give Tracey's murder a run, she was more or less home and dry. But they may not. She needed some inside info on what was happening there.

'You're right, Anne, as always. I'll check up on him when I get back. Find out what he's up to.'

Chapter 9

THE PORTACABIN THAT SHE HAD been given for the squad was at the rear of the force headquarters, hard up against the boundary fence, about as far away as it could be from the centre of power. She had deliberately arrived early to prepare herself for the first meeting with her team, a very generous word to describe the mix of non-starters that she had been given. The large storage box she was carrying made opening the door difficult. Once inside, she deposited it on the table opposite the door and looked around her domain. Apart from the table, there were four desks arranged along either side of the length of the room. There were piles of document folders on three of the four desks. The heating, such as it was, was provided by three storage heaters. They must have been on a timer as the air inside the room had the chill taken off. She went to her office which was a glazed partition at the far end of the room. It had Venetian blinds which would allow her some privacy. There were two piles of document folders on her desk. She adjusted the blinds so that she could see out into the office but she could not be seen from it and picked up the smaller of the two piles. They were the team's personnel files. She quickly glanced through them.

DS Barbara Dyer, a schoolteacher before joining the job, a very promising early career which seemed to come to a halt around 2006. Rumour was she had a drink problem but no one had ever caught her out. DC Colin Shepherd, twenty-eight years in and two to go, his annual appraisals and sick record said that he had retired but just hadn't told the Chief Constable. Finally, DC David 'two brains' Sharpe, six years in the job, a high IQ and a good degree but never quite able to fit in.

At 8.30 a.m., the door of the portacabin opened tentatively and three figures made their way inside. First in was Shepherd, a big, burly man, with thick grey hair, wearing a wax jacket over a tweed suit. Next was Dyer, a dull greying blonde dressed in a grey wool trouser suit. Coming up in the rear was Sharpe, a tall rangy man wearing a well-cut woollen topcoat with a scarf knotted at his neck. Shepherd looked around the room then quickly made his way to the desk nearest the storage heater in the corner and her office, and furthest from the door.

'Age has privileges, gents, you two can have your choice of the other three.' He touched the top of the heater and felt its dull warmth. 'At least someone's switched the bloody things on although you'd never know it. It's as cold as charity in here and about as welcoming as a witch's tit. How fucking appropriate is that?' He gave a dry, mirthless chuckle at his own wit. The others didn't react.

As he was finishing, Stone opened the door to her office and came into the main room.

'And just how is it appropriate, DC Shepherd?' she asked, placing their personnel files on Shepherd's desk.

The others smirked but, unfazed, Shepherd replied, 'Just a manner of speaking, boss. And I can't see any kettle. Not a proper squad office without the makings, is it?'

Stone turned to Sharpe. 'DC Sharpe, you're the youngest so you get to run the tea club. There is all we need in that storage box over there. Set it up and make us all a cup. Mine's a coffee, a proper one, there's a cafetière in there too.' When he didn't move instantly, she followed on with, 'Come on, lad, get a bloody move on. We've got work to do here.'

Sharpe got slowly to his feet, made his way to the table and began to organize the coffees. When they all had a mug in hand, she began her briefing.

'I want to put my cards on the table with you all. Just so there's no misunderstandings. First off, I know that none of you want to be here. The squad is a handy place for the Chief to put me while the brouhaha from the murders settles. You lot are collateral damage.'

She looked around the group to see how they were taking this. They all sat, impassive.

'But you should all know that it works both ways.' She picked the personnel files up from the empty desk. 'None of your previous bosses were desperate to hold on to you, in fact, chances are they couldn't wait to get rid of you for all sorts of reasons which you will know,' she held up the three files, 'and now you know that I know.' She tucked them under her arm. 'I don't want to be here. My only way out is to get some results out of all this crap.' She indicated the piles of files on the desks. 'I've never failed at anything in the job and I don't intend to start now. So your job in the next few days is to work through all of these files – they are undetected murders and stranger rapes. Each of you will find one worth following up. I've got my own pile in there. When that's done, we'll get together and compile a list in order of likelihood of success. OK? Let's get on with it.'

She picked up her mug and went back into her office.

As she entered the little wine bar, Stone saw Tricia Downing sitting in a booth in the corner, leafing through a magazine. She had had to work hard to get her here. They had little in common except the bond of women working in a world dominated by men. Tricia's tall, blonde good looks were complemented by an ability to make everything she wore match, maximizing the effect of the central, expensive items of her wardrobe. She was attractive but there was no edginess to her, she could only ever play the good cop. As the door closed behind Stone, Tricia looked up and gave a brief, worn smile of welcome. Stone signalled with a drinking motion and Tricia raised a nearly full glass of white wine to show that she had already got one. When she had her wine, Stone joined her in the opposite bench of the booth.

'Thanks for coming, Tricia, I really appreciate it.'

'I'm not quite sure why I'm here at all. And I'm not comfortable with it.'

'I appreciate that. I really need to know how the case is coming on. What's happening?'

'You could ask Superintendent Bradshaw yourself. It's not as if you don't know him.'

'That's the trouble, Tricia, I do know him. I don't want to know what he is willing to tell me. I want to know what he isn't willing to tell me.'

'I won't be your spy!'

Rachel sat back and took a sip of her wine.

'Tricia, my career is on a knife edge at the minute …'

'I did warn you about that but you just ignored me.'

Rachel sighed. 'I know. And you were right. But I believed that I had to do it,' she paused, 'and I did tell you how to safeguard yourself, didn't I?' Tricia nodded. 'And it worked. You're still on the team.' Another pause, another sip. 'Has Tony come on to you yet?'

They exchanged smiles.

'In a half-hearted sort of way,' Tricia said. 'You know, almost as if he feels that he needs to rather than wants to. More than a flirt, but only just.'

'He must be getting old, then. Or maybe this Jane is the real thing – for now anyway.' She took another drink, a long one this time. 'Anyway, enough of my paranoia about Tony. What's happening?'

Tricia gathered her thoughts, selecting what she would say and what she wouldn't.

'You know what it's like after an arrest. Putting the case together, writing up the statements, and dealing with all the bloody disclosure issues. But it's going well and we're trying to put it to bed before we get another one.'

Stone nodded her encouragement.

'There has been a development from the defence,' said Tricia.

'A development?'

'Yes. They've come back to the CPS and said that they are willing to plead to Emma's murder.'

'Too bloody right – he's bang to rights on that one.'

There was a silence that shouted that Tricia had something to say that she knew Stone didn't want to hear. The only thing to do was wait her out.

'The thing is,' said Tricia, 'he'll only plead to Emma if the charge against him for Tracey Gibbons is dropped.'

'What!'

'They say that if we go ahead with both, he'll plead not to both.'

'The bastard!'

Stone looked across the table at Tricia, who had suddenly found that her wine glass held all the secrets of the universe.

'But that's not all, Tricia, is it? What else is going on?'

'Well, Bradshaw thinks we should drop the charge.'

'I knew it. That bastard is grabbing the chance to fuck up my life yet again.'

Despite herself, she knew her voice was getting louder and she had great difficulty in resisting the desire to smash her fists on the table. Tricia held up her hands to quiet her, looking around the bar to see what effect Stone's outburst was having. When she was sure that no one had noticed, she sat back in her seat.

'It's not such an unreasonable decision, Rachel. It'll save the cost of the trial and would ensure that the families wouldn't have to go through the ordeal of one.'

'But what about Tracey's parents? Where's the justice for them?'

'You must have thought that this was a possibility when you let him take you to her grave?'

'No, I bloody didn't. He was talking. He volunteered to take us there. We found her bloody body. The court has never excluded evidence like that before.'

Tricia's face took up that tight-lipped well-I-told-you-so-nanny-look that Stone's mother often used to great effect, then sat in silence to let it sink in.

Stone was the first to crack. 'But Cartwright, he still going on with it, isn't he? It's not Tony's decision. Cartwright promised me he'd give it a run.'

'Times change, the attitude to the police is changing all the time and you're not there to push it any more, Rachel. And Bradshaw is putting a lot of pressure on him.'

'Shit, shit, shit – shit.' She paused to take a breath and think. 'But he hasn't dropped the charge, has he? Or you would have told me. What is he going to do?'

'He's referred it up to the DPP. They're putting it out to a QC for advice. When they get that they'll decide.'

When Tricia had finished her drink and gone, Stone stayed on. The bar did enough fiddly tapas things to let her tell herself she was having a proper meal, letting her have a bottle of Rioja to go with it. Everything was going to hell in a hand cart. She was stuck with some deadbeats and she knew in her soul the CPS would take the easy way out if the brief gave them half a chance. Everyone was focused on budgets rather than reasons for existing these days and the CPS were no different. Trials were expensive. And they would have the wonderful excuse that they were only doing it to save the families the horrors that the trial would bring – the need to describe the deaths – the state of the bodies – the speculation on what else Fleming might have done. Fleming was only in his thirties; unless someone killed him in prison, he'd be out in fifteen years, maybe even ten.

And if the CPS didn't go ahead with Tracey, it was only a matter of time before Naeem would be looking for her head.

Chapter 10

'I'VE LOOKED AT ALL THE possibles and decided that we are going ahead with these two,' began Stone.

The other three CCU members were gathered in a horseshoe around the whiteboard at the end of the general office.

'A series of rapes in 1991 and a murder in 2006. The rapes because there is outstanding DNA, and the murder for reasons that I'll come to. David, you ID-d the rape cases so take us through it.'

Sharpe got to his feet and moved to one of the briefing boards. It had three sets of photographs showing the victims, three women in their early twenties and the bedrooms which were the scenes of the rapes.

'In the late spring going into the early summer of 1991, there were a series of three rapes in the university district of Granby. The houses were all traditional terrace houses, subdivided into bedsits, mainly used by students and low-salaried workers. The investigating team were certain that it was the same offender because of the M.O. He always broke in while the occupant was out and lay in wait. From this they deduced that he must have cased the target and carried out some sort of surveillance.'

'Were there any sightings of him doing this?' asked Shepherd.

'No, so they thought that he may have been posing as a workman of some sort, you know, gas, electricity, water.' He paused to collect his thoughts then continued. 'He was always masked and for that time was very forensics aware, maybe he been caught by them before. He was gloved and always wore a stocking over his head. When the victim came home, he lay in hiding until it was clear that they were alone; then he'd emerge and threaten them with a knife. All the victims described it as a large and intimidating knife, probably a hunting or combat knife. He forced the victim to strip, bound their hands behind their back then raped them vaginally and anally. He always wore a condom and took care to comb out their pubic hair to ensure that he did not leave any of his.'

'Why did he stop at three?' asked Dyer.

'When he was in the act of raping the last victim, there was a noise at the front door and the victim had the sense to say that it must be her boyfriend. This panicked him and on leaving through the bedroom window, he grazed his forearm on the window frame. The investigating team think that this probably spooked him, and may be why he stopped.'

'Any description at all?' Dyer again.

'He was slim, quite small, 5'4" or 5'5"; but fit and very strong, so probably either worked out or did a manual job. His intelligence points to the likelihood that he worked out.'

'Why is it worth following up after all this time?' Shepherd asked Stone.

'There's really nothing much to do with this other than ask for a rerun of the DNA. His M.O. points to a reasonable level of intelligence and the crime, burglary, tends to run in families. So even if he's given up, his siblings may not. I've asked for a familial DNA to be done. You'll see that I'm going to do the same with our main cold case, but it has other lines of inquiry that will take up our time. If we get nothing on the DNA on this one, we've got nothing else to work on. Now on to our main case,' she said, moving to the other briefing board and pointing to the picture of a middle-aged Pakistani male. The name Bashir Rana was written alongside it.

'On Monday 24 April 2006, two men wearing ski masks entered the premises of Granby Taxis. Witnesses identified them as being Pakistani from their skin colour and accents. They spoke in English but it was heavily accented. We're pretty sure they had been brought over from Pakistan for the job. The pictures we have from CCTV were poor and our facial recognition systems couldn't find a match. One of them produced a sawn-off shotgun from beneath his coat and they shepherded the dispatcher and a driver who was waiting for a job into the toilet at the back of the premises and locked them in. They then went into the office of the manager and part owner of the firm,' she pointed to the picture, 'Bashir Rana, age forty-two. He'd been running the firm for about ten years. He had no criminal record but was known to police. I'll come back to that in a minute. The gunman shot Rana using both barrels, killing him instantly. Both men then left and got into a car that was waiting outside for them and drove off. The car was found half an hour later, burned out, about five miles out of town in the grounds of a derelict factory. It wasn't immediately connected to the murder.'

Stone turned to Dyer. 'Barbara, you were on the murder squad, weren't you?'

'Yes, I was. But only for three or four weeks. I fell ill and was off for quite a long while. When I got back to work, the squad had been closed down – it just hadn't been able to get anywhere.'

'That's ridiculous,' said Sharpe. 'Two guys walk into an office in the middle of town, in the middle of a working day, shoot someone and walk out and we can't get anywhere. There must be something worthwhile; forensics, CCTV – if nothing else, there had to be a motive that we could have worked on.'

'I'll come to that in a minute, David,' said Stone, 'but first the SIO, Detective Chief Superintendent Fowler. He'd retired by the time I came up here. What was he like, as a detective, Colin?'

Shepherd nodded his head. 'He was a good detective. A bit old school but did the business. I think that the Rana killing was the only murder case he didn't clear up.'

She looked at Dyer. 'Barbara, what did you think of him?'

She squirmed in her chair and avoided eye contact. 'I was a fairly new DS then. Pretty low in the food chain. I never really had much to do with him.'

Funny reaction, thought Stone, but decided to press on, time enough later to explore the foibles of the team. She turned to Sharpe. 'Getting back to the points you raised, David. The CCTV that we managed to get identified the car. But it was stolen and on bent plates. There was nothing on the driver, he wore a baseball hat with the visor pulled down. From his hands, he was Asian, probably Pakistani, too. It's more than likely he was a local as he would need to know the area. If he was, he managed to stay under the radar as the investigation got nowhere with him.' She consulted her briefing note. 'There were no prints at the scene and the car was completely burnt out. It was well gone by the time the fire brigade got there and since it presented no danger, they didn't bust a gut putting it out. But there was some DNA.'

She pointed to the picture of a brass figure.

'When the gunman came into the office, Rana must have thrown this brass paperweight at him. It was found lying in a corner opposite his desk. He must have been a good shot as there were traces of blood on one corner. There were no matches against the national database and there have been no hits on it since the murder. This tends to confirm the theory that they came from Pakistan specifically to do the job.' She looked at Sharpe. 'David, all this talking is making me thirsty. How about some coffee for us all?'

Before he could react, Dyer got up saying, 'I'll get them, David. I was part of the squad so I know the background.'

She went to the table and began setting up the coffees.

Stone continued, 'There were four lines of inquiry re-motive: a turf war with a rival taxi firm; that he may be skimming the books; a drugs connection; and finally, a connection with child sex trafficking, what we now call Child Sexual Exploitation, CSE. The turf war lead ran dry almost immediately. There was no apparent connection with any rival Asian-run firms and the few white-run ones had given up the ghost by the mid nineties.'

'Why drugs, boss?' asked Sharpe. 'Was that how he was known to police?'

'No, it wasn't. But almost all the heroin that comes to Britain comes from Afghanistan. Most of it is brought overland through Iran or the old Soviet republics. Some of it comes out through Pakistan. The police and security services there are very corrupt and have a weird relationship with the Taliban. So it was a possibility.'

'But?'

'But it got nowhere. SOCA, the Serious Organized Crime Agency as was, now the National Crime Agency, NCA, probably have another name before we finish this inquiry, could find no connections – certainly none that would justify a killing. The original investigation also did a forensic audit of the books; minicabbing is a cash business in the main so it was worthwhile looking, but they didn't find anything of any note.'

'So that left the CSE?'

'Yeah. At the time of the murder, a DS Mark Dryden ...'

'He's a DCI at the regional CTU now,' from Shepherd.

'As you say, Colin, now DCI at the Counter Terrorist Unit, was leading an inquiry into possible abuses against young girls, aged twelve to fifteen, all either in care or under care orders.'

'I heard about that,' again from Shepherd, 'it all came to nothing.'

'You're right. It did. It concluded that the girls couldn't be believed and that what, if anything, had happened to them, was voluntary, part of a lifestyle that they had picked for themselves.'

Dyer began passing the coffees around and Stone checked her notes.

'Four of the drivers at the taxi firm were suspects in that inquiry. Rana was not a suspect. The trouble was that all the girls in the inquiry were white so their families – assuming they had the brains and the money to hire a hitman, and looking at the families that's a hell of a big assumption – would hardly have the connections to hire Pakistanis to do the job.'

There was a long silence while they sipped their still too hot coffees and looked for inspiration at the board. Finally, Shepherd broke the silence.

'OK, boss, I give in. Why are we looking at the case that the previous inquiry dead ended? Have you seen any obvious flaws in the investigation?'

'No, but then again I didn't expect to. It was audited twice by an outside team, one from GMP and the other from Notts. They both gave it a clean bill of health.'

'So why then?'

'Three reasons. The first is the DNA. We now do a check on a much bigger number of sequences so we may get a hit. And I'm asking them to search as broadly as possible in case there are some familial possibilities. We do that much better now than we did then.'

'You said three reasons,' said Sharpe.

'The second is that with the shit hitting the fan nationally about the police failure to deal properly with CSE in the noughties, I think the Chief will give us some support if we have a look again at that aspect, just in case there are some time bombs ticking away. Finally, Rana was related to our PCC, Mrs Naeem. If I can find his killers, maybe, just maybe, she'll be so grateful she'll get off my case and let me get back to the Met.'

She looked at her watch.

'I've an appointment with the ACC in five minutes. Maybe get some help to open up the local Pakistani community and find a few more leads.'

'How are you going to manage that?' asked Shepherd.

'I'll tell you if I'm successful,' she replied as she went out the door.

'I did do my best for you first time around, Rachel, you know the pressure we're under these days. I ...'

'Come on, sir. It's only the one man. And he's not even a trained detective.'

'But he has been selected for the department. He's only waiting for a place at the training school.'

'And this will be really good experience for him.'

ACC Jackson sat back in his chair. Stone took that as a good omen, he hadn't said no, not yet.

'And I know the guy. I used him in a difficult domestic violence case last year. He managed to get the woman to talk to us and helped her to stand up for herself.' She decided to change tack. 'I really need a success for the squad, sir. We both know I'm a good enough detective to get one. But Ahmed would give me an edge, a line of inquiry that the original team didn't have.'

Jackson pursed his lips. 'OK, but not as well as. I can only give you three so you need to give up one of the others.'

'Sharpe,' she said, without hesitation. 'I know he's supposed to be bright but he doesn't have Shepherd's experience. And Shepherd was around at the time of the first investigation so he knew the players and what was going on at the time.'

'He's certainly all that, but not exactly Mr Dynamic, is he?'

'Let me worry about that, sir, I'm a good motivator. I'm sure I can get the best out of what is there.'

'Your call, Rachel. Arrange the change with HR and get the paperwork to me ASAP.'

'Thanks, sir, you won't regret it.'

'I bloody well better not,' he muttered to her retreating back.

Chapter 11

She had broken the news of Sharpe's transfer back to division as diplomatically as she could and was disconcerted by the look of relief on his face, and the speed with which he gathered up his gear and left. Her little squad was more of a leper colony that she had believed. She had asked Iftikhar Ahmed to report to the portacabin at 8 a.m., before the others arrived, so that she could give him a basic briefing. She knew he would be early so she got there at seven thirty. Sure enough, at 7.45, his head poked tentatively round the door.

'Come in, Iftikhar, come in.'

He was tall, just under six foot, slim, clean shaven, his dark good looks complemented by an aquiline nose and full lips. The last time she had seen him he was in uniform, the modern one of baggy pants, stab-proof vest and a loaded equipment belt that makes it impossible for anyone to look smart. Now he was in what was clearly his natural element; a dark, well cut suit, a gleaming white shirt, the whole image that of a successful man on the make, made complete by a muted red silk tie and highly polished plain black shoes. He had a black wool overcoat slung over one arm. Whether he thought that this was how a detective should look or just to ensure that he made a good first impression, only time would tell. He had certainly made an impression, she thought, oh, to be twenty again.

'Good morning, ma'am. I'll just hang this up,' he said, crossing to the clothes rack in the corner.

'You can have either of these desks,' she said, pointing to the two spare desks. 'That one's DS Dyer's and that one is DC Shepherd's.'

He nodded.

She walked across to the table where the cafetière stood, already full.

'Coffee?'

'Please.'

She filled two mugs.

'Help yourself to sugar and milk. Welcome to the Cold Case Unit. What have you been told about us?'

'Practically nothing. At the end of early turn yesterday I was told to report here, to you, in plain clothes, and that I would be attached to this unit until further notice.' He shrugged. 'So here I am.'

'You do know why I'm here?' she asked.

He smiled. 'I think everyone in the force does and, not that it means much, everyone I know thinks you made the right decision.'

'Thank you, it does mean much.' She took a sip of her coffee. 'What I need now is for the CPS and the judge to agree with you.' She moved across to the whiteboard. 'Meanwhile I need to make a success of this job. I've decided to reinvestigate two cases. One is a serial rapist and depends on a new run at the DNA. The other is this.' She pointed to the picture of Bashir Rana. 'He ran a minicab company back in 2006. He was murdered by two Pakistani hitmen. We're pretty sure they had come across from Pakistan to do the job and imme-diately returned there. We think it was because of something going on in the family. It may have been related to an investigation going on at the time into the sexual exploitation of some young white girls by some of his drivers. As far as we know, he himself was not involved. That's why I asked for you. I won't be able to take this any further forward until I can establish a motive for killing him. Last year, you showed me that you can think like a detective and that you understand the dynamics of policing in the community.'

He shrugged. 'I can't say I'm totally comfortable with being selected for a job just based on my ethnicity.'

She smiled. 'Can't have it both ways, Iftikhar. Part of the rationale for trying to get the force to reflect its communities is to ensure that there is someone in the force who has some idea of what the hell is going on in those communities. But anyway, I didn't pick you on the basis of your ethnicity. This is an old case, the evidence will be difficult to find. I need people who are good at the job if I'm going to get a result. And that's what I do, get results.'

He was still considering this when they were disturbed by the arrival of Dyer and Shepherd.

Stone turned to them, saying brightly, 'Barbara, Colin, meet the new addition to the team.' She waved an open hand towards Ahmed. 'Iftikhar Ahmed – he's replacing David. I would have liked to have kept David as well but the ACC will only allow me two DCs.'

She looked at Shepherd who showed no reaction to being the one she had selected to stay.

Dyer gave a nod of acknowledgement then moved to her desk. Shepherd stopped in front of Ahmed and smiled.

'Iffy, isn't it?'

'Actually, it's Iftikhar.'

'Oh, I thought they called you Iffy on the section?'

'Not to my face, they don't.'

Shepherd sustained the smile. 'Sorry, no offence meant.'

Ahmed returned the smile. 'None taken – this time.'

Well, thought Rachel, ethnicity clearly had no effect on testosterone, but they're still smiling and that gets some of the alpha male issues out of the way early on.

'I've got some housekeeping to do. I've no doubt you all do, too,' she said, nodding at Dyer and Shepherd. 'That'll give Iftikhar here a chance to read through the file summary and get up to speed. Then we'll meet again to discuss how we take this forward.'

Chapter 12

AN HOUR LATER, THEY WERE gathered in a horseshoe at the whiteboard.

'So, it's breakout time,' said Rachel. 'Now it's the backbreaking bit when we check everything out.' There was a groan from Shepherd. 'Not all of it, Colin, just the main players. To start with at least. The DNA, when we get it, may give us something new to work on. But till then, we go back and look a few people in the eye.'

'I'm going to start with Frank Fowler, the SIO. There's only so much you can put on the record and there may be more that he can tell us. Barbara,' she looked at Dyer, 'you come with me. Colin and Iftikhar will go back to the taxi firm. Speak to the new manager there, Gohar Jat, and the dispatcher, Ellen Benson. She was doing that job on the day of the murder. Looking at the file, she seems to be the only one who's still working for the firm.'

'Do you think that's a good idea, boss?' asked Dyer. Rachel looked questioningly at her but Dyer went on. 'It's just that, knowing him a bit, he might not like the idea of his ability being questioned by two women. Especially with me being on the original squad.'

'There's no doubt about that. He'd hate it,' said Shepherd, a smile on his lips.

'That's what I thought too, Colin,' said Rachel. 'Get him on the back foot.'

'There's also the fact that I dealt with Benson in the original inquiry,' argued Dyer. 'She's a really difficult woman to handle, mouthy cow with a couple of oak trees on her shoulders. I could make sure that she cuts out the crap and cooperates from the off. It would be quicker and easier.'

Rachel took the time to think it over then said, 'OK. We'll do it that way. I'll keep you back in case I need to see Fowler a second time. Up the ante. Let's get to it.'

*

As she entered the minicab office, Dyer thought that there must be a blueprint for them somewhere to ensure that they all looked the same. All small shops converted to the same pattern. A little foyer with the dispatcher behind the glass fronted partition and counter. A bench running down one wall, stuffing coming out of the cushion, an optional extra which Granby's had taken up. Two drivers were sitting on the bench, reading the local newspaper.

The dispatcher looked up as they entered. Ellen Benson had been in her mid-thirties at the time of the shooting. Then she had coarse features, lank hair and was going to fat. The only change was that she had now reached the end point as far as getting fatter was concerned, at least if she still wanted to be able to reach the radio mike from her chair.

Shepherd began to dig his warrant card out of his inside pocket when she said, looking at Dyer, 'It's OK. I know who you are. He's expecting you. Through there.' She nodded at the door at the side of the counter.

Jat was sitting behind a beaten-up metal desk in the small office at the rear of the premises, working on a laptop. There was barely room for the desk and Shepherd's bulk seemed to fill all the remaining space. Dyer took up a position by the door. Shepherd began to introduce himself but Jat looked up sharply from the laptop and cut across him.

'I know who you both are, but I don't know why you're here. I wasn't here when Rana was shot. I don't know what you expect to learn from me.'

'So you don't want us to find out who murdered your cousin?' asked Shepherd.

'Of course I do. I just don't know what you expect to learn from me.'

'You're aware of all the facts of the case then, all of the lines of inquiry?'

'No, but—'

'You see, Mr Jat, I am. And I think it's worth my while talking to you. So, can we go forward on that basis?'

Jat shrugged.

'Did your cousin have any enemies that you knew of?'

'Look, I hardly knew Rana. The firm is owned by the family. I was one of the directors and I took over when he was killed. You have to ask people closer to him for that sort of information.' He looked at his watch. 'This isn't the only business I run, you know. I'm really busy at the minute. I don't think I can give you much more of my time.'

Shepherd gave a sigh, edged down the side of the desk and sat on the corner, his leg touching Jat's chair.

'Getting old,' he said by way of an explanation. 'Can't stand for long. All right if I perch here for a couple of minutes?'

It was clearly not all right for Jat. He had already pushed himself away from Shepherd as far as the wall would allow. And now he had the detective's bulk towering over him with no way out. The desk was no longer a defence. It was now a prison. Dyer smiled inwardly at the way that Shepherd had managed the situation. Still a very effective cop when he chose to be. Instead of continuing with Jat, Shepherd turned laboriously to talk directly to Dyer.

'Did you notice all those cabs parked on the double yellows outside this office?'

'I did.'

'One of them was even double parked, here, in the city centre.'

'Yeah, I saw that too.'

'Now if I did that, I'd have a ticket in no time.'

Dyer nodded.

'When we get back to the office, I must find out which traffic warden works this beat. Do a background check, find out how many minicabs are actually ticketed in this area, check out his performance, finance, you know—'

'All right. All right.' Jat raised his hands in surrender. 'How can I help you?'

Shepherd smiled. 'Thank you, Mr Jat. Now at the time of the murder, were there any turf wars going on with any other taxi firms?'

'What do you mean?'

'I mean was there any repeat of the turf wars that went on in the early nineties when the Asian firms muscled the white firms out – that sort of thing?'

'I don't know what you're talking about.'

Shepherd sighed again. 'I've been a cop for nearly thirty years. I was in Granby back then. I know all about the slashed tyres, the misdirected calls, the radio eavesdropping so as to get to the customer first – that sort of thing.'

As he was talking, he leaned over Jat, their faces only inches apart.

'So, were there any turf wars going on?'

Jat was now slumped in his chair. 'No. Business had settled down. Everyone got on OK.'

Shepherd nodded. 'What was going on, eh? Why did two Pakistani hitmen, and we do know that they were Pakistani, walk in that door,' he pointed to it, 'and blow Rana, your cousin and business associate, to hell and back with both barrels of a sawn-off shotgun?'

'I don't know – how could I?'

'Was he skimming, Gohar? Was that it? Taking too much off the top, more than his share, more than you and the family could tolerate?'

Jat wriggled in his seat, his frustration with not being able to move beginning to show.

'No, there was nothing like that. You should know, your people audited the accounts. That happened as soon as I took over so I know.'

'So it must have been because some of your drivers were fucking thirteen-year-old white girls. Was that it?'

Jat was sweating now, desperate to get up and get some distance between him and Shepherd but he was trapped until Shepherd thought that he'd had enough.

'I don't know, I'm telling you. I know nothing about that. By the time I had taken over, weeks after the murder of my cousin, the drivers involved had already left and I was told that the inquiry about the girls had found nothing wrong.'

'Where did the drivers go?'

'I don't know,' he said, looking pleadingly at Shepherd. When he could see that this would never be enough, he shrugged and added, 'Birmingham, Yorkshire, I think. I know one of them went back to Pakistan.'

'But you don't know where?'

'They are all self-employed. They don't need references or anything like that. How could I?'

Shepherd gave him a long hard look, stood up and edged his bulk back down the side of the desk. The look of relief on Jat's face was palpable.

'Thank you for your cooperation, Mr Jat. We'll be back if we need any … clarification. Now, we need to borrow your office for a few minutes so that we can speak to your dispatcher, Ellen Benson.'

'But she's busy.'

'Aren't we all,' said Shepherd with a benign smile. 'I'm sure you or one of the drivers can fill in for a few minutes. Or do I need to start making enquiries at the traffic office?' Another smile, this time less benign. 'But we don't want to go through all that again, do we?'

Jat got quickly to his feet and scurried out of the door. A few moments later, Benson waddled into the room. Shepherd indicated with a wave of his hand that she could sit behind the desk. She looked at the space and gave him a cold look.

'You're taking the piss, aren't you? I'm happy enough here,' she said, perching herself on the edge of the desk. 'The boss said it would only take a couple of minutes.' She looked Dyer up and down. 'I know you, don't I, from the first time?'

'That's right,' said Dyer. 'Describe to us what happened on the day of the shooting.'

'But I already did. It's all in the statement you lot took from me at the time.'

'I know, but humour me. Tell me again.'

Benson pursed her lips as if to go on with the refusal, but sighed and began.

'Not much to tell. It were all over in seconds. I were at the dispatcher's desk, one of the drivers were sitting on the bench. It were mid-morning so it were quiet like. Then the two Pakistani men came in, one of them shut the door and turned the closed sign on. I was just about to say something when the other one pulled a sawn-off shotgun out from under his coat.'

'Did you recognize them? Had you seen them before?'

'No, they were Pakistani Pakistani, you know, not from round here. You can always tell when someone has just come from there. They had really strong accents, all the locals sound just like us.'

'Go on.'

'Well, they pushed Basra and me into the toilet at the back and locked us in. Then we heard the shots and them running out of the office.'

'Did you hear them saying anything to Mr Rana?'

'No, there were some shouting but I think it was in Punjabi and I'm sure it was Bashir's voice, then the shots. Then the running.'

'How did you get out of the toilet?'

'Basra tried to get out through the window but it were nailed shut. So when we were sure they'd gone, we started banging on the door and shouting. Next thing, you lot were here and let us out, and took us to the station.'

'At the time, was there any trouble between this firm and any of the other taxi companies – any bad blood you know of?'

'No. Nothing like that. There had been a long time ago between the Pakistani firms and the older ones – but they all went out of business.'

'Because of the turf wars?'

'A bit, maybe, but the Pakistani guys work longer hours and for less money as well – that was the cause of most of the trouble. They kept undercutting the locals' prices.'

'You didn't resent that?'

Benson shrugged. 'They all need dispatchers and most of the customers are white. And that's what they want to hear on the phone. I'll always have a job no matter who runs the firms.'

'What happened to Basra, he left, didn't he?'

'Yeah. A few weeks after the shooting. Maybe it spooked him.'

'But not you?'

'I had three kids and no man. I needed the job. I couldn't afford to be spooked.'

'Basra was one of the drivers involved with the girls, wasn't he?'

'I don't know nothing about that.'

'No gossip even?'

'Look,' she said, standing up. 'They all speak Punjabi when they don't want me to know what they're saying. I didn't know anything until you lot came to question me about it. And I said then what I'm saying now. I knew nowt then, I know nowt about it now.'

Dyer looked to Shepherd who gave a slight shake of the head. Benson picked up the signal and began to waddle back to her post saying, 'So I'll get back to what I'm paid to do if that's all right with you.'

Chapter 13

EX-DETECTIVE CHIEF SUPERINTENDENT Frank FOWLER lived out in Brickstock Hill, the decidedly posh end of Granby. The house turned out to be a large mock Georgian detached, with a wide semi-circular drive. A side drive led to a detached double garage. If Stone had been in London, it would have screamed bent cop but here in the Midlands, house prices were different, so she found it harder to guess. She still thought it was a lot of house for a retired chief superintendent.

The knock was answered by a tall, austere-looking woman who did not return the introductions that Stone made, but merely opened the door to allow them to enter. Once in the hallway, she pointed to a door at the far end and said, 'He's through there, in his conservatory.'

They found him as directed, sitting in a comfortable reclining armchair, reading a newspaper. He set it aside as soon as they entered. Even sitting, it was obvious that Fowler was a big man, well over six foot tall. He had been muscular at one time but had now gone to fat. His big round head was topped by a thick layer of white hair. The fat of his face squeezed his alert grey eyes into little gleaming stones. How he spent the time was evidenced by his boozer's nose and the almost full ashtray on the small side table. Despite the size of the room, the air was thick with tobacco smoke. As soon as he put the paper down, he began to light a cigarette taken from the pack by the ashtray. He signalled them to sit in the two other armchairs opposite him.

Before Stone could speak he said, 'She won't let me smoke in the house – so I built this.' He indicated the conservatory. 'Do what I bloody like in here.'

A clear statement of intent. Stone introduced herself and Ahmed. Fowler focused on her, ignoring Ahmed, even in the introductions.

'So, Miss Stone, what do you want from me?'

'As I said, we're reopening the Rana case and I need to get your views on it as the SIO.'

He pulled long on the cigarette, almost as if he knew how much she would have liked to join him, then blew a long plume of smoke towards the glass roof.

'My views as the SIO are where they should be. In the policy book and the case notes. It's all there. The case just ran into the sand. We followed up every lead. Even tried to get the Pakistani police involved. A complete waste of time that was,' he said, looking for the first time at Ahmed.

The column of ash on the cigarette looked as if it was going to join many of its predecessors by littering his shirt front, but he knocked it off into the ashtray with a timing born of practice.

'It was the only murder I never cleared up, you know. The only one. The investigation was audited twice, once by Manchester, then by Notts. Clean bill of health both times.'

'With the benefit of hindsight, is there anything else you think you could have done?'

'If there was anything I could have done, I would have done it. I don't like to fail. This isn't the Met, you know. We like to clear up our murders.'

Stone nodded as if agreeing. Taking her time. She hadn't been expecting a warm welcome but had thought that she would get a more professional, considered reply.

'How about the inquiry into the taxi drivers grooming and trafficking the girls? That was going on at the same time and you supervised it too, didn't you?'

'I did. Do you have a problem with that?'

'No, it's just that it seemed to be wound up quite quickly. Completely discounted the girls' evidence.'

He grimaced. 'Christ, are you another one of those bleeding-hearts liberals who thinks that the girls must have been victims – that they had no choice in what they did?'

He stomped out the stub of the cigarette he had been smoking and then lit another. Stone could feel Ahmed's discomfort. Even for an almost-ex-smoker, the air in the room was becoming difficult to breathe and had her eyes smarting.

'I think that we're all a bit more sceptical now about thirteen- and fourteen-year-olds making free and informed choices, sir. That more weight should be given to what they say was done to them. They were still just girls after all.'

'Absolute bollocks. Look, it wasn't just my decision. Everyone forgets that. It was a joint investigation with the Children's Services of the county council. It was overseen by the bloody CPS. We all agreed that the girls were out of control – that's why they were in care in the first bloody place. They just couldn't keep their knees together.'

'But what about the drugs and the alcohol?'

'The allegations of drugs and alcohol. Look at the evidence. They kept going back. Defending the men who were supposedly "abusing them."' He bracketed the words with his fingers. 'They were not credible witnesses. Any prosecution would have been a complete waste of time.'

Stone could see little point in taking the matter any further. Fowler was in complete defence mode and was clearly confident that any review of the case papers for either the murder or the CSE would bear him out. She was still trying to think of a way forward when Ahmed intervened.

'Do you think that the murder was payback for the alleged trafficking, sir? The families of the girls must have been upset by what had been going on. Some of them at least.'

Good question, Stone thought, gives Fowler a chance to calm down, come off the defensive.

'Look at the policy book, son. We did follow that up but the problem was that they were all white and the gunmen were Pakistani – we were sure about that.'

'Do you think Rana was involved in using the girls?'

'There was no evidence against him and if he was screwing around, we couldn't find any evidence of it. The only names the girls would give were those of the drivers. They said there were other men involved, but they either couldn't or wouldn't give us any names.'

He took another cigarette from the pack and rolled it between his fingers as he picked up the lighter. Before lighting it, he looked condescendingly at Stone.

'I've been a cop in Granby, man and boy. I know the local communities, even the Pakistani one, as far as any outsider can know them.' Another look at Ahmed. 'The problem in dealing with the Pakistani community is that we have no idea what is actually going on. Some of the women still don't speak any English and never leave the house without their husbands. Getting access to them is a nightmare.' A pause. 'You can see from the policy book; at the end of the day, we were pretty certain it was a family matter. The problem for us was that we didn't know if it was a family matter to do with something here in England, or still going on from something in Pakistan. Your boy there will tell you, these families, more clans really, are all intermarried and the ones in England still have close connections through marriage and business

– sometimes they're the same thing. We just couldn't break through. And you won't either, not unless you can find some point of weakness where you can get some leverage. Find someone who doesn't like the outcome. We didn't have any coloured officers on the team then. Constable … Ahmed here might find you a way in. Good luck to you. I couldn't.'

Back in the main office, the group were gathered around the whiteboard.

'What did you find out at the taxi office, Barbara?' asked Stone.

'Nothing that wasn't already on the file.' She looked at her notes. 'The gunmen were Pakistani Pakistanis, not British Pakistanis. No turf wars, no drug connections. He didn't appear to be skimming, or if he was, it wasn't enough to be noticed. Not long after the shooting, the four drivers who were suspects in the CSE investigation moved away. We don't know where because the inquiry was wound up at about that time.'

'Fowler wasn't at all helpful, was he, Iftikhar?' He nodded agreement and she went on. 'He says it's all in the policy book and the case notes—'

'He would, wouldn't he?' interjected Dyer. 'He'd rather a woman failed than the murderer he couldn't detect was caught.'

'I thought that you said you didn't know him,' said Stone.

Dyer shrugged. 'I don't, but I know the type only too bloody well.'

'He does seem to tick all those old boxes of misogyny and racism,' added Ahmed, with a conspiratorial exchange of smiles with Dyer.

'No matter. Fowler thought that it might be domestic. There was no evidence that Rana was screwing around so it doesn't look like an honour killing. He wasn't skimming and we've no drugs connection. All we have is the fact that there was a CSE inquiry going on and that shortly after the murder, it was wound up. Fowler refused to accept that there could be a link with that inquiry, which he also headed. That it was a coincidence. Well, I don't believe in coincidences in murder inquiries. So that's where we're going to look.' She turned to Dyer. 'Barbara, get all the case notes out of the archives. Colin, Iftikhar, start finding out what happened to the suspect drivers. I'll get in touch with this DCI Dryden who headed it. At some point, I'm going to have to talk to our precious Commissioner. Rana was her cousin and now that she's also part of the police family, she may be able to tell us something we don't know.'

Chapter 14

DESPITE THE FACT THAT THEY had made an appointment, Naeem kept Stone and Shepherd waiting for over twenty minutes. Just to show her authority and their place in the food chain, thought Stone. She had thought of bringing Ahmed, get his view on the commissioner, but she didn't know him well enough yet and there was the nightmare scenario where the commissioner spoke to him in Punjabi, excluding her. She was not confident that he would know how to handle that. In the end, she decided to play safe and use Shepherd. They used the time for a final hushed talk through the interview plan and were up for it by the time that they were ushered through by her secretary.

Naeem remained seated behind her desk, going through the ritual that busy people adopt when faced with an unwelcome interruption, continuing to reread and finish off correspondence on the desk in front of them. There were no chairs on their side of the desk, prolonged conversations clearly taking place at the conference table, or on the settees arrayed in the centre of the enormous office. Stone and Shepherd looked at one another, Stone nodded and they quietly walked over to the conference table, easy on the thick carpet, picked up a chair each and returned to the desk. When Naeem looked up, expecting to find the two cops standing, waiting for instructions, she found instead both of them comfortably ensconced on the other side of the table. It was funny, thought Rachel, how people with power were always surprised by the fact that cops took over an interview. Common sense would tell them that whilst they knew nothing about police powers and procedures, and might be questioned by a cop once in a lifetime, cops questioned people for a living. A no-brainer really, but it seemed to happen every time.

'Oh,' Naeem said, 'we could move to the conference table if …'

Get out of that one, thought Rachel, you're caught between the rock of your bad manners and the hard place of your affronted dignity.

'No,' said Rachel, 'we're fine here.'

'This is about Bashir Rana, isn't it? How do you think I can help you.'

Rachel had been going to use the title Commissioner but as an ex-Met officer, it stuck in her craw, so she found herself saying 'ma'am'. 'Yes, ma'am, I think that the Chief Constable has already spoken to you about it.'

'Briefly.'

'You weren't interviewed in the first investigation, were you?'

'No – and to be honest, I'm not sure why I'm being interviewed now.'

Rachel nodded as if in agreement but made no attempt to address the point directly.

'The first investigation couldn't find any substantive motive for the killing. They ruled out all of the more obvious ones, then all the less obvious. That left them with the most common reason for murder.' She paused. 'Some domestic difficulty, usually sex or money. But they had nothing to back that theory up so it went no further.'

'I still don't know what you expect to learn from me.'

'Mr Rana was your cousin.'

Naeem replied with a politician's cold smile. 'Chief Inspector, sometimes I think that half of the people from the Punjab are my cousins.'

'Were you close?'

'We met now and then at family gatherings, you know, weddings, funerals, big birthdays – that sort of thing. But no, we were not close.'

'The thing is ...' Rachel paused. 'The thing is we now want to follow up on two possible lines of inquiry that we don't think were adequately examined by the first investigation. The first is the domestic issues.'

'And how do you think I can help?'

'You'll be aware now, after working with us for three years, that we have some difficulty in making inquiries in the British Pakistani community.'

Another politician's smile, colder this time. 'All you need to do is recruit more of them into the service.'

Stone decided tactically not to mention Ahmed joining the team. Something maybe for another day, and she was already sure from Naeem's attitude that there would be another day.

'That may well be, ma'am. But I'm in CID, not recruiting, so that can't help me now.' She moved forward in her chair and rested her hands on the edge of the desk. 'But you're now part of the police, part of our family too.' She ignored

Naeem's dramatic raising of her eyebrows and ploughed on. 'So I'm asking you in that role if you can cast your mind back to 2006. Were there were any domestic issues that might have been causing problems, disputes about money, business, sex – those are the lines we usually start with.'

'No, there were not.'

'You're certain? It was some time ago and you didn't take much time to think about it.'

'Absolutely certain.'

Rachel sat back in her chair and looked at Shepherd, who picked up the cue.

'There is another way you could help us, Commissioner,' he said.

Naeem turned to him with a guarded smile. 'And how could I do that?'

'As the Chief Inspector says, we have real difficulties in finding out what goes on in British Pakistani families. Could you do some asking for us?' Naeem's jaw dropped but Shepherd plodded on. 'Or put us in touch with someone who is willing to.'

'As I said, Detective …' She paused, clearly struggling to remember his name.

'Detective Constable Shepherd, ma'am.'

'As I said, Detective Constable Shepherd. There were no difficulties in the family that could have led to this killing. I am, as you say, now part of the police "family", so you can take that as authoritative.'

'But you said you weren't close.'

'No, but the murder of Bashir was a major event in the family. We talked of it for months afterwards. There was nothing going on, believe me.'

'And you won't ask…?'

'I will not spy on my family for you.'

'We are not asking you to, Commissioner. This was a brutal murder. All we are asking for is your help.'

'And I am helping. There was nothing going on. Don't waste your time and my budget following this line of inquiry.'

'Mrs Naeem,' Rachel took up the reins again, 'there is another, associated line that we are following up.' Naeem turned to her, stony faced. 'At the time of the murder, the force was carrying out an inquiry into a case of CSE. It involved four drivers from your cousin's firm—'

'Bashir was not a suspect in that inquiry,' Naeem quickly interjected.

'How do you know that?'

'I know that, as you will be well aware, Chief Inspector, because I was the lead for child protection in the county council at the time. As such, I was privy to the conduct of the inquiry.'

'Our problem is that if there is no domestic motive, as you insist, it looks to us like the only other line worthy of further inquiry. As you will also be only too well aware, attitudes to the victims of CSE have changed considerably since 2006.'

'I don't need you to lecture me on that, Chief Inspector. It was my decision to increase the size of Granbyshire Police's Child Protection Unit, and I have personally assisted in ensuring better working protocols with the county council.'

'I'm aware of that, but all the same, we think that it's a line of inquiry worth pursuing.'

Naeem smiled ruefully and shook her head. 'I think that you are wasting your time, and, if you'll forgive me, I do not want you to waste any more of mine.' She picked up her pen and took some papers out of her in-tray. 'We both know why you want to re-open the CSE inquiry, Chief Inspector, don't we? You're hoping for some sort of revenge for me calling for you to be sacked after the mess you made handling the murder cases of those two poor little girls – well, I can tell you that the CSE inquiry was carried out by a very competent detective who was much, much more experienced than you – and he found nothing wrong.'

Rachel signalled Shepherd and both stood up, returned their chairs to their places at the conference table and walked towards the door.

'That may be so, Mrs Naeem. But then again, he didn't find your cousin's killer, either, did he? Thank you for your time.'

As they walked towards the door she heard Naeem say, 'Chief Inspector?'

Stone turned to face her, finding her now standing behind the desk. 'I will be asking for reports on the progress of your inquiry. If it looks to me as if your approach is anything less than professional, I will intervene.'

'If that's the test, ma'am, I've nothing to worry about.'

Chapter 15

THE TEAM WAS GATHERED BY the briefing board at the end of the portacabin, coffees to hand.

'Today,' Stone began, 'we go to work on the CSE part of this case. A quick recap so that you know where I'm coming from on this. In April 2006, a fourteen-year-old girl in care, Brittany Selby, had a good go at killing herself. She slashed her wrists in the bath. The only reason she didn't succeed was because she had left the taps running and passed out. The bath overflowed, alerting the staff in the care home, who got her to the hospital just in time to save her life. It was her second attempt in six months. This sparked off a major case review which revealed that she and two other girls, Kelly Brooks and Liz Ryder, now Libby Grainger, both a bit older than Brittany, were engaged in what was described at the time as child prostitution. It appeared to have been going on for about eighteen months.'

'How could they be prostitutes?' asked Ahmed. 'They were under sixteen, they couldn't legally give consent.'

'When did you join?' this from Shepherd.

'2013, but what's that got to do with it?'

'You'll find over the next thirty years that attitudes change to lots of things, just as they have in the last thirty. Look at how we deal now with porn, domestic violence ...'

'Usually where women are the victims,' Dyer chipped in.

'Not always – attacks on gay men for instance.' He waved his arms. 'Look, I'm even saying gay men for God's sake.'

'Enough,' said Stone. 'This is a bloody briefing, not a social history class.' She looked down again at her notes. 'The girls had a common history of running away and then being recovered two to three days later, often clearly suffering from the effects of drink and/or drugs. They refused to say where they'd been or who they'd been with. The most they would say was that they had been with friends or their "boyfriends". After Brittany's second attempted suicide, they were questioned much more aggressively and persistently, this time by police and not social workers. You've all read Kelly Brooks' and Brittany's statements. It's clear now that they had been very efficiently groomed and then trafficked. Liz Ryder refused to cooperate throughout the inquiry. We need to follow up on that.'

'Can't really blame her when no-one believed them,' said Ahmed.

'That's not quite right, Iftikhar. The investigators may have believed them, they just didn't think that a jury would. At first, they had denied that anything had happened and only reluctantly told the truth. They went from nothing to nuclear. From denying that anything had happened, to describing gangbanging, spit roasting, orgies. And nobody seemed to recognize how they had been manipulated, not the girls themselves, not the cops, not the CPS and definitely not the social workers. Everybody focused on their lack of credibility and the fact that they were "out of control" and had made "lifestyle choices".'

'At fourteen?' said Ahmed.

'Thirteen in Brittany's case,' said Dyer.

A sombre silence fell on the group, then Stone picked them up again.

'Awful I know, but we've got the chance now to revisit that decision, maybe give the women, for that's what they are now, some degree of justice, closure.'

'Do you think that the CSE and the murder were connected?' asked Shepherd.

'Well, the CSE inquiry began about three months before the murder and all of the named suspects worked for the taxi firm. And they all disappeared into the wind within weeks of the murder. That could be a coincidence. But as I said, I don't believe in coincidences in murder inquiries. And it's the only line of inquiry we've got until the DNA comes back.' She turned to Dyer. 'Barbara, tell us about the girls.'

'There were three in the inquiry; Libby Grainger, the oldest of the three and we think the first to be groomed, when she was fourteen. Then Kelly Brooks, also fourteen, probably recruited by Grainger; finally, Brittany Selby, only thirteen when she started going missing. Brittany committed suicide about eighteen months after the case was closed. Same method as the attempt, but this time she remembered to turn the taps off. I contacted both Brooks and Grainger. Grainger was always going to be hard work. She wouldn't make a statement to the original inquiry, always insisted that she was with a boyfriend and that there was nothing going on. The other two insisted that she was with them on the game, but she stayed schtum. She is now Libby Grainger, seems to have turned her life right round. She moved to Birmingham, became a teaching assistant and she's now married to a deputy head. That's the good news – the bad news is that she gave me a flea in my ear and told me that she still has no intention of cooperating with any police inquiry.'

'That's a bugger, why wouldn't she cooperate?' asked Stone.

'They've got her down as a "stroppy cow" who wouldn't answer any questions.'

'And Brooks?'

'The good news is that she's still living in Granby and is willing to cooperate with us.'

'And the bad?' asked Stone.

'She hasn't worked since leaving school. She now has two kids by two different, and very indifferent, fathers. She's living on benefits in social housing in The Carleton, and we all know what everyone thinks of anyone who lives on that estate. She's not going to be a great witness.'

'Is it worth my while trying to talk to Ryder?'

'You could try, boss, the rank might work. But she seemed pretty adamant to me.'

'OK. I'll try. Meanwhile set up a meeting for us with Brooks for this afternoon. You two can keep following up on the drivers.'

Rachel went back into her office and dialed the number that Dyer had given her.

'Hello, am I speaking to Libby Grainger?'

'Yes.'

'Good morning, Mrs Grainger, I'm Detective Chief Inspector Rachel Stone. I believe my colleague, DS Dyer, has already spoken to you. We're following up on the case you were involved in back in 2006.'

'I told your colleague I wanted nothing to do with any police inquiry.'

'I know but I was hoping you would give me the chance to persuade you otherwise.'

There was a long pause and just when Rachel was about to break the silence, Grainger spoke.

'Chief Inspector, I've made a new life for myself. I have absolutely no intention of allowing what may or may not have happened to me nearly a decade ago define what happens to me for the rest of my life.'

'But I—'

'Goodbye, Chief Inspector.'

She heard the click of the cut-off, then a dialing tone. Not a great outcome, she thought. She was still noting the conversation in the case notes when Dyer came back through.

'There's a Thomas Wyatt on the line, Grainger's solicitor. Take care, ma'am, they're very anti-police.'

Stone nodded and picked up the phone. 'DCI Stone, how can I help you, Mr Wyatt?'

'I'll make this very brief, Chief Inspector. I've just had a very upset client on the phone. Mrs Grainger has told you she does not want to be involved in this rehash of an investigation. That is her right.'

'Yes, but—'

'I'm not here to discuss it or negotiate it in any way. Please do not contact her directly again. Any contact must be through me. If she is contacted by you, or any of your team, or anyone from the Granbyshire Police, I will treat it as harassment and act accordingly on her behalf. Am I clear on that?'

'Crystal clear, Mr Wyatt. May I ask why she does not want to cooperate?'

'You may not. The police forfeited that right in 2006. Good day, Chief Inspector.'

Another dialing tone. A great start to the inquiry, she thought. One dead, one as good as, and one who probably wished she was.

Chapter 16

LEAVING THE TWO MEN TO trace the taxi drivers and follow up on the getaway driver, Stone and Dyer made their way to see the only victim willing and able to talk to them, Kelly Brooks. She lived in Carleton Meadows otherwise known as The Carleton, a council estate well past its best, built when owning a car was a dream as likely as winning the pools. Now, its narrow streets were an unofficial one-way nightmare, with every verge and spare space taken up with parked cars, many of which did not look as if they had moved in a long time. The gardens were default open plan, any fences that had been there having been knocked down or rotted away long ago. On the edge of the estate stood three high-rise blocks, now only half-full, waiting till the council could summon up the courage and the money to knock them down. A previous chief constable had said that he could halve the crime rate in Granbyshire if he could drop eighty families from The Carleton into the North Sea.

They parked close enough to Kelly's address to be able to keep the car in sight from the windows of the house. As they walked up the broken path, Stone noted that although there were no plants other than some scrawny grass, there was no rubbish either, no broken pram, no rusted bicycle frames. Kelly clearly had some standards. They were a couple of metres away from the door on the side of the house when it opened and Dave Bates stepped out.

'Shit,' said Stone.

'What's the problem?' asked Dyer.

'That's the reporter who tried to doorstep me.'

'The flower shower.' Dyer smiled. 'A good story always gets around.'

'The same.'

Bates had half turned away from them, still talking to someone inside the house. He didn't notice them until they were right up on him.

'Mr Bates,' said Stone, 'what are you doing with my witness?'

He stepped back, creating a space between them.

'Helping her to get the justice you failed to give her first time around, Chief Inspector. You lot had your chance back in 2006 and blew it. I'm helping Kelly to get her case across, get the justice and compensation she deserves.'

He finished with a knowing grin to Kelly, whose bulk now filled the doorway. Stone eyeballed him, saying nothing in reply, partly because of the truth of what he had said and partly to ensure that she kept Kelly onside. To do that, she needed to find out what 'compensation' Bates was talking about. The last thing she needed was her only witness to be compromised by a bit of cheap cheque-book journalism.

'I'll be in touch soon, Kelly,' said Bates, stepping round the two police officers. 'Don't believe anything this lot tell you about me. You know now who believes you and who doesn't.'

With a wave, he walked off down the path. Stone waited till he started to get into his car before turning to face Kelly. She was a big girl in every sense, completely filling the doorway. The step up also meant that she towered over the two policewomen.

'We need to talk to you, Kelly,' said Stone. Getting no reply, she added, 'Inside would be better. It may take a bit of time.'

Kelly turned and walked down the hallway, speaking over her shoulder to the two women.

'Well, you'd better get a move on. Me mam is looking after the kids but she's bringing them back in half an hour.'

'Couldn't you phone her and make that a bit longer?' asked Stone.

'No, she's doing an afternoon shift in Asda. She only agreed to do it in the first place because she is hoping for some money out of it from the papers.'

They followed her down the hall to a small, neat living room. Two storage boxes, piled high with toys filled one corner and a large flat screen TV another. It was on but thankfully muted. Kelly sat on the armchair facing the TV, leaving the two policewomen the only remaining seat, a small sofa. There were two empty mugs on the small coffee table between the TV and the armchair. Bates had clearly been made at home.

'What did Bates want?' asked Stone.

'Bates? Oh you mean Dave. He said he wanted to give me the chance to give my side of the story this time.'

'How did he know we were reopening the case?'

She didn't answer immediately and Stone knew that she had to take care as to how she took this next bit forward. Threats would be counter-productive. Just as she was about to move it up a gear, Kelly spoke.

'Me mam told him. When I told her you were coming, she said that this time we should get something out of it. Got his name from one of her mates.'

'And has he promised you that you would get some money out of it?'

'He says we will – says he can sell it to one of the nationals.'

'You need to be careful dealing with people like that, Kelly. He's only got his own interests in mind.'

'He said you'd say that. But he's bringing me a contract, all proper and above board.'

'When he does, be sure to read it. Better still, get a solicitor to read it before you sign anything.'

'A solicitor? How the fuck do I afford a solicitor?'

'Well, try Citizen's Advice, anything, but get somebody else to read it before you sign it.'

'Right,' said Kelly, crossing her arms and settling back into the armchair.

There didn't seem to be anything else to say on this and Stone knew that it was going to be hard to move forward from such a shaky start – bloody Bates. She was still thinking of how to go forward when Dyer spoke.

'How do you feel about it, Kelly, about opening it all up again?'

Well done, thought Stone, the good cop.

'Depends, don't it?'

'Depends on what?'

'On whether you lot believe me this time. No point in going over it all again if you don't believe me, if you're not going to do anything about it, is there?'

'We do believe you,' said Stone. 'We've read your statement. Times have changed. The service has moved on since back then. You must have read about other cases in the papers. And neither DS Dyer nor I had anything to do with the original investigation. We believe you were telling the truth.'

Kelly looked at them long and hard, arms still crossed, defences still up.

'Won't make any difference anyway.'

'What do you mean?'

'It were years ago and all the blokes I could identify, the one whose names I know, they've all left Granby, haven't they? Gone back to bloody Pakistan, I bet. And the guy who ran it all, he got shot, didn't he?'

'You mean Bashir Rana?'

'Aye. As soon as that happened, you lot lost all interest in us. Told us that we had changed our minds too many times. That no one would believe what we said.'

Stone and Dyer exchanged puzzled looks.

'So, was Rana one of the men who had sex with you?' said Stone.

'Aye, lots of times. He preferred Brittany and Liz but he did it lots of times, so did the white bloke he brought.'

Another exchange of looks. Stone was sure that there had been no mention of either Rana or any white man in Kelly's statement. Dyer's shared puzzlement confirmed her belief.

Chapter 17

'WHITE BLOKE? WHAT WHITE BLOKE?'

'There was only the one, all the rest were Pakis. I don't know what he looked like 'cause he always wore a mask, one of them ski-mask things. He were the only one who did that.'

'Can you tell us anything else about him?' asked Stone.

'His voice, it were local. And he had soft hands.'

'You're sure about all this, Kelly?'

Kelly angrily uncrossed her arms and opened them in supplication. 'See, there you go again. Not believing me. This is a bloody waste of time.'

She started to heave herself out of the armchair but Stone waved her back into the seat saying, 'No, wait a minute, let me explain. OK?'

Kelly harrumphed but sat back in the chair.

'The reason I asked if you were sure is that you don't mention either Rana or this white man in your statement. I've read it, more than once. Neither you nor Brittany do.'

'But I did. I told that detective, the really good-looking one …'

'DS Mark Dryden?' Dyer chipped in.

'That's right, Mark. I told him and he wrote it all down.'

'Then you signed it?'

'Not right away. He took it away and got it all typed up then brought it back and I signed it.'

'Did you read it again first?'

Kelly's hesitation was enough to tell Stone that she had not re-read the statement but had taken it on faith from the 'very good-looking' detective. Why shouldn't she? He was a cop, he was taking an interest in her. Before

81

Kelly could reply, Stone said, 'You didn't do anything wrong if you didn't read it, Kelly. But it's really important that you tell us exactly what happened so that we can get it right this time. You see, we're not just reopening your case, we're also reopening Bashir Rana's murder. We think that they might be linked.'

'Truth is I couldn't read very well then, always bunking off school, wasn't I? I'm better now, took lessons when my eldest was born. Thought I'd better. But not then. He told me that everything I had said was in the statement so I signed the bottom of all the pages.'

She reached down the side of the armchair, picked up the handbag that was lying there and pulled out a pack of cigarettes and a lighter. Stone could see that her hands were shaking, not much, but perceptible – the first indication she'd given that this revisiting of her past was not as easy as she made it out to be on the surface. Stone only just managed to stop herself asking for one of the cigarettes, the excuse that a shared smoke would help to take the interview forward was almost enough to break her resolve. Why did everyone she interviewed these days smoke?

'That's a laugh, isn't it?' Kelly said shakily, drawing deeply on the cigarette. 'I told the truth and no one believed me. He lied and everyone believed him, even me.'

She was crying now, no sobs, just tears running down her cheeks. She wiped them away with the heel of her hand. Dyer got a packet of tissues from her bag and gave it to her. She struggled to open the little tab and Dyer gently took it back, opened the tab, passed her a couple of tissues, then stood up, picking up the mugs.

'I'll make us all some tea,' she said.

Kelly started to get up from her chair but Dyer waved her back. 'It's all right, Kelly. I can manage. You sit there and talk to the chief inspector. Milk and sugar?'

'Yes, two sugars.'

With that, Dyer disappeared into the kitchen. Stone waited until Kelly had composed herself again.

'I do believe you, Kelly. It's important that you know that. That you believe me.'

Kelly nodded, snuffling into the now soggy tissues. Stone pulled another couple from the packet that Dyer had left on the coffee table and passed them to her.

'I'll have to take a proper statement from you again but can you tell me a bit more about Rana and the white man now?'

Another nod.

'Where did they do it?'

'Bashir had a little flat, above a shop, in White Street. It wasn't very clean but it had a bed and a sofa and a little kitchen bit.'

'And he took you there?'

'Yes. He'd meet me with his car down the street from the home.' She blew her nose, wiped her face clean of tears and took another deep drag on the cigarette. Her composure was returning now. 'Bashir was all right really, always gave me a bit of money. And he weren't rough like some of them. Not rough at all really. And it was usually just him. Except when the white bloke came.'

'How many times did that happen?'

'Four or five times with me. I think he preferred Liz, she was prettier.' She gave a grim smile. 'And she had bigger tits.'

'I know you didn't see his face but what impression did he leave?'

'He was a big fella, you know, big built – not fat.' A bitter laugh. 'He was strong but had soft hands.'

There was a brief interruption when Dyer brought three mugs in from the kitchen and placed two of them on the coffee table, one in front of Stone and the other in front of Kelly. She sat beside Stone who continued. 'How were the meetings with the white guy organized?'

Kelly took time to think about this, taking herself back. 'Just like the ones with Bashir. I'd phone him and he'd pick me up near the home and take me to the flat. We'd have a drink, usually something with vodka in it.' She said nothing for a few moments then continued. 'Of course, I know now that his were all orange juice or whatever and mine were nearly all vodka.' She laughed. 'Wish someone would do the same for me now. Anyway, the first time he told me that he needed a favour from me. That someone he needed to keep happy was coming, and that he would be wearing a mask, but that I shouldn't let that worry me. Made it a bit of a game.'

'And what did he do with you?'

'He always did it the same.' She paused. 'He always did it over the back of the sofa, you know, with me bending over. And he had these big hands, but soft, not hard like a labourer or that.'

As Kelly described the sex, Stone could feel Dyer stiffening in her posture on the sofa beside her.

'Always the same way?' Stone asked.

'Yes, first he'd get me to give him a blowjob to get him hard, he'd fuck me normally like, then he'd fuck me up the arse, that seemed to be the only way he could come.'

As Kelly was describing this, Stone could see from the corner of her eye Dyer putting her mug on the coffee table, her hand shaking.

'What about his voice?' Dyer asked; her voice now had a noticeable tremble.

'He didn't say much, enough to know he was from up here. But every time when he was finishing in my arse, he'd say, "and now one for his nob" – and he'd laugh. Every time.'

Dyer sprung to her feet with her hand over her mouth and ran out of the room. Stone could hear the clatter up the stairs then the bathroom door slamming shut. The two women looked at one another, as if the other could explain why Dyer had reacted so violently.

'Back in a minute,' Stone said to Kelly, getting up and following Dyer upstairs.

Outside the bathroom door, she could hear Dyer dry-retching. She tried to go in but the door was locked.

'Barbara, are you all right?'

No reply.

'Unlock the door and let me in – Barbara!'

'Give me a minute. I'm all right.'

She heard the door being unlocked and it opened to reveal a grey-faced Dyer, her hands shaking as she used some toilet paper to wipe her mouth.

'There,' Dyer said, turning to throw the paper into the bowl and flushing it, 'much better.' She turned back to Stone. 'Sorry about that. It must have been something I ate.'

'Funny time of the bloody day to be reacting to something you ate, lady. You're sure you're all right? Nothing you want to talk to me about?'

Dyer forced a laugh. 'Well, I'm not pregnant unless it's a virgin birth. It's nothing. I'm fine now.' She looked down at her hands and could see that they were still trembling. 'I'm just a bit shaken up with all that bloody spewing.' She looked at Stone and gave a worn smile, some colour returning to her face. 'I'm fine, really. Poor Kelly, we should get back to her.'

'No, I'll do that. I've only got a couple more questions for her. You go and get some fresh air and wait for me in the car.' Dyer started to protest but Stone cut across her. 'I mean it, Barbara. Wait for me in the car.'

Dyer nodded and made her way back downstairs holding onto the banister, then went out through the side door. Stone returned to the living room.

'Is she all right?' asked Kelly.

'Yes. Something she ate, she thinks,' said Stone, sitting down again, facing Kelly. 'I've got a couple of questions more.' She paused to allow Kelly the opportunity to object and then ploughed on. 'You always call Rana 'Bashir'. Did you like him?'

'I thought I did at the time. He was kinder than the rest, gentler, and more generous.'

'Did his murder come as a surprise?'

'Of course. Come on, this is Granby, not exactly the murder capital of England, is it?'

'I mean, can you think of anyone who wanted him dead? Any of the drivers involved with you girls? Anyone trying to muscle in on his territory or on the trafficking that he was doing with you three?'

Kelly shook her head. 'No, it was always OK. I mean, I was wasted a lot of the time so I can't tell you much, but he seemed to get on with everyone.'

'Even the white guy that he had to keep happy?'

'Yeah, I think so.'

'He never mentioned any problems he had, anyone giving him a hard time?'

'No, not that I can remember anyway.'

'I'll leave it at that for the minute.'

She rose to leave. 'Thanks for your help, Kelly. I'll get back to you once we've rounded up all the men who abused you back then. In the meantime, be careful around Bates. No matter what he says, he's only in it for what he can get. I'd hate to see you misused again.'

Kelly heaved herself out of her chair and walked with Stone to the door.

'He's a man, isn't he – all the same. I've never met one who wasn't in it for what he could get from me.'

Chapter 18

'I THOUGHT WE WERE GOING back to HQ.'

'We are, but I want to show you something first,' said Stone.

They had been driving in silence since leaving Kelly Brooks' house. Dyer's face now had some colour, but the dark rings around her eyes left her with a haunted look. Within minutes, they arrived at the car park at Frankton Park. Rachel turned off the ignition and got out of the car. Dyer waited for a few moments, shrugged, then did the same. By the time she had, Rachel was strolling over to the edge of the car park where it looked out over the moor. The winter's day had a sharp edge and the silhouettes of the trees on the distant ridge were etched against the skyline. A curtain of rain was being drawn along its length.

'I couldn't get used to this when I first came here,' said Stone, 'being in the country in a matter of minutes. I'd always lived in London, just south of the river.' She gave a little laugh. 'Clapham Common was my idea of countryside.'

Dyer said nothing, wouldn't meet her eyes, looked out towards the ridge with a thousand-yard stare.

Rachel pointed down to a small copse about 200 metres away.

'In those trees there, that's where my career began to unravel; where it all started tumbling down; where I let Mickey Fleming take me to the second body.'

There was a long silence, more comfortable than either expected.

Dyer turned towards her, pulling her fair hair back from her face. 'Why are you telling me this?'

'I need you to know how powerfully I react to my instincts, even when I know it's going to get me into trouble. I knew that Fleming would tell me, all I had to do was get the context right.' She turned her body to face Dyer. 'So, what happened back there at the house? And don't tell me it was something you ate.'

Dyer said nothing. The problem in questioning cops, thought Stone, is that they know all your tricks. In fact, as junior ranks, they get more practice, so they're usually better at it than you. A prompt was needed.

'Come on, Barbara, what was it? You can tell me and it'll go no further, I promise you that.'

Dyer gave a wry smile. 'It didn't take me long in this job to work out that senior officers' promises were as empty as a beggar's purse. And that the women were no better than the men.' A pause. 'It was something I ate.' She looked Stone directly in the eye. 'And I'll make sure it doesn't happen again. So that makes it my business and no one else's.'

'Maybe, but, you know, I've been a cop a long time now, most of it in the Department. You know what it's like working your way in as a detective, as a woman. You get all the so-called women's work to start with – the rapes, the domestic violence, the child abuse. You have to do a lot of that before you get to do the "proper" detective work.'

Dyer nodded as she spoke.

'So, I may be crap with the men in my life but I do know women. Not just because I am one. I've seen what's been done to them and the effect that it has. That wasn't something you ate back there, Barbara. That wasn't a coincidence. That was a bloody trigger – I've seen that gun fired too often to miss it.'

Dyer turned and began to walk back towards the car. Stone followed and as they walked side by side towards the car, Dyer spoke.

'When we started the squad you said you'd read my file. What does it say?'

'That you were a promising young detective, got promoted quickly to DS then went off sick for five months due to stress. You had some counselling, but that was confidential of course, there's nothing about it in the file. There was no reason given for the stress so it was assumed that you had had difficulty in adjusting to the promotion.' She gave a small smile. 'You are a woman after all and it was men making the judgement.'

By now they had reached the car and were looking at each other across its roof, Stone by the driver's door, Dyer by the passenger's.

'But it wasn't that, was it, Barbara? So, what was it?'

'Have there been any complaints about my work since then?'

'No, but I would have expected you to have got to DI by now, with the start you made.'

Dyer gave a bitter little laugh. 'What, with "can't cope with the stress of being a DS" on my file? Fat chance.'

'What was the reason then? Tell me. You owe it to me – not least if it's getting in the way of this investigation.'

Dyer opened the car door.

'Do you have any complaints about me not being able to do my job?'

'No, but—'

'Then it's my business, and only mine.'

'But if it does get in the way—'

'It won't.'

'Please, Barbara, talk to me about it. I promise it'll go no further.'

Another bitter laugh from Dyer. 'You don't know just how empty I know that promise is. With all due respect, ma'am, I think we're done here.'

With that, she got into the car and closed the door. Stone stood for a few moments, looking at the space across the car roof then followed suit.

Chapter 19

WHEN THEY GOT BACK TO the portacabin at HQ, Stone found Shepherd in conversation with a tall, strikingly handsome man of around forty. The quality of his dark business suit, shoes and haircut made her think immediately of a banker, or a high-pressure salesman of bonds or Bentleys. Dyer went to join the pair, but Ahmed came out from behind his desk and cut Stone off before she could do the same.

'Yes, Iftikhar?'

'I don't want to bother you, boss, but I need your help to get past some twit in West Yorkshire intelligence.'

'What's the problem?'

'You know we're having difficulties chasing up the taxi drivers.' She nodded and he continued. 'Some of them may have gone back to Pakistan. They were all either Pakistanis with the right to reside in the UK or had dual nationalities, and of course, Immigration or is it Border Agency – the names politicians give those poor buggers – don't keep a record of people leaving, only those coming in.'

'Go on.'

'Well, I managed to trace one of them to Rotherham and got hit on their intelligence system but the content is blocked and the DI in charge refused to give me access without speaking to you first.'

'Did he say why?'

'No, only that he needs to speak to you first – even then I'm not sure that he'll give us access.'

She thought about the problem for a few moments. She could understand, if there was an ongoing inquiry, that whoever was investigating it would not want a foreign force coming in, stomping all over potential suspects or witnesses.

'Get back onto the DI, get the name and number of the officer who's in charge and I'll speak to him, cut out the middleman.'

Stone turned to join the trio by Shepherd's desk.

'Boss,' said Shepherd, 'this is DCI Mark Dryden.'

As they shook hands Dryden said, 'I got your message and since I was coming to HQ today to brief the ops team, I thought I would kill two birds.'

'Thanks for coming over, pretty perfect timing actually, we've just been interviewing Kelly Brooks.'

He didn't appear to recognize the name.

'One of the girls in the CSE inquiry back in 2006.'

He thought for a second then said, 'Of course, a big girl if I remember right.'

'If she wasn't then she certainly is now. You know Barbara of course?'

'We go back a long way, practically joined together and sort of dogged each other into and through the Department.'

'Good. How long have you got?'

'As long as it takes. The unit's based in Birmingham so I like to use my time back in force to see as many people as I can.'

'Let's go to my office. Do you mind if Barbara joins us? She's leading on the CSE element.'

'No, no problem.'

Once in the office, they ranged themselves around Stone's desk.

'You know we're reopening the Rana murder,' Stone began. He nodded. 'As part of that, I've decided to reopen your investigation into the CSE that his drivers were involved with—'

'I've got to say,' Dryden interrupted, 'before we go any further, that I was very unhappy with the way that that investigation was handled.'

'In what way?'

He took his time before answering, then sat back against the chair with his arms open, palms up, a mute plea for understanding.

'To start with, the girls were a nightmare to deal with. I mean, we all knew what had been going on but they refused point-blank from the start to cooperate. Always said that they had been with their "boyfriends". Denied the involvement of any other Pakistani guys.'

'But there was other evidence?'

'Bags of it, but all circumstantial. Disappearing for days at a time. Coming back to the home clearly under the influence of drink and/or drugs. Clothes in a state of disarray. But no names. No definite suspects. That was why it was so frustrating.'

'How so?'

'I felt that I was having to investigate with both hands tied behind my back. As I said, the girls were refusing to cooperate, the social workers were clueless, didn't seem to have any influence, had given up on them. No one wanted to prosecute, or even give it a run.'

'No one?'

'Not the children's services, not my governors, not the CPS – in fact, their decision that the girls weren't credible made it impossible for me to get my bosses to take the case seriously.'

'I don't think that Granbyshire was any worse than anywhere else at that time.'

'That's exactly my point. I wanted to try something different.'

'What would have been different?'

He paused to think. 'What we're talking about was rape. These girls were only thirteen or fourteen when it started. They couldn't legally give consent. But everyone was treating them as if they were adults. How can a damaged fourteen-year-old give consent for God's sake?'

'If you felt so strongly about it, why didn't you do something?'

'I tried. I did eventually get the girls, well, two of them anyway, to make a statement describing most of what had been going on. But by then they had denied everything so often that the CPS took the view that they wouldn't be credible in court. It would have been too easy for any defence counsel to completely undermine them and their evidence.'

'I can understand that.'

'Yes, well, I wanted to come at it totally differently. When the girls denied everything, I wanted to put them back in the home and run a surveillance on them, find out what was going on independently. Maybe even catch some of the bastards in the act.'

She had to admit to herself that his earnestness was becoming attractive but …

'Why didn't you?'

'I was told not to. The case conference with the CPS and Children's Services effectively ended my investigation. Then Rana was murdered and the drivers scattered to the wind, so any surveillance would have been a waste of time. I would have had to start all over again.'

'But Rana wasn't a suspect.'

Dryden looked hard at her. 'What do you mean, wasn't a suspect? Of course he was. In fact, if I remember rightly, Kelly was one of the girls he abused and you've spoken to her, you say. She must have mentioned him.'

Stone looked at him long and hard. This was not what she had been expecting him to say. She needed a quick change of game. Ensure that she was playing him and not the other way around.

'You're right. She did.' Stone opened the file in front of her at Kelly's statement. 'This is her statement. So why isn't he in here?' she said, tapping the papers with her index finger.

Dryden gave her a puzzled look. 'But he is. I took her statement. He was one of the names she could give. And he was the one who organized most of the trafficking. Took the girls to an address in Birmingham if I remember rightly.'

'Not according to the statements in this case file. She was taken to Birmingham more than once, but not by Rana.'

She passed the file across the desk to Dryden who picked it up and quickly read through Kelly's statement. When he finished, he looked up at Stone.

'There must be some mistake. This,' he stabbed a finger at the papers, 'this is not the statement that I took. There's nothing at all in here about Rana, or the white guy.'

'The white guy?'

'Yeah. I remember him clearly because he was the only white man involved. All the rest were British Pakistani. Made him stand out. That and the fact that he was always wearing a mask so that they couldn't identify him. At the time, I thought he had to be a local politician, someone whose face was regularly in the local press.'

'But you never ID-d him?'

'Never got the chance. They held the case review and it was decided that it wasn't worth attempting to prosecute. Then Rana was murdered.'

'Were you part of the review?'

'No. I was too far down the food chain. I think...' He paused. 'No, I'm sure that Frank Fowler did it – him, the head of Children's Services and the local head of CPS.'

Stone moved the file to her side of the desk. 'Who do you think changed the statements?'

'God only knows. It would depend on when they were changed. It must have been after I had submitted the case papers. When the decision was made not to proceed, they would be in the system; so it could be anyone who had access to the files. That really means any detective and most of the civilians who work in CID. Go in for one reason and then take them out. There's not much of a check, is there, from memory? The system is fairly open, it relies on trust, especially out of office hours. And if it was after they were archived, it's even worse. They've always been a mess, not enough space, too many unchecked movements.'

Stone knew only too well how right he was. It had taken hours of work for them to find the case files, and even then, only a photocopied version. The original signed statements had disappeared, as had the digital copies. So there was no way of finding out when they had been changed. This case went from bad to worse by the second. She had started with a murder, that had gone on to include a historic CSE investigation, and now she was into a conspiracy to pervert the course of justice and some sort of cover-up. She was still thinking about how to go forward, what role Dryden might have played in it all, when he cut across her thoughts.

'Look, Rachel, I can see only too clearly the difficulty you have in going any further on this with me. I think that the best way forward may be for you to check it all out with Jill MacLean.' He saw the questioning look on her face. 'The DC who worked with me on the case. She was with me in all the interviews, helped put the final report together. She retired shortly after the case and moved to some island in Scotland. Talk to her first.'

He got up and moved towards the door. 'I'd like to help if I can. Talk to Jill then come back to me. Anyway, I'll probably see you both at Phil Mason's retirement do tonight. I think half the force will be there, certainly most of CID past and present.'

'I don't think so. I hadn't planned to be there and you're right, there'll be a lot of people there so I won't be missed.'

'Well, you will be now – by me. Let me buy you,' he included Dyer with a turn of his head, 'buy you both a drink.'

After he had gone, Stone turned to Dyer.

'Let's see what we've got here, Barbara. We've got a murder, a CSE and now a conspiracy to pervert the course of justice.'

She started to enumerate them using her fingers for emphasis.

Index finger. 'We know that Rana's murder was done professionally by two Pakistani nationals, but we still haven't got an obvious motive.' Middle finger. 'We now know for a fact that the drivers working for Rana's firm isn't a coincidence. He was the organizer.' Ring finger. 'Someone has had access to the case papers and has edited both Rana and this mysterious white man out of them.' Little finger. 'The white man is local and must be the key. So we need to split the inquiry. Colin and Iftikhar will follow up on the drivers. We should have access to at least one of them very soon. I'll see if I can hurry that up. I want you to follow up on the CSE, find out who's had access to the case papers.'

'Shouldn't that be done by Professional Standards?'

'We don't know that it was done by a cop – at least not yet.'

'But shouldn't the Deputy Chief decide that, decide who investigates that element at least?'

'I've considered that but he was ACC here at the time, he may have been involved in the case, so might Bob Jackson.'

'I'm really uneasy about this, boss. Someone in ACPO needs to know, needs to decide.'

Stone looked across the desk at Dyer, knowing that she was right. But who could she trust? She decided.

'The Chief's going to be at Phil Mason's do tonight. I'll grab him there, arrange to see him. Are you happy with that?'

'That'll work. He's only been here a couple of years, he's got no connection.'

'I don't want you to speak to anyone about this for the minute, Barbara. Not even Colin and Iftikhar. No one. Agreed?'

Dyer nodded.

'Good. Now all I've got to do is find a way to talk to the chief in private.'

Chapter 20

A FEW MINUTES LATER, AHMED CAME into her office with the name of the detective in charge in West Yorks, a DCI Glass, who answered as soon as Stone called, obviously having been alerted by the DI in intelligence.

'DCI Glass, I'm DCI Rachel Stone from Granbyshire. I'm trying to make inquiries on a nominal in your system but we've been blocked. My understanding is that he's subject to an ongoing inquiry.'

'Yes, Basra Chaudhry. Our intelligence people have told me about your inquiry. How can I help you?'

'I'm reopening an inquiry that was first done here in 2006. Chaudhry was a suspect and I need to know where he is now and what he's doing.'

'Can you tell me first what the inquiry was about?'

'I'll be very disappointed and annoyed if it isn't already on your system, but for the sake of brevity, it was an inquiry into CSE concerning a British Pakistani taxi firm and abuse of local white girls in care.'

There was a long pause on the other end of the line.

'Look, before we go on, Ms Stone, I need to know that you're not going to do anything that will put my case back, you know, like come over here without telling me and arresting Chaudhry just when we're going to move on him.'

'I can understand that but we're still at the point of information gathering, we're a long way from arresting anyone. This is a historic case. It'll take us weeks, more like months before we'll be in a position to do anything. I've got to find the other three suspects for starters. I won't do anything about Chaudhry without consulting you first.'

'Including interviewing him?'

'That as well. Now, where is he and what's he up to?'

There was another long pause on the other end of the line, but this time Stone was reassured by the sound of papers being rifled through. Eventually Glass came back on the line.

'He's working for a taxi firm here in Rotherham. It looks like he came here from Granby and got back into his bad habits almost straightaway. We're building a case against him and ten others, some historic and some relatively current offences, so you can imagine the size of the investigation. We'll probably be making arrests in the next few days. I want to lift them all in one swoop to maximize the chances of turning some of the minor players into prosecution witnesses.'

'I can see that. I can't see that we'll want to talk to him until after you've arrested and processed him. When we do I'll make sure you're involved. You never know, the extra pressure might make him roll over, TICs are always better than convictions when the judge is considering sentence.'

'You'd do that?'

'Processing him would be a lot of work for us and I'm primarily interested in what he knows about the murder of the guy who ran the taxi firm here, Bashir Rana. The CSE inquiry is a means to an end for me. And anyway, I don't have the manpower to do a full-blown historic CSE inquiry.'

'OK, you've got a deal. I'll pass through all we've got on him and call you when we make the arrests.'

Stone hung up the phone and walked into the main office, punching the air.

'First giant leap forward, gang. West Yorks are going to arrest Chaudhry in the next few days and they'll give us access to him as soon as they've processed him. I think that there'll be a good chance that we can cut a deal with the bastard if he has anything on the Rana murder.'

Stone was tidying her desk, ready to leave when her door opened and Dyer stuck her head in.

'I've managed to talk to Jill MacLean on the phone. She's living on the island of Harris.'

'No chance of seeing her face to face then?'

'Be easier if she lived in bloody Timbuktu. I talked her through the case. She confirms everything that Mark Dryden said. Remembers the white guy and that Bashir Rana was ID-d by at least one of the girls.'

'Did she have any thoughts on who would have wanted to make the changes?'

'No, but she did confirm that Dryden wanted to set up a surveillance. That he was unhappy with leaving it at a lifestyle choice by the girls. Even did a bit on his own time. But it was blown out by the case conference, then there was the murder and everyone seemed to lose interest.'

'That seems to put Mark Dryden in the clear.'

'It certainly goes a long way towards doing that.'

'What's the score on him, Barbara? He looks too good to be true.'

'I haven't had a lot of contact since working as DCs together, but what you see seems to be what you get. Good-looking bloke, ambitious as get out. Never been married.' Dyer caught Stone's look and laughed. 'No, I'm sure he's straight.'

'I was thinking that when I go to the do tonight, as well as grabbing the Chief, I might take the chance to touch base with a few people.'

'Of course,' said Dyer, smiling, 'base touching is always a good idea. See you in the morning, boss.'

Chapter 21

POLICE RETIREMENT PARTIES DIVIDE INTO four basic elements. Firstly, there is a drink at the bar on the retiring officer; then there are the speeches and presentations by a senior officer and one or two 'best friends in the job'; then there is a finger buffet and the senior officers leave. Finally, comes the serious boozing and exchanging of war stories that don't need to be censored for political correctness and/or the threat of prosecution. Phil Mason had been a long-time detective, been in the Department since his third year in the job, spending it in equal thirds as detective, detective sergeant and finally detective inspector. He was acknowledged as the best office manager in murder inquiries in the force and as a result knew, and was known by, every detective, old and young, junior and senior. He had watched a number of now very senior officers cut their teeth in the job. Like a lot of cops, he was a born storyteller. The fact that he had the black on so many people and knew which stories could be told, when, and to whom, made a lot of people happy to be in his company. Stone knew that the event would be packed out and her arrival and departure were unlikely to be noticed. When she arrived, the Chief Constable was on the platform with Phil Mason, finishing his piece.

'I've only known Phil for a relatively short time and I think it is only right that those who have known him longer get their chance to reflect on his long and interesting career. So, I'm just going to wish Phil a long and happy retirement on behalf of the force and leave the stage to those who have known him all his career to get their revenge – I mean, sing his praises.'

He got the expected senior officers' laugh here and stepped down from the stage. There was the usual hiatus as the chief left and two of Phil Mason's mates joined him. Rachel had positioned herself close to the edge of the stage.

She took the opportunity that this gave her to grab the Chief's attention as he walked past.

'Sir, could I have a few words? It's very important,' she added in response to his raised eyebrows.

'Can't you arrange it through my PA?' he said.

'It's very sensitive. It concerns the reputation of the force. And I need to tell you without anyone else knowing what the subject is. Then you can tell me what you want done.'

He thought for a few moments. 'Tomorrow morning, 7.45 in my office. My praetorian guard doesn't get there until 8.30, so we'll be private. If anyone asks what you want to talk to me about, it's about going back to the Met.'

'That would be great, sir. Seven forty-five tomorrow.'

He walked away to join the other senior officers standing immediately in front of the stage. As her eyes followed him, she saw that Mark Dryden had noticed the exchange. He smiled and waved his glass in greeting.

As the presentations ended, the laws of group gravity began to apply to the mass of people in the room and they gathered naturally and spontaneously into their social groups of senior officers, serving and retired officers. Stone spotted Dryden in the middle of a serious conversation with Fowler, on the edge of a group of retirees. Within a few moments he saw her, acknowledged her again with a wave of his glass, had a few final words with Fowler then made his way through the throng towards her.

'I thought you weren't coming.'

'I just wanted to show my face. I've got enough problems at the minute without being labelled as the moody cow from the Met.'

'True, cops are quick to rush to judgement.'

Now that the discipline of silence during the speeches had been removed, the noise in the low-ceilinged room was making any kind of normal conversation very difficult. They were having to lean into each other's ears as they spoke. She could feel the heat of his face and the faint smell of his Paco Rabane after-shave, their own little island of intimacy. He clinked his glass on hers.

'We're both empty, would you like a refill?'

They both looked towards the crowd at the bar which was now three or four deep with the people released from the speeches and tasked with refuelling their groups.

'Not this side of Christmas,' she said.

'Look,' he said, 'we've both been seen to be here and I've spoken to everyone

I need to or want to. I've been on the go all day and would love something good to eat, not this buffet crap. And I'd like to do it sitting down. There's a really good Italian place about ten minutes' walk from here. Do you fancy joining me?'

She thought about it briefly. As far as the Chief was concerned, she was now mission accomplished. She had only intended a flying visit in any case. There was his little *téte-à-téte* with Fowler – and he was a very attractive man.

'I'd like that. I know the place.'

'We both know how people talk so it's probably better that we make our way there separately. I'll leave first and get us a table. See you there in fifteen minutes.'

With that, he broke away and went to say his goodbyes to a couple of other exiles from the regional squad.

Chapter 22

'So,' said Dryden, sitting back from the table, the remnants of the lasagne and salad lying between them. 'What's next for you?'

They were well into their second bottle of Chianti. Most of the first had disappeared while they were deciding what to eat and waiting for the meal to appear. Stone had that mellow glow which comes from good food, enough wine and enjoyable company. And Mark Dryden was enjoyable company. Good-looking and charming in its very best sense, that mix of dry humour, self-deprecation and active listening that she seemed to come across very rarely.

'Back to the Met, if they'll have me after this fracas on Fleming. It would help if I could get a result on this cold case.'

'You think you will? Frank Fowler couldn't do it and he's a bit of a legend in Granbyshire.'

'Do you know him well? I saw you talking to him at the do.'

'Not really. I had only just been promoted to DCI when he retired.'

'So, just checking out what retirement feels like?'

'Not even that. I don't think Frank finds much fun in retirement. Always feels the need to know what is going on, and we're going through big changes now with all these joint force squads working at regional level. He did a bit of time in the old Regional Crime Squads and keeps telling everyone that we are doing the usual re-invention thing. And he's much worse when he comes to anything here at headquarters. I think it's because he has to give up his fags for too long. Can't do without them and hates going out in the cold. A bad mixture.'

'I know what you mean. I interviewed him at his house. I didn't think you could build up that much smoke in a room on your own. And that's from a hoping-to-be-ex-smoker.'

'You don't seem to be too bothered this evening by not being able to.'

'I'm trying to give it up – I had been using one of these e-cigs as a prop when I was desperate but I'm now going cold turkey. But that aside, interviewing him was no fun, he is a truly miserable old git who thoroughly deserves his equally miserable wife.'

'I don't know about her, but he always was a miserable bugger, even at the best of times, and he would hate having his work questioned by anyone. In spades if it was by a woman.'

'A bit of a misogynist?'

'Certainly a believer that a woman's place is on her back or in the kitchen. But a good detective nonetheless.'

'So everyone has been at pains to tell me,' she said with a laugh.

'Well,' he said, smiling, 'you are from the Met after all. Not a force with a great reputation for respecting their country cousins.'

'That's a bit of an old stereotype, surely?'

'Every stereotype has some basis in fact. And you are keen to leave us and get back there, aren't you?'

'Touché,' she said. 'But it's a lot more complex than that, than just wanting to go back to London.'

There was a brief silence. Him waiting for her to explain the complexity; she unwilling to go further, in fact already regretting showing a chink in her armour; blaming the wine and the ambience. She would need to be careful around this guy as he would be through her armour and into her knickers before she knew it. It was time to make a move, on or out. She looked at her watch.

'Time to go, I think.'

'I'll get the bill.'

'No, Mark, we'll both get the bill.' To his questioning look she added, 'I mean it, Mark, I came here as a colleague.'

He shrugged and signalled the waiter for the bill.

They stood on the pavement outside the restaurant.

'I live ten minutes' walk that way,' Stone said, pointing down the road away from headquarters.

'I'll walk you home.'

'I'm a big girl, Mark. I don't need an escort.' She held out her hand. 'It's been a really enjoyable evening, thank you.'

He took her proffered hand, then stepped forward and kissed her cheek.

'I'm back in a couple of days' time. It would be great to do it again,' he smiled, 'as friends rather than colleagues.'

'I think I'd like that.' With that she stepped towards him and kissed him briefly on the lips.

'You know where to find me.'

She walked off, confident that she didn't need to turn and check that he was looking after her. Definitely not as colleagues was a thought that she kept in her mind during the walk home.

Chapter 23

'THAT'S THE ONLY PROBLEM STARTING before the team gets here, I've got to make my own coffee.'

Stone and Chief Constable David Hill were standing in the little kitchen area which lay off the secretarial office, waiting for the kettle to boil. She had offered to make the coffee but he had insisted that he would do it quicker and make it exactly to his taste. Once made, she agreed. One sip of his morning caffeine hit nearly stripped the enamel from her teeth. They made their way into his office, sitting at one end of the conference table.

'So, DCI Stone, what more bad news have you got for me?'

'When I did the initial review of the Rana murder, there appeared to be three possible lines of inquiry. That it was a domestic, concerning the family in some way. The powerful indicator for this was the fact that the hitmen, and that's undoubtedly what they were, were Pakistani, not British Pakistani, so probably imported for the job and immediately returning to Pakistan. The Pakistani connection would have been difficult enough to follow up at the time; I think impossible now.'

'That's fair,' said Hill, 'even if it was safe to send an investigation team there, I wouldn't agree to the cost.'

She sipped her coffee, wishing she had put more sugar in it when she had the chance.

'The second line of inquiry was through the DNA recovered from the paperweight that Rana hit one of the gunmen with. There were no hits at the time, nor on anyone arrested since, but I have asked for the widest possible search to be made and I'm expecting to get the result any day now.' Another sip of coffee. 'I can't say that I'm all that hopeful but there have been developments in that field and it's a line that I need to follow up.'

Hill looked at his watch. 'We've not got long before the outer office team arrives, Rachel, and I don't see why this needed all the secrecy.'

'It arises out of the third line of inquiry. The CSE investigation into some of Rana's drivers.'

'Go on.'

'According to the murder policy book and the CSE case notes, the only suspects were four of Rana's drivers. He was not identified as being involved. I've now spoken to one of the two surviving victims and she states that Rana was the main organizer of any trafficking that took place. She also states that there was a mysterious, unidentified white man involved. There is no mention of either in the CSE case papers.'

Hill had been chewing on the leg of his glasses as she spoke. He stopped and placed them on the table.

'How can we be sure that she did raise this with the investigators? The impression I've got was that the victims were not cooperative. Maybe she didn't raise it then.'

'I agree, but I've checked it out with DCI Dryden, who was the DS leading the CSE investigation. And with his partner Jill MacLean, then a DC, now retired. They both insist that Rana's role and this unidentified white man were in the statements and in the case papers.'

Hill picked up the glasses and resumed chewing the leg. She took this as an indication to go on.

'The person heading the murder investigation, and who led for the police in the CSE review with children's services and CPS, was Frank Fowler. According to Dryden and MacLean, he, or his office, was given the original case papers which described the role of Rana and this white man.'

She paused to give him time to digest the facts, then continued. 'That's the reason I asked for this meeting, sir. The combination of these factors indicate that it is more probable than not that Fowler was involved in purging the CSE case papers. He was pivotal to both inquiries and if the CSE link had been made to the murder inquiry, it should have been followed up. It wasn't. That link, other than the purported coincidence of the drivers, was not made.'

'Why didn't you take this to the Deputy? He's responsible for the professional standards department. This is clearly a case for them.'

'I thought, in the circumstances, that should be a decision for you, sir. At the time of the murder inquiry, he was ACC Ops and was Fowler's immediate line manager. The current ACC Ops, Mr Jackson, was head of the HQ/CID and may have had a role in supervising the CSE inquiry.'

'Jesus wept,' said Hill, pushing back his chair and beginning to pace the room. 'That's a serious allegation you're making there, Miss Stone. That my top team is bent.'

'I'm not alleging anything, sir, at least not against anyone but Fowler. Everything else is a mere statement of the facts. But you must see why I had to bring the decision to you.'

'What decision exactly?'

The thought flashed through her head that at least he didn't say 'I didn't get here today by making decisions like that' but she said, 'Who does the investigation into the cover-up? Do I continue with it or hand it over to the Deputy and Professional Standards? Or do you want to bring in an outside force?'

Hill had reached the window of his office at this point. It overlooked the HQ sports ground and the town of Granby beyond. He stopped and stared out of the window, initially saying nothing, then speaking without turning back into the office.

'I don't want to call in an outside force if I can help it.'

'Maybe leaving it with me, for the meantime at least, is the middle way.'

'How so?'

'I was in the Met when all this happened. I have absolutely no connections with Fowler. He had retired before I came here.'

'And what about the Deputy? Leaving it with you is an implied questioning of his integrity.'

'That would be the same outcome if we brought in another force. In his position, I'd prefer if it was kept in-house. And we know from bitter experience what outside enquiries are like. They always demand wide terms of reference. In this case, they would want to cover the murder as well. And we wouldn't be able to restrict the size of the team they used. My experience is that they're like Topsy. And it will all come out of our budget.'

Hill turned back into the office, nodding.

'I think his pride could be assuaged with that argument, if necessary. I want you to keep the inquiry at present. You will report directly to me, and only to me. That means I need to know what is happening before anyone else. Either ambush me at this time of the day if I'm in force, or get to me through Mary, my PA. I'll tell her to make sure that you do get through. If all that fails,' he fished a card from his wallet and handed it to her, 'this is my mobile.'

Stone pushed her chair back, stood and began walking towards the door.

'Do your best to keep this to the smallest number of people possible,

Rachel. If anyone asks about this meeting, we stick to the transfer to the Met story.'

With that, he made his way back to his desk and she left the office, passing the PA coming in with a cheery 'good morning, Mary' to her questioning look.

Chapter 24

'Boss,' said Shepherd, 'there was a call from Dr Greville at the lab. It's some sort of result from the DNA and he wants to talk you through it.'

'Some sort of result?'

'That's what he said – said he would explain it to you.'

She looked at her watch. 'OK, we'll meet in ten minutes to talk through what we've got and where we go from here.'

In her office, she dialled the number that Shepherd had given her.

'Dr Greville.'

'Dr Greville, DCI Stone, Granbyshire. You asked me to call you – you've got some sort of result on the DNA according to my sergeant. Have we got any hits?'

'Yes and no. It's complicated.'

'I'm all ears, Doctor.'

'There were no hits against the national database but you asked me to do as wide a search as possible. Since the initial profiles were done, we've made big leaps in familial comparisons and of course we now use a much longer number of STRs, short tandem repeats.' He paused, perhaps waiting for her to comment. She felt the need to reassure him that she really did understand.

'STRs, that's what you call the locations on the DNA that you check against one another?'

'That's right. Good. I'll deal with the rapes first as they are the more straightforward. We have had a hit on someone who is the son of the rapist. He was arrested last year for burglary. The DNA definitely identifies him as the son. I've checked his record and there is no mention of a father in it but it is only a matter of identifying the father and getting a confirmatory sample.'

'That's excellent, at least we've got one result. What about the other sample, from the paperweight?'

'We had no hits, but I can say with some certainty that the person hit by the paperweight is related to the victim in some way. Not a sibling but a cousin. There's quite a strong match.'

'First cousins?' She could feel her excitement build. First cousins were a limited enough number to make getting DNA from them worthwhile.

'I can't say. The difficulty is that in the Pakistani community, here and in Pakistan, there's quite a lot of intermarriage at cousin level, including first cousins. Most marriages have been arranged and it's easier to be sure of the past of the parties—'

'And if there are dowries involved it keeps the money in the family,' interrupted Stone.

'Just so. The problem that it presents is that there will be a large number of people, here and in Pakistan, who could come within the target group. Normally the genes of subsequent generations are diluted by marriage. Each parent contributes half the genes to a child so that in subsequent generations, that element is diluted by the next generation of parents.'

'But if they intermarry at cousin level—'

'You get my point entirely. The genes of the cousins will have much in common. It's not a new thing nor is it unique to the Pakistani community. European royalty did much the same up until fairly recently. At the time of the Great War, the Kaiser, Tsar of Russia and the King of England were all first cousins.'

'So all we can say is that the gunman was someone in Rana's family clan?'

'Just so. If I can be of any further help, Chief Inspector, please call me.'

Back in the main office, the group was gathered in a horseshoe around the whiteboards.

She went to the rape board and in the box headed suspects, wrote *Father of Kevin Howard, burglar arrested Birmingham 2015.*

She turned to the group.

'Barbara, I want you and Colin to track down young Kevin here and find out who his father is and arrange to get his DNA.' She smiled. 'This is great news guys, a hit. Now our friend Rana.' She crossed to that board and wrote *related to the victim* in the empty square titled *suspects.* She described her conversation with Dr Greville then said that she would have to brief the Chief as it meant that Naeem could also be related in some way to the gunmen.

'Well, you'll be able to tell the ACC about it, boss,' said Shepherd. 'His

PA called while you were on the phone. Wants you to go across to his office. Straightaway.'

'Did she say what it was about?'

'Nothing she would tell a mere constable.'

'Bollocks,' she said under her breath as she made her way across the office and out, the door clattering closed behind her.

As she entered the secretarial office, Jackson's PA stood up from her desk, knocked on the ACC's door, opened it and waved her through. Stone had been expecting to find him alone and was surprised to see her ex, Tony Bradshaw, sitting at one of the two chairs on her side of the ACCs desk. She stopped at the door.

'Sorry, sir, I didn't mean to interrupt ...'

'Come in, Rachel, sit down,' Jackson said, waving her to sit in the empty chair. 'This involves you and I thought it better that Tony was here to explain what's happening.'

'I think I can guess what that is, sir,' she said, sitting on the edge of the chair.

Bradshaw began to speak, directing his conversation to the ACC. Stone glared at him, knowing what was to come.

'As you know, sir, the CPS—'

'You and the CPS,' she interrupted.

'Rachel,' Jackson said, failing to keep the sigh out of his voice, 'we'll get on much quicker if you let him speak.'

'Sorry, sir,' she said, slumping back into the chair, looking now at the surface of the desk.

Bradshaw readdressed the ACC. 'The CPS had decided that the best way forward with the charge against Fleming for the murder of Tracey Gibbons was to refer it to a QC for advice on whether or not we should proceed. There was no problem with the charge regarding Emma Bolton, Rachel did a great job with that one.'

'Don't bloody patronize me, Tony, just get on with it.'

Jackson smiled ruefully. 'Get on with it, Tony.'

'The difficulty with Gibbons is that basically we've got nothing ...' Stone made to speak but Jackson silenced her with a raised palm. 'We've got nothing other than that he took her to the grave. If that isn't admissible then we're left high and dry. There are no forensics and no witnesses, and on advice of counsel, he said nothing when he was brought to the station and was formally interviewed.'

He paused, as if expecting another interruption; when it did not come he continued. 'The defence have indicated, informally, that if we only proceed with the case against Emma then they'll plead. But if we go on with both, they'll fight it. It's a simple question of whether or not we should put Emma's and Tracey's family through a trial.'

'And there's always the cost,' Stone added.

Bradshaw grimaced. 'And there's always the cost. Is it worth the risk when there is, according to counsel, a high probability that the confession and finding of the grave will be ruled inadmissible?'

'We can surely appeal this to the DPP herself?' Stone said, speaking to Jackson and not Bradshaw.

'She's been involved in the decision already, I think,' said Jackson, looking to Bradshaw for confirmation. He nodded and Jackson continued, 'so that would be a waste of everyone's time and effort.'

'But where's the justice for Tracey's family? And it means that Fleming could be out in as little as fifteen years. That can't be right.'

'That's a matter for the judge and the justice system, Rachel. We've done our bit.' He shrugged. 'We can't do any more than that.'

'And where does that leave me, sir?'

'What do you mean?'

'We both know this leaves me exposed to criticism at least, and maybe even discipline.'

Jackson templed his hands, the tips of his fingers almost touching the end of his nose. 'Fleming hasn't made a complaint and, I can only speak for myself of course, but I don't intend to take it any further. It was a decision for the CPS. They've made it and we all need to live with it.'

Stone began to say something else then stopped. There was a short silence broken by Bradshaw.

'If that's all, sir?'

'Yes. Thank you both for your time.'

Even though she knew that this was a possible outcome, Stone could barely contain her fury. The decision on giving it a run was a marginal one. If she had remained as SIO, she knew that she could have convinced the CPS to at least give it a go. She knew that if she did say anything now she would lose it completely. Her only option was to get the hell out of it and away from Tony as quickly as possible. She rose quickly out of the chair and, leaving the door open behind her, strode out of the office past the secretaries and through to the corridor, trying to put as much distance between her and him as she could.

'Rachel.' She heard his call to her back but kept going. 'Rachel, please, a minute of your time.'

She stopped and turned, only because there were witnesses and she did not want to be labelled as 'that hysterical woman'.

'Please,' said Bradshaw, catching her up. 'A minute, in the conference room,' he added, pointing to the door.

Once in he said, 'Would you like to sit down?'

'You said it would only take a minute.'

He shrugged. 'OK, look, I only wanted to say I tried my best to get Cartwright to go on with the Gibbons case.'

'Don't bullshit me, Tony. Your lies worked once, too bloody well. But I know you've wanted to drop the Gibbons charge from the start. Roger was willing to give it a run when I left the squad.'

'Tricia's been speaking out-of-school, hasn't she? Another woman scorned.'

'Don't kid yourself on either count, Tony. She would no more come on to you than she would to Fleming. The fact is I know you and what you're capable of.'

She turned and put a hand on the handle of the door.

'But don't worry, I'll get through this. We both know I'm the better detective. I'll clear up this cold case then get back to the Met – where I belong, even if you don't.'

She swept out of the door, leaving both it and Bradshaw swinging in the wind.

Commissioner Naeem marched past the chief constable's PA, knocked peremptorily on his door and entered the office, ignoring the PA's call that he was busy, on the phone. David Hill was indeed on the phone, but he waved her to the chair beside his desk and continued speaking. She ignored the invitation and paced the room.

'Doug, something's just come up here. Can I call you back?' A pause. 'Great, later this afternoon.' He hung up and looked at her. 'Akila, I didn't know we had a meeting.'

'We don't, David, but I had to see you or explode. When were you going to tell me? Were you going to tell me at all?'

'Tell you what, for God's sake?'

'That the CPS is dropping one of the murder charges against that child killer, Fleming!'

'Oh, that. I was going to tell you tomorrow at our scheduled meeting. It isn't a big deal. He'll go on trial for the murder of Emma Bolton and now he'll probably plead guilty. That'll save the families the hell of going through a trial.'

'And the CPS the expense of one. But the important issue is that they are dropping the charge because of how that woman Stone mismanaged the investigation, aren't they?'

He paused before replying but then said, 'That's one way of describing it.'

'So, what are you going to do about it? I assume she's already been suspended.'

'No, she hasn't, nor will she be.'

'I can't live with that, David. She's got to go. A family has been denied justice because of her high-handed behaviour. Think how that will look in the press.'

'The families also got the opportunity to bury their daughters. Got to know how they were killed.'

'That is as may be. I demand that she be disciplined and sacked.'

'I don't think that's a very good idea. The families will support her. They'll get the press on her side. Trust me, the best thing to do is keep our heads down for a couple of days and it'll all go away.'

'I'm sorry, David. That's not good enough. She's got to go and she must be suspended, immediately.'

Hill paused, pursed his lips then said, 'I don't like to fall out with you, Akila, but there's no doubt that the decision on discipline is mine to make and not yours. Your disciplinary powers are restricted to the ACPO team. You can try sacking me for not disciplining her but that's all. But I'm sure you know that already. You would have checked it out before coming over here. Or you can go for a judicial review of my decision, but that would look ridiculous, cost a lot of money, and almost certainly fail.'

'You're right. I did check it out before coming here. I wanted to give you the opportunity to do the right thing. I thought that you had to agree with me. I can see I was wrong in that. If you won't discipline her, I demand that you refer the case to the IPCC. I can do that.'

'You can. I think it's a bad idea, but you can make that demand. You can even refer it to the IPCC yourself.'

She was now standing on the opposite side of the desk, hands on hips.

'I think it's better that it comes from you for all sorts of reasons. I will confirm my request in writing if you want.' She tapped the top of the desk with her fingers. 'Now I want her suspended while the IPCC investigate the case.'

Hill got up from his desk and walked over to the wide bay window that overlooked the playing fields attached to the headquarters. He looked out for a few moments before turning.

'I won't do that. The incident was a one-off. The case she's working on now is highly unlikely to lead to a situation where she would even need to consider doing the same thing again. She's a good detective, a good police officer, with a fine record. Her motives were sound. Suspension wouldn't fulfil any useful purpose.' He walked back to the desk and stood close to her. 'Why are you so desperate to get her suspended? Don't you want your cousin's murderers found? Because if I suspend her I'm effectively suspending the CCU. I haven't got anyone else I can put in there.'

'Of course I want his killers found. But I think that it looks bad for the force if no action is taken against her.'

'But that isn't the case. We've agreed, I'll refer the case to the IPCC. But I refuse to use suspension as some form of discipline. I'm paid not just to manage this force but also to lead it. The officers have got to believe that I'll back them if I can.'

'You think because I'm going for mayor that I'm a dead woman walking, don't you, David? But I'm not. And I don't like being crossed like this.' She stared hard at him for a few seconds then left the office without another word.

Chapter 25

'I've asked the ACC to join us, Rachel, so you can bring us both up to speed.'

The three were sitting at the head of the conference table in the chief's office, a tray of coffees at their centre. Hill picked his up and the other two followed his cue. Stone sipped hers tentatively, hoping it had been made by the PA this time. If it had, she used the Chief's recipe; it was no better.

'In our trawl through the cold cases, we selected two, a serial rapist in the early nineties who suddenly stopped. And the murder of Bashir Rana. The good news is that we have made progress on both through DNA. In the rapist, we have positively identified him as the father of a Kevin Howard, arrested last year in Birmingham for burglary. We're following that up and I'm confident that we'll get a clear up out of it.' She paused. 'In the Rana murder, there were traces of DNA on a brass paperweight which we're sure is that of one of the gunmen. It's come back with the conclusion that the gunman it came from was related in some way to Bashir Rana.'

'What do you mean, in some way?' asked Jackson.

'You'll both be aware that it's now possible to establish familial links, not just immediate family like parents and siblings.'

'Yes,' they chorused.

'The analyst is certain that the DNA from the paperweight shows that the gunman was a cousin of some sort of Rana's.'

'Frank Fowler was right then,' said Jackson with a grin, 'he always thought that the killing was family-related.'

Stone looked at Hill for a lead on whether or not she could share her suspicions of Fowler with Jackson. He played his part and took it up.

'I think any experienced detective would have looked for that in this sort of case, Bob,' said Hill, 'but there's no doubt that this takes us forward. It's a concrete piece of evidence, not just a suspicion.'

'The additional difficulty that it presents us,' Stone said, taking up the baton again, 'is that the gunmen must also be related in some way to Mrs Naeem. When I interviewed her, she was adamant that there were no "domestic" issues, that I was wasting my time and her budget in exploring that line of inquiry.'

'Oh, it's her budget, is it?' asked Jackson. 'You don't think she was involved, surely?'

'I don't think anything yet, sir, only that we now know it was a "family" matter. The problem is that the family is more like a clan, and the practice of intra-familial marriage means that the gene pool we're looking at is necessarily a very big one – and mostly located in Pakistan.'

Jackson looked across at Hill. 'I don't think I could agree to sending an inquiry team to Pakistan. It'd be expensive, dangerous for the team, and I don't think we get anything out of it.'

'I agree, Bob,' said Hill. 'On what we've got, I doubt that the Foreign Office would agree to it, either, and they need to if we are to get the cooperation of the Pakistani government.'

'I'm not proposing that, sir,' said Stone. 'At least not at this stage. My difficulty is that Mrs Naeem has made no bones about the fact that she wants me sacked, wants me suspended at least, because of the CPS decision on Tracey Gibbons. The combination of that and the DNA result is a poisonous cocktail for me. I need to know that I have your support in taking it forward. Mrs Naeem needs to be re-interviewed.' On seeing Jackson's reaction to this she added, 'Not by me, of course. I'll get Barbara Dyer and Colin Shepherd to do that. They're both experienced detectives and will do as good a job as I could.'

'That's agreed,' said Hill.

Stone went on. 'Meanwhile, West Yorks have told me that they've arrested a Basra Chaudhry, one of Rana's drivers and a main player in the CSE that was going on back in 2006. I'm going to Bradford to interview him tomorrow both on the CSE and to find out if he knows anything about Rana's murder. Now that we've got him locked up and bang to rights, he might be willing to talk to us about it. I'll be taking Iftikhar Ahmed with me. He comes from up there – I think that the combination of being deep in the shit and being interviewed by a fellow countryman might just be enough to push him over the edge.'

'But if you think that the killing was domestic in some way, why are you following up on the CSE?' Jackson said, looking to Hill for support. 'Surely that part should be handed over to our Family Protection Unit now? Cost us enough to expand it. And it is their job.' Then, addressing Stone directly, 'You don't have the resources for that. You should be concentrating on the murder.'

Stone had discussed how they would handle this with Hill. He did not want anyone else to know about her inquiries into the changes made to the CSE case papers. The fact that the ACC clearly didn't want her to follow up on the CSE added to her difficulties. The practicalities made his point difficult to counter.

'I think it's too early to say that there's no connection, sir,' she said. 'I'll have a better idea of that once I've spoken to Chaudhry, assuming of course he's willing to talk to me.'

'If you must, you must,' said Jackson with poor grace.

'I think that the murder and the CSE investigation happening around the same time is more than a coincidence. We need to establish what, if any, connection there is before we split the investigation.'

'I'm just thinking of you and your team, Rachel,' said Jackson. 'I don't want you so stretched that you end up doing both investigations badly or superficially.'

'I realize that there seems to be a lot to manage, sir,' she said, looking to build on this slender statement of support. 'But since the other drivers are still in the wind and any investigation in Pakistan is out of the question, for the time being at least, I only need to focus on a relatively small number of people. I'm sure we can manage.'

Before Jackson could say anything in reply, Hill came in with a 'Good. Well done with what you've achieved so far, Rachel. Leave the Commissioner to me. I'll tell her about the DNA and the need for another interview. I'm sure she'll do her best to cooperate.'

'I still don't know that I'm totally happy with that,' said Jackson. 'It seems daft to set up a specialist unit, give them the extra training to do the job, then not give them the sort of inquiry that they were specifically set up for.'

He's hanging on to this, thought Stone, despite the Chief's prompt. Does he know, or suspect, more than he's saying?

'On the face of it, I agree with you, Bob, but I don't think that they're sitting on their thumbs waiting for work at the minute.' There was a pause, enough for Jackson to mutter 'true enough'. 'I'm sure that Rachel will involve them as and when necessary.' He turned his attention back to Stone. 'Be sure to keep us both up to speed on what's happening.'

Taking that as her cue to leave, she gathered up her papers, nodded to both, then left thinking that she achieved what she thought was impossible, managing to get up the nose of yet another person with power over her future.

Chapter 26

THE SECOND INTERVIEW WITH NAEEM presented Stone with a problem. As DS Dyer would lead, should she play safe and use Shepherd, or use Ahmed and hope to put her off-balance? The fact that Naeem would not be able to retreat behind a vague 'you do not understand my community' swung her in favour of using Ahmed. His role would be to look and assess, only contribute when invited to do so by Dyer or when addressed directly by Naeem.

There was no game-playing this time. Naeem received Dyer and Ahmed exactly at the time appointed and there were chairs for them on the other side of the desk. Dyer introduced them both. If Naeem was in any way disconcerted by Ahmed's presence, she did not let it show.

'Constable Ahmed,' she said, 'I don't think we've met. You're not from Granby, are you?'

'No, Commissioner, I'm from Bradford.'

'And what brought you to Granby?'

'It isn't Bradford.'

She gave a little laugh. 'So, Detective Sergeant, the Chief Constable has told me about the DNA development but I have to say to you, as I said to him, that I don't know that I can help you at all.'

'Thanks for your time anyway, Commissioner. You appreciate that the DNA does show us that the killing is in some way connected to the family.'

'Of course, but, at least as it was explained to me by the Chief Constable, the gunman – how dramatic a description that is – is not that closely related. I'm sure you're aware that Pakistani families tend to be quite big, by English stand-ards at least. My mother was one of three sons and five daughters. Multiply that out by three generations and you are literally into hundreds of people.' She laughed. 'In the Pakistani community, the concept of six degrees of separation is laughable. You are lucky if it is only two or three. As I said before, sometimes I think I'm related to half of the Punjab, especially if they are looking for something to be done.'

'The DNA does indicate a strong link with your mother's family.'

'My mother has four sisters and three brothers that she knows about.' Naeem paused, carefully selecting her words. 'In Pakistan, at that time, the culture allowed a degree of latitude to men to have more than one wife, and concubines were not uncommon, certainly not in my grandfather's time in Pakistan. It is possible that this was only a coincidence. I understand that both the gunmen were thought to be from Pakistan, not British Pakistanis.' She shrugged. 'God, yours and mine, only knows how many "cousins" I have who could fit this DNA profile.'

She's very smooth, thought Dyer, she's had the time to think through how to handle this. She's probably done a bit of research on what a familial match can mean and knows exactly how far we can take it.

Dyer persisted. 'It doesn't prompt you to have any second thoughts on who the gunmen might be – or what may have caused your cousin Rana to become the target?'

'No second, third, or fourth thoughts. No, Detective Sergeant, I can only say what I told your chief inspector. There was no discord in the family in England, no reason why anyone in the family would want to take such drastic action. They are all engaged, one way or another, in running businesses; making profits; employing people of every race and colour; making a positive contribution to the English economy, the English way of life. They are not primitive Kashmiri tribesmen pursuing some obscure vendetta.'

'What about his involvement in the CSE?' Dyer asked, speaking softly.

'What do you mean, "his involvement in the CSE"? He wasn't. Some of his drivers were but he was not. If he had been, I would have known. I led for the council on it at the time.'

'I know that. So, in your conferences on the CSE with,' she checked her notes, unnecessary as she knew the name, 'Detective Chief Superintendent Fowler, your cousin's name didn't come up?'

'Of course not. If it had, I would have needed to recuse myself from the decision making. If you don't believe me, check the minutes of the meetings.'

Dyer checked through her notes again, long enough for noises outside the office to become noticeable. Then she looked up and across the desk at Naeem.

'We have, of course. But they're not at all helpful. They're very sparse and only record the outcome, the decision not to proceed with its supporting rationale. Not the discussion.'

Naeem sat back in her chair, looking first at the ceiling then back at Dyer.

'I'm sure that we had copies of the police case papers. That was what we discussed. That discussion should be in the police reports. You must be able to access them.'

'You would think so, wouldn't you?'

'You mean you can't find them?'

'We found some case papers. Not the originals. The trouble is that we've also found that they don't contain all of the information that they should have. When we went back to the key witnesses and the investigating officers, we found that they appear to have been tampered with.'

'In what way?'

'In that the only surviving victim of the CSE who is willing and able to talk to us now tells us that your cousin Bashir Rana was THE main player. That he organized the trafficking. This has been confirmed by the officer who led the CSE investigation. You were involved in the decision not to take the case forward. Your cousin was a main player and you're saying that you knew nothing of it?'

She said nothing more, only looked expectantly across the desk at Naeem.

'This is ridiculous. The decision was based on the evidence presented by the police, I'm certain of that. Why is all this coming up now?'

'Because of the re-investigation of Rana's murder. His part in the CSE was never fully explored in the original murder inquiry because, at some point, the statements had been altered to exclude him from any involvement in the CSE. That investigation was not pursued because it was decided that the girls would not make credible witnesses. Until we reopened the murder, there was no possibility of this tampering coming to light. That decision was made by you, your chief officer Chris Jenkins, Chief Superintendent Fowler and the CPS. We now need to explore that link.'

'Are you are alleging that I had some part in this 'tampering'?'

'We're only going where the evidence is leading us, Commissioner.'

'So suddenly I'm a suspect?' said Naeem, her voice rising.

'I didn't say that.'

'You didn't need to.' Naeem stood up. 'I know what's behind this. Chief Inspector Stone thinks that she can avoid her culpability for messing up the investigation into Tracey Gibbons' murder by undermining me.'

'I don't think—'

'I don't care what you think, Sergeant. I will not say anything more without my lawyer being present. I may be the Police and Crime Commissioner but I'm also a member of a minority community that knows from bitter experience exactly what the police are capable of. I'd like you to leave – now!'

Dyer looked at Ahmed.

'I'm also a member of that community, Commissioner,' he said, speaking stiffly. 'All we're trying to do is find out who murdered your cousin Rana.'

There was a brief exchange between the two in Urdu. They had anticipated that this might happen and thought that the balance of advantage lay with Ahmed replying in the same language, but that he should keep it short. At a nod from him, they both got to their feet.

'I don't know what you just said, Commissioner, but I can assure you that we're only going where the evidence leads,' said Dyer. 'We'll be in touch again to arrange another interview when you can have your lawyer present. But it won't be here. It'll be over there,' she said, pointing out of the window towards the main headquarters building. 'And it will be taped. Just to ensure everyone's rights are protected. Especially those of the victims.'

Once outside the office, Dyer asked Ahmed what had been said.

'She told me to remember how important family was …'

'I thought I recognized *Biradari*, that's family, isn't it? What did you say?'

'That I know how important family is – just as I also know how important my oath of office as a constable is.'

After the officers left, Naeem sat thinking over what had happened. Had she overreacted? She needed advice and took her phone from her handbag. It was answered after a few rings.

'They've been to interview me,' she began without preamble. 'They've found a link between the gunmen and Bashir.'

'What sort of link?'

'DNA recovered from the scene shows that they were related to him, cousins of some sort.'

'That's all?'

'Yes. I told them that Bashir probably had lots of cousins he would not know of, especially if they came from Pakistan.'

'Was that enough to satisfy them?'

'No. They've also found out that the case papers in the CSE inquiry had been altered, leaving Bashir out. And they've now got a Pakistani officer on the team.'

'Who?'

'His name is Iftikhar Ahmed – he's from Bradford.'

'That's not good – given the decision not to take the case forward.'

'That's what I thought so I brought the meeting to an end.'

'How?'

'I told them I would only continue with my lawyer present.'

There was a long pause. 'I'm not sure that was the best way forward, Akila. It makes it look as if you have something to hide.'

'But I don't know what they know.' Her voice rising. 'They say they don't have the originals of the case papers at this time and that the only note of the meetings describes our conclusions, not the evidence.'

'I think they're fishing, probing to get a reaction. I doubt that they know what actually happened. What about Hill? What is he doing? He is your man after all.'

'Not any more. He knows I'm standing for mayor and that I'll be gone in a few months' time.'

'Maybe we need to move that up, resign and distance yourself from the police completely. Say you need to focus on the up-coming election, that it would not be right to do so while still holding the office of PCC, something along those lines.'

'I think I should wait until the IPCC make a finding. Stone admits what she's done so they must make a finding against her. Then she'll be out of my hair at least; and I think without her the inquiry will go nowhere.'

'Up to you, Akila. You've usually got a good nose for these things. But get your parachute ready, just in case. Meanwhile, I'll find out what I can about this Iftikhar Ahmed.'

'Thank you, uncle.'

She slowly hung up the phone and sank back into her chair, her mind no easier, but at least he hadn't criticized her, hadn't found anything wrong with what she was doing.

Chapter 27

As she drove up to Bradford, Stone mused on what awaited her. She had decided, for obvious reasons, to take Ahmed with her for the Chaudhry interview. If he got funny about speaking English, she would let Ahmed get on with it in Urdu and then get it translated – after making sure that Chaudhry was made aware of the cost of pissing her about. And Bradford was his home territory.

He had told her that he intended going up the night before, by train, so that he could fit in a visit to his parents. She agreed that would be a good idea. Just as she was packing up for the night, he had come into her office looking a bit sheepish.

'I wonder if I could have a quick word, boss?'

She waved him in and he closed the door behind him. 'What's the problem, Iftikhar, are your parents away?'

'No, no such luck.'

'What's the problem then?'

He sighed. 'It's my mother.'

Stone was enjoying his discomfort too much to help out. She said nothing but looked at him expectantly.

'You see, when I finished my law degree, my parents were certain I was going to become a lawyer, a solicitor. My joining the police came as a bit of a shock. Policing is something that white people's kids do. And then I didn't join the local force but came here to Granby. Moved away. God only knows what she thinks I get up to.'

'And?'

'And when I told her that my chief inspector would be picking me up on the way to the station, she insisted that I invite you to stop by for a coffee.'

Stone was about to agree that that would be a good idea but he rushed on. 'It will be her first chance to meet a senior officer. Maybe reassure herself that I do in fact have a career.' Again, before she could speak, 'Be fair, boss, I am forewarning you. If you don't want to, I can make my own way to the nick and meet you there.'

'What's she like, this mother of yours? She sounds quite formidable.'

'She is. She's not your average mother. To start with, she's a local councillor. Did that a couple of years ago because she said the men weren't making a good enough job of it.'

'That must have been tough. My impression is that Pakistani men see politics as being their fiefdom.'

'That used to be the case,' he shrugged, 'but like everything, times are changing.'

'She's not going to question me on how good, bad or indifferent West Yorks police are, is she?'

'No, I think I can guarantee that. All she is going to talk about is me,' he said dolefully.

'In that case,' she said with a laugh, 'I would love to meet your mother. I'm only too delighted to join her for a coffee. I'll do my best to reassure her because I know where you're coming from. My mother didn't think too much of my career choice, either.'

'But you've made chief inspector. She must think differently now.'

'She's a mother, Iftikhar, I'm her only child. I haven't produced any grandchildren. Until I do that, all judgement is on hold.'

He laughed. 'My sisters have produced more than enough of them to take that pressure off me at least.' He opened the door. 'So I'll tell her, tomorrow, around ten.'

'It will be my pleasure, I'll even try hard not to take the mickey out of you too much in the process.'

Ahmed's family lived in the street that had clearly been developed in the fifties by independent builders, free of any modern planning constraints. There seemed to be a variety of everything from bungalows, small and large semis and a few redbrick and concrete rendered detached, all sitting in modest plots. The family lived in one of the latter. Stone parked in the street and made her way up the short path. Before she could knock, Ahmed appeared in the doorway and invited her in, leading her through to a large open plan kitchen diner at the rear of the house.

His mother was standing by a worktop, a kettle in hand, having clearly just filled the cafetière that was in front of her. She was wearing a dark red floral Abaya dress, her thick black hair hanging loose to her shoulders. Stone could see immediately where Ahmed got both his looks and his height. She crossed the floor toward Stone, smiling, holding out her hand. They shook hands.

'Chief Inspector Stone, I'm very pleased to meet you. You must call me Fatima. Iftikhar tells me you like proper coffee so I hope mine comes up to scratch.'

'I'm sure it will. And you must call me Rachel – with two biblical names like that, we should get on well.'

'I'm sure we will. I hope you'll forgive my forwardness in inviting you but Iftikhar, in the way of all sons, tells me nothing. And now he lives away in Granby, I worry. I just couldn't resist a chance to meet his boss, especially when I learned that the boss was a woman.'

By now she had seated Stone at the table. She brought the cafetière across and joined her. Iftikhar stood by the table until his mother signalled that he should join them. On the table lay a tray with the most delicate coffee cups and saucers. Stone's first thought was how breakable they looked.

'You have a lovely home,' Stone said, looking around as Fatima poured the coffees.

'Thank you,' she said, placing the cafetière on the tray. 'Look.' She paused. 'Rachel. I know you have an appointment at the police station shortly. So I'll come directly to the point—'

'Mother,' Ahmed interjected.

She held up a hand to silence him, leaning conspiratorially towards Stone.

'Do you think he has made a wise choice, joining the police? It's not too late, he could still be a solicitor!'

Stone took a sip of the coffee.

'I'm not sure I'm the right one to answer that, Fatima. I did a couple of years as a teacher when I left university, but I've loved this job from day one.'

'Even with all the trouble that Iftikhar tells me it is giving you now?'

'Even with that. The other side of the coin is that the job puts me in a position where I could put a family out of its misery. That makes it all worthwhile.'

Fatima nodded as Stone was speaking.

'But what about all the racism in the police? It's still there, isn't it? He can't have a future in that sort of organization.'

'I would be a fool to try to tell you that there isn't any racism in the police, but I don't think it's worse than most organizations and it's better than some.' She paused. 'I think the best way to describe how things are changing is to look at it from my perspective as a woman. We are the largest visible minority group in the police. There's been equality of pay and opportunity in theory since 1975 but it's only in the last ten to fifteen years that there's been anything like real equality. It's the same with race, ethnicity. When I joined, the hostility and discrimination was much more prevalent and more openly practised. But now, especially with people like Iftikhar joining, it's much less.'

She took a long drink of her coffee.

'And I think it's fair to say that the rate of change is quickening. I mean, look at you. I'll bet that ten years ago the suggestion that you should be a councillor would have been laughed at. But you are one now.'

'True. But it was not a change that came about easily. The local Labour party were very hostile when we women raised the idea. But they were not getting done the things that we women needed done.'

'And you changed that. Think of how much easier it will be for your daughters. It's the same in the police – the more Iftikhars there are, the less discrimination there'll be.'

'You think it is a good choice for him?'

'I think it's a good one for the service. Only he can say if it is a good choice for him personally. He's intelligent and hard-working, he's already been selected for CID, and I do know he's good at what he does. He'll go as far as he wants to.'

Fatima sat back in his chair and sighed. 'I suppose I'll have to live with that.' She looked up at the kitchen clock. 'But I've kept you too long. I mustn't make you late.'

They got up from the table and moved to the front door.

As they shook hands again Stone said, 'Thank you again for the coffee, Fatima.'

'Take care, Rachel – and look after him for me.'

'I don't know how to thank you for that, boss. The fact that she's met you and likes you will make life much easier for me.'

'You can thank me by getting something worthwhile out of Chaudhry,' she said as they pulled into the visitors' space in Bradford nick's car park. 'I really need a result on this one.'

Chapter 28

DCI GLASS HAD ALERTED THE front office and she and Ahmed were taken directly to the major incident suite. It buzzed with the success of the previous day's arrests, officers now focused on getting the paperwork done. Their man Chaudhry had been one of the first to be processed and there was enough time running on the PACE clock for Stone to come at the interview in a measured way. Chaudhry's lawyer, a Mr Jawanda, had been alerted to the fact that Granbyshire wanted to interview his client. Their first task was to find out if he was going to be a realist or a pain in the arse. Glass had said that he had developed a good working relationship with him. But then again, having captured Chaudhry bang to rights had helped him with that.

Having made the introductions, Glass left them to it in the office he had found for their use. Mr Jawanda's well cut suit and tall frame both did their best to hide the fact that he was very fat, but in the end his sheer mass made that task impossible. He had a ready smile and an easy manner which Glass had said disguised a sharp mind and a rock-hard resolve. Rock-hard could work both ways if Stone could convince him that it was in his client's best interest to cooperate with them.

Stone gave Jawanda a brief summary of the case they already had against Chaudhry, emphasizing that he was the first of the suspected drivers to be arrested. That put him in pole position as far as negotiating a deal with the prosecution was concerned. If he held out, he would lose that when any of the others were arrested.

'Mr Jawanda,' said Stone, 'we both know that your client will get ten or twelve years for the charges he faces.'

'I think you underestimate my powers of persuasion in mitigation, Chief

Inspector.'

'In the current climate, I doubt that even God Almighty could get him less than that. We also know that if we attach our charges onto the West Yorkshire list, it won't make much, if any, difference to the sentence. We both know there's a limit on how far the judge can go. Anything he gets for ours is likely to be concurrent. He might end up with an extra year.'

'Maybe so,' he said with a sideward tilt of his head.

'However, if we hold off until we've arrested everyone else involved in our case, and that might take a year or so,' Jawanda gave her questioning look at which she shrugged, 'we've only got a small team, it's historical and your client isn't exactly going anywhere in a hurry. By the time we get to court, he'll have served eighteen months to two years of his sentence, and the judge might feel able to tack on a more sizeable lump, three, maybe as much as five years.'

'And your local CPS has been consulted about this?'

'I discussed it with them before coming here. It's one less hit on their budget and should make it easier to make a case against the others once we've arrested them.'

Jawanda sat like a well-dressed Buddha, nodding his head as she spoke, conducting his own internal dialogue before speaking.

'I can see the benefit to you, and your CPS. But all I see for my client is risk. I have not had the opportunity to examine the strength of the case that you have against him.'

'Look, Mr Jawanda, my main focus is on the murder of Chaudhry's employer in Granby, Bashir Rana. He, Rana, was the main player in the CSE set up. If Chaudhry cooperates, I'm willing to allow that cooperation to go forward in mitigation. The more he cooperates, the better that mitigation will sound. Probably enough to ensure that he gets no more than he will anyway under the West Yorkshire charges. May even get them reduced. Depends totally on the level of his cooperation.'

Jawanda grasped the edge of the desk to help him get to his feet. He picked up his briefcase from the desk and moved to the door.

'I will discuss your offer with my client.'

As he opened the door Stone said, 'Time is of the essence, Mr Jawanda.'

'Maybe for you, Chief Inspector. For me it is my client's interests.'

At first sight, Chaudhry looked shell-shocked. For good reason. One minute he had been a cab driver, wife and three kids at home, some easy sex on the side. The next he was locked up, the details of what he had been up to with a group of fourteen and fifteen-year-old girls in Bradford being described to him at some length. Then a quick appearance at the nearby magistrates' court for a three-day lay down and back to the police station for more questions. Just when he thought it couldn't possibly get any worse, these other cops appeared from the past with even more allegations, including murder. He was clearly bemused by the whole process and leaned heavily on the advice and directions he was getting from Jawanda. Stone's job was made easier by the fact that most of the law had already been explained to him by the Bradford squad and his lawyer.

She began by rearresting him for rape and cautioning him. One complaint with the IPCC was enough. Ahmed then went through the allegations that were in Brooks' statement where Chaudhry could be identified. He began to reply in Urdu to Ahmed, who immediately held up his hand to stop him.

'Mr Chaudhry, you have been questioned at length by the police here. All in English?'

'Yes.'

'Good, then that is how we'll conduct this interview.' He looked at Jawanda, back to Chaudhry, then Jawanda again.

'Your client should understand, Mr Jawanda, that I am an English police officer, this interview is taking place in an English police station. I am not *baradari na banda*. He has dragged our community and our religion through the dirt. I have more in common with a piece of dog shit on my shoe than I have with him.'

Jawanda shrugged, whispered in Chaudhry's ear then said, 'Carry on, officer.'

Ahmed repeated the last of the allegations and invited Chaudhry to comment. Chaudhry initially tried the line that the girls knew what they were doing and had not been forced to do anything they didn't want to. This defence faded very quickly, however, when he was reminded that he knew that they were under sixteen and so could not legally consent. Stone knew that he had been through all this with the Bradford squad but also knew that he would have to give it a try. Once the ground rules were established, neither Stone nor Ahmed were surprised that his replies were limited to 'she was a fat one, wasn't she?'; 'I don't remember'; and finally, in resignation, 'if you say so.'

Having gone through all of the CSE allegations, Ahmed concluded, 'The detailed charges you face will be added to those that West Yorkshire are bringing and they will all be dealt with at the same time. Do you understand that?'

'Yes, Mr Jawanda has explained it to me.'

Ahmed having dealt with the CSE issues, Stone now took over to deal with the murder. She felt that this would help to separate the two in Chaudhry's mind and may make him more cooperative.

'Mr Chaudhry, I'd like to come now to the murder of Bashir Rana.'

'I had nothing to do with that.'

'No one is saying that you did.' She picked up some papers from the pile in front of her and glanced through them. 'I read your statement to the murder inquiry. You don't seem to have been asked anything about Rana's involvement with the girls.'

'They didn't ask me anything about it.'

'Don't you think that's a bit strange?'

'No, not at all. It was not anyone involved with the girls who killed him. The killers came over from Pakistan, everyone knows that,' he smiled, 'even the police.'

'Do you have any idea who brought them over and why?'

He sighed. 'Look, Chief Inspector, Bashir Rana was not my friend. He was my boss. My employer. His family have lots of money, run lots of businesses here and in Pakistan. His wife's family are also rich. They have many businesses in Pakistan. I work for him, that is all.'

'Not all, you were both having sex with the same underage girls.'

Chaudhry looked to Jawanda before replying. Taking silence as a direction to go on, he said, 'That is true. But he saw the girls separately. He didn't join in with us drivers. We got them after he was finished with them. Never before.'

'Did you resent that?'

'There is no point. It was a fact of life, isn't it? He was the boss. It was his right.'

'The killers had come over from Pakistan. Could it have been his wife's family who hired them if she had complained to them about his involvement with these English girls?'

'I don't think so.'

'Why not?'

'His wife is very traditional. It was an arranged marriage. He brought her over from Pakistan. Her English is not very good. She stayed home and only went out with him or other women like her. I don't think she would have known.' He shrugged. 'He was only fucking these girls. He wasn't going to divorce her or anything like that. He did not dishonour her.'

'What about his own family, here or in Pakistan?'

'I told you. I was only a driver. The taxi business was successful, made money. The girls, I think, were a little extra he kept for himself.'

Stone looked through her notes again, marshalling her thoughts. What he said was believable. It was time to move on.

'Who was the Englishman that Rana gave the girls to?'

Chaudhry looked aside at Jawanda then leaned across and whispered something in his ear, covering both his mouth and Jawanda's ear with his hand. Jawanda pursed his lips then waved his hand, indicating that Chaudhry could speak.

'I don't know who you are talking about.'

'But you do know something, don't you? You didn't ask him,' she pointed to the lawyer, 'for permission to say that you know nothing.'

Chaudhry looked again at Jawanda who waved a second permission.

'Rana's family are very well connected, very important in the local Pakistani community. He has an uncle who is a Lord – Lord Gohar Malik. And your Police Commissioner, she is also his cousin. I think you know that.'

'I do. But how does all this relate to this Englishman?'

'Bashir was always telling us how well-connected he was. How easy it was for him to get things done. Sometimes he used it to help drivers, you know, visas, work permits, favours that he could call in if he needed them.'

Stone wanted to get to the point but was aware of the need to let him get to it in his own way, at his pace.

'Once, when I was taking two of the girls to a place in Birmingham with him – they were drinking and listening to their iPods in the back of the car – I said that I was a bit worried about getting into trouble with the police. We had been using the girls for a while by then and too many people knew about it. I thought it was only a matter of time before someone in the police would come after us.' He looked again at Jawanda who gestured for him to go on. '"Basra," he says, with a great big smile and patting my arm, "Basra, don't you worry about that. I've looked after everyone as far as that's concerned. There will be no problems with the police. No problems at all." And he laughed, a great belly laugh. I asked him how he could be so sure and he laughed again. "Don't worry, Basra," he said, "the English have a good saying for it. We are all pissing in the same pot. Well, we are all putting our pricks in the same holes."'

'Did he tell you anything more?'

'No, but he obviously meant that he had influence with someone, someone he had let fuck the girls.'

'And you think that someone was, who?'

She was anxious not to put words into his mouth, to allow him to say the word.

'A police officer, isn't it? And he would need to be high up, someone who could give Rana a lot of protection, I think.'

'Did he ever mention a name?'

Chaudhry shook his head.

'A rank? Detective or uniform?'

Another shake of the head.

She tried another line. 'Do you know anyone else who might be able to tell us, point us in the right direction? You haven't given us much, Basra. Hardly anything at all.'

Jawanda stepped in. 'I don't think that is quite accurate, Chief Inspector. My client has done his best. He has cooperated completely with the CSE element of your inquiry and he has told you as much as he knows about the murder. At some danger to himself, if I may say. You now know that you have at least one bad apple in your police force. And at a senior level. For all my client knows, he is still there. Maybe there are others he doesn't know about. All of them could present a danger to him.'

'The quicker I can identify this police officer, the safer your client will be, Mr Jawanda. We both know that.' She looked back at Chaudhry. 'You're certain you can't give us any idea who this police officer might be?'

Chaudhry shook his head. 'I've told you all I know.'

Stone signalled to Ahmed to end the recording of the interview. As he went through the ritual for the tape, she looked hard at Chaudhry. He refused to meet her eyes. The trouble with that was that she couldn't tell if he was still holding something back, or was frightened, or was just being polite to a person with power; cross-cultural inquiries were a real bugger for that. She was certain that he knew more but would only give it up if she could be seen to be taking the allegations about the senior officer seriously. She could not tell them that she was already doing exactly that. She took two cards from her bag and gave one to Chaudhry and one to Jawanda.

'If you remember anything more, you'll get me there.'

At her signal, Ahmed stood and accompanied Chaudhry and Jawanda from the room, leaving her to ponder on how to positively identify this bent and perverted cop.

Chapter 29

'WHAT DO YOU THINK ABOUT Chaudhry?' asked Stone as they drove back to Granby.

'I think he was telling the truth as far as it went. He knows more, maybe not that could be evidence, but he knows more. I think that the point that Jawanda made, about not knowing who else may have been involved, was a good one. If we do make an arrest, it would be worthwhile going back to talk to him.'

'I agree.'

'And we've got two powerful indicators now, the interference with the case papers and then this, according to Chaudhry, protection for Rana – at a senior level. It must be the same person, surely?'

Stone had come to the same conclusion. She had decided, reluctantly, that she needed to tell Shepherd and Ahmed about the changes that had been made in the case papers. Her main concern had been Shepherd. He was long time CID and would be the more likely to let it slip, deliberately or accidentally, to his old mates in the Department. But there had been no option. The murder and the CSE were clearly entwined. The interview with Chaudhry had just proved that pretty conclusively.

'I agree. And all the arrows seemed to be pointed in the same direction.'

'Fowler?' asked Ahmed.

'He must have been involved somehow. But there could be more than one. We need more, not much, but more before I can bring him in.'

Her phone rang, the caller ID said Tricia Downing – a surprise as at their last meeting, she had made it clear that she did not want any more contact.

'Patricia, what can I do for you?'

'The IPCC team are here. I'm seeing them tomorrow morning.'

'Good. The sooner we get that out of the way, the better.'

'I need to tell them what happened. I've no option.'

'Of course you don't. You must tell them exactly what happened; the advice you gave me. That's what I'll be doing when they eventually get around to me.'

'I just thought I'd give you a heads up.'

'And I'm grateful for that, Tricia. Relax about it. I told you at the time that I'd take the consequences. That still applies. Don't worry. Tell them exactly what happened. That's what I intend to do. Bye, Tricia.'

After she hung up she sat quietly, thinking about the arrival of the IPCC and what it meant. Ahmed was astute enough to catch on and focus on his driving. Their inquiry would not take long. The facts were known. And she would not be disputing them. There comes a time in every complex job when you wonder if it is worth carrying on, keeping all the plates spinning. The irony of course is that the complexity is also the challenge, managing it brings the job satisfaction. Twenty years ago, when she joined the job, there would have been no difficulty in what she had done – the opposite, in fact. Now she found herself in exactly the position of the detectives she had scorned for their inability to live with the growing constraints on how suspects had to be handled. Now she was the one who had decided that the law was inadequate in the face of someone like Fleming. Maybe she should go, pack up her tent and find another career while there was still time. Become part of the gig economy. But she still loved the job. All she could do, or wanted to do, was to ensure that all the factors she had considered, when taking Mickey Fleming to the graves of the girls, were taken into account. If, after that, they wanted to sack her – so be it.

The phone went again, this time with a message. *I'm in Granby today/ tomorrow. Meal? I'll be in the restaurant. 8 p.m. Hope you can make it. Mark*

She smiled to herself – not all bad today then. He must have tried to get through when she was speaking to Tricia. A relaxed meal in good company sounded too good to be true. *Great. See you there,* she texted back. And if Ahmed put his foot down, she might have time for a nice relaxing bath as well.

Ahmed did his part but she still didn't get her bath. Megan Freeland was waiting for her in the portacabin office.

'I've come to see you about some proverbial that's about to hit the fan,' she said, 'and to make sure you don't overreact.'

'To what?'

'This,' Freeland said, handing her a printed email. 'It's the draft text of the story the *Guardian* are going to run tomorrow.'

The headline was *Crime Commissioner Clashes with Chief Constable*.

She looked up at Freeland. 'I see that their alliteration expert is on the case.' This did not get even the smidgen of a smile in return, so she knew it was going to be bad. She went on to read the text.

Sources close to the Granbyshire Police and Crime Commissioner Akila Naeem say that the relationship between her and the Chief Constable, David Hill, has completely broken down. She disagrees with his decision not to suspend DCI Rachel Stone whilst the Independent Police Complaints Commission (IPCC) investigates the complaint against the officer concerning her handling of the investigation into the murders of Emma Bolton and Tracey Gibbons.

DCI Stone was responsible for the arrest of the girls' alleged killer, Michael Fleming. In the course of the arrest, it is alleged that DCI Stone refused Mr Fleming his rights and protection under the PACE codes of practice. As a result of this, the CPS have decided not to proceed against Mr Fleming for the murder of Tracey Gibbons as they believe that the evidence of Fleming allegedly taking Stone to Tracey's grave would be ruled inadmissible. There is apparently no other evidence against Fleming for this murder. This decision reflects a welcome tightening of the CPS's approach to evidence gained illegally or in contravention to the PACE codes of practice.

PCC Naeem has requested that the IPCC investigate this and they commenced their inquiries in the force today. It is surprising that DCI Stone has not been suspended as, if the allegation is made out, it would constitute gross misconduct. The normal outcome of such a finding would be that she be sacked. The Chief Constable's office has been asked for a comment and will only confirm that the IPCC has been asked to investigate the matter. They do not make comments on cases under inquiry.

Stone looked up at Freeland. 'I assume that "sources close" are a.k.a. that bastard Peterson.' Freeland shrugged. 'And look at the by-line. It's that other bastard Bates. Is there anything I can do about this, Megan?'

'You could bring in the Federation. In fact, I'd advise you to do exactly that. They've a lot of experience in this and they've got deep pockets when it comes to paying for advice.'

'But that'll take forever. And I don't want them involved in the IPCC inquiry. I know how I want to handle that.'

'The trouble is, even if they reacted immediately, the sad fact is that the

Guardian piece is all a matter of fact. There's not actually much to refute.'

'How do I get my side across?'

'You don't. You're just as hamstrung as the Chief.'

'But …'

Freeland raised a hand to silence her. 'But, of course, the families aren't. They can say what they like.' Freeland said this with the most po of po-faces. 'A little bird tells me that they are now aware of the *Guardian* article and have managed somehow to get in touch with the crime correspondents in *The Mail* and *The Sun* to give their views on the detective who found their girls and gave them closure. How brave and clever she is '

Stone grabbed Freeman in a bear hug.

'Thanks a million, Megan. I owe you. I really do.'

Freeland managed to extricate herself the bear hug. 'I can't think what for, Rachel. It's all being done by the families.' She gave a little flip of her hair. 'We had absolutely nothing to do with it.'

Chapter 30

DYER SAT IN HER CAR, parked about fifty yards away from Libby Grainger's house, a bright, red brick, barely detached one on a new estate. She needed time to finalize her approach. Libby Grainger had moved on since being Liz Ryder, the girl in care. She had transformed her life, and her future, since 2006. A very experienced foster couple, living well away from Granby had taken her on. She had made the most of the new opportunity, gaining an NVQ, getting a job as a teaching assistant, then marrying a teacher at the same school. His promotion to deputy head had brought them back to live twenty miles away in Derby, far enough to make it unlikely to meet anyone from those days, but near enough for place names to prod her with reminders. She now had two children of her own, a boy aged four and a girl of two. She still worked part-time as a teaching assistant but had one morning a week to herself, when both children were being minded and she was not working. Dyer knew she was at home as her people mover was parked in the driveway. The husband cycled to work.

Since the interview with Kelly Brooks, Dyer had rehearsed again and again what her approach would be. There was no risk-free way of doing it. But it had to be done, she had no doubts about that. Libby had returned from delivering the children to their carers about ten minutes ago. Long enough to let her take her coat off and put the kettle on. Not so long as to be engrossed in some other task important enough to add to her excuses for not talking to Dyer.

She reluctantly left the warmth and comfort of the car to walk to the house. The estate had a bleak newness, emphasized by the absence of mature trees and bushes. All the front gardens were open plan patches of scrubby winter grass, broken by the occasional piece of low ranch fencing. As she approached the half-glazed front door, she saw Libby's mottled figure in the hall, going towards the back of the house. She rang the bell and saw the figure stop, turn and come to the door. The figure turned out to be a slim, pretty, blonde woman, dressed in jeans and a pale blue woollen top, her blonde hair just long enough to make a ponytail.

'Mrs Grainger,' a short pause as she showed her warrant card, 'I'm Detective Sergeant Barbara Dyer, Granbyshire Police. I know …'

'I'm not saying anything to the police. My lawyer has told you that. In fact, I think I should phone him now.'

She began to close the door. Dyer had guessed that this would happen. Libby was an intelligent woman. She had a good lawyer and was clear about her rights. A real foot in the door would only have antagonized her. Dyer needed a virtual one.

'I know about Fowler. I know why you wouldn't cooperate back then.' Libby hesitated, giving Dyer the opportunity to finish. 'I just want to talk to you. If you still don't want to help after that, I'll go away. No one from the force knows I'm here. If you do complain, I'll probably lose my job. But I need your help. Not the police, not Kelly or Brittany – me.'

As she spoke, the hand that held up her warrant card dropped to her side. In speaking, her shoulders had drooped, anticipating rejection. They both stood still, Libby half-hidden by the door, Dyer resigned.

'Just ten minutes of your time – please.'

Libby said nothing but turned, leaving the door ajar. Dyer pushed the door open and went in. As a cop, she had gone into a lot of strangers' houses. They all had an instant feel; told you what was coming. This one's warmth belied Libby's cold back, gave her some hope. She followed her into the neat kitchen at the back of the house. The evidence of the children was everywhere from framed photographs, drawings magnetized to the fridge, to the tiny back garden strewn with over-sized toys.

'I was making myself a coffee, would you like one?' said Libby.

'Thank you – may I?' Dyer indicated a chair by the table and sat without waiting for permission. She was in and would only have this one chance. As Libby made the coffee, Dyer sat in a silence broken only by a 'milk, no sugar' response to Libby's enquiry. The sound of the radio drifted in from the living room, the faint beat filled the background. Coffee poured, Libby joined her on the opposite side of the table.

'Ten minutes,' she said, putting the mugs down and looking pointedly at the clock on the wall.

The aroma of the coffee was clearly the only element of a welcome that Dyer was going to get. She used up thirty seconds of her time looking around the room, taking it all in.

'You've done well,' said Dyer, indicating the kitchen with a wave of her hand, 'this, your job, your marriage, your kids. You've really got your life sorted. We've spoken to Kelly, gone through the whole case again. We would really like to put away the people who put the three of you through all that. But as I told you, I'm here for myself and I need to focus on one person. Kelly told us about an English guy who always used a mask. She doesn't know who he was. But he did rape you all at some time.' She paused to sip her coffee. 'You were always much cleverer than the others. You would have wanted to know who he was, what was going on. I don't think you would have lived with the mask nonsense. I think that you would've got past it. I think that you know who that man was.'

'You said you needed my help. I don't see how knowing that helps *you*.'

'I know the man was a police officer. A Detective Chief Superintendent Fowler.'

'Then you don't need me, do you?' Libby said with a cynical half-laugh.

Undeterred, Dyer went on. 'Somehow or other you identified him, I'm sure about that. He was probably the main reason why you didn't cooperate with the inquiry. You were a clever girl. I say that because I think it was the intelligent thing to do.'

Libby frowned. 'So, it was right then when I had nothing, but wrong now when I have all this.' She mirrored Dyer's earlier gesture.

Her logic was grindingly effective, momentarily paralyzing Dyer's thought process. She had thought that exposing Fowler would have been enough for a breakthrough. It clearly wasn't. She needed to move up a gear, explain why it was important to her, her personally, not the investigation. She made a couple of false starts, couldn't get herself to say the words, found her throat too tight, the control of her voice, her emotions, momentarily beyond her capabilities. She spooned some sugar into her coffee, took a long sip, then put the mug back on the table with trembling fingers.

'He raped me too.'

They looked across the table at each other. The beat of the music audible again. In the deeper background, she could hear the rumble of the traffic on the bypass.

'But you're a police officer. How could that happen? How could you let him do that to you?'

Dyer took a deep breath then blew it out slowly between pursed lips.

'I'd just been made DS, been posted to the murder squad investigating Rana's killing.' She was in testifying mode now, getting her facts lined up, bringing them out in their logical, case-making order. 'There'd been a bit of a do, celebrating someone's promotion, I think. I was still on a bit of a high from my own promotion, drank more than I would normally. Anyway I 'coincidentally' found myself outside the pub looking for a taxi home at the same time as him. He offered to share it and buttered me up on the way. You know, how much he was looking forward to working with me, how good it was to get a woman on the management team. I was the only woman sergeant although there were a couple of detective constables on the squad.' The sudden thought flashed through her mind that they must have known what he was like, yet never warned her. No female solidarity there then. 'When we got to the flat, he more or less invited himself up for a coffee.'

Libby said nothing but that didn't stop Dyer answering the unasked question.

'I know. I should've known better. But he was a chief superintendent, a legend in CID. Saying no to a coffee would have looked so small, so ungrateful, so bloody timid. And I was a bit pissed. That didn't help, then or later.'

'But you're a police officer,' Libby repeated, unable to keep the disbelief out of her voice. 'You get training in self-defence. How could he …'

'Police training in self-defence is basically crap. Trust me. And I didn't have a Taser or CS spray, or an extending baton in my bag.' She took a sip of the coffee, her hand steady now, her voice more matter-of-fact. 'Even if I had, it wouldn't have done me any good.' She breathed deeply again, a couple of breaths, then carried on, getting the images right. 'As we go into the living room I feel his hand on my shoulder. He turns me and begins trying to kiss me. I push him off and slap him. Then he hits me. Unbelievably hard. In the stomach. He's a big man, over six foot. I'm really badly winded, nearly unconscious, can't breathe. I only stay standing because he's holding me up. Then he drapes me like a broken doll over the back of the sofa, pulls down my pants and fucks me. First in the vagina. Then in the anus. As he puts his prick in there, he says, "And now one for his nob." Just like Kelly said he did to her.'

As she said this, she looked Libby in the eye and saw the look of recognition flash over it.

'I can't believe it's happening. I feel so bloody helpless. I still can't get my breath. The pain in my gut is crippling and he's holding my head by my hair, with his other hand over my mouth. When he's finished, he leans over me and says "it would have been easier if you'd played along. Put this one down to experience, girl – you've got a bright future if you play it right." Then he pulls back my head by the hair, forcing me to look into his eyes and says "but if you say anything about this, I'll destroy you. And we both know that I can.'"

Her voice was trembling again and she was barely managing to keep back the tears.

When Dyer had finished, Libby got up and went into the living room. Dyer was certain that she had blown it, that the next sound would be Libby on the phone to either the lawyer or Complaints. Instead, she came back a few minutes later with a bottle of vodka. She dolloped a healthy measure into each mug, put the bottle on the worktop and came back to sit at the table. They toasted one another with the new mix.

'So you didn't report it?' Libby asked.

'I had the next couple of days off. I didn't do anything for two days except wash. I was obsessive about the need to get clean. Get him out of me.' She gave a half-laugh. 'If I'd had one of those bottle washing brushes, I think I'd have done myself some permanent damage.'

'But you're police. You know what to do. How to get the bastard.'

'You're right. But by the same measure, I knew what was going to happen. How I'd be judged. I had destroyed all the forensics. Didn't report it straight-away. And he's a legend in the same department that would be investigating the crime.' She looked across the table at Libby. 'You know how it feels. You've been there. The people you need to trust are the very people you know you can't. Catch-22.'

'What happened when you went back to work?'

'I didn't. Not for a while anyway. When my leave was up, I phoned in sick. He was my boss, no-one would question it if he didn't. A couple of days later, I went to the doctor's. She took one look at me and signed me off for a month with clinical depression. She tried to get me an emergency appointment with a psychiatrist, but the wait was something like two months. So I went privately.'

'Did that help?'

'A bit, not much. I was making her fight with one hand tied behind her back. I wouldn't discuss the rape. I couldn't. Not even with her. You're the only person I've ever said this much to.'

She drained her mug, got up, crossed to the sink, ran it under the tap and put it on the draining tray, then turned back to face Libby.

'But I'll tell the world now if I think that we can get that bastard.'

'We?'

'You, me, Kelly. Trust me, the combination will work. His M.O. is the same. If we all testify, he's meat.'

'But you and Kelly would be enough. Why do you need me?'

'The conviction rate for rape is still pathetic. Kelly's moved on a lot since you knew her, but she's still a bit of a space cadet, still easy to undermine as a witness. And as for me, you've said it yourself, I'm a police officer, a detective sergeant for God's sake. I knew what had to be done. I've probably waited too long. But you knew back then that he was a police officer, didn't you? You had the perfect reason for saying nothing. With all three of us it would work.'

'You're asking a hell of a lot.' Libby got up from the table and joined Dyer by the sink. 'I'd be risking all this. All that I've built up for myself.'

'You'd be given anonymity. No one would know.'

'In Granby? Fat chance.' She rinsed her mug, picked up a tea towel and began to tidy both away. 'I'm sorry. I can't do it. I won't risk it. You're asking too much. I want my future, my children's future, to be safe – much more than I need some sort of revenge for the past.'

'Not revenge, Libby – justice.'

'You call it what you like. If you want your "justice", you'll need to get it without me.'

Chapter 31

STONE ARRIVED AT THE RESTAURANT a little late. Only ten minutes, but late. She pathologically hated that; always thought it put her at a disadvantage that she never quite overcame. She hadn't had time for that bath, but after four hours in a custody suite, she felt that her hair and body reeked of other people's sweat and fear, so had made do with a shower. For some reason, her hairdryer seemed to be working at half-power and took forever to dry her hair. Mark Dryden was already at the table, halfway through a glass of red wine. He rose to greet her and kissed her demurely on the cheek while she babbled her apologies. There was a plate of bruschetta in the middle of the table and a glass of Chianti already poured at her place.

'I took the liberty of ordering these,' he said, pointing to the bruschetta and the wine. 'Is that OK? It's easy enough to change them.'

'No,' she said, picking up a slice, 'brilliant idea. You must have known I'd be famished.'

They both knew what they wanted without the need for the menu: lasagne and green salad. The rapid depletion of the bottle of Chianti with the bruschetta indicated that it was going to be another two-bottle meal. He was an easy man to talk to, a good listener. It had only taken a couple of prods to get her to take him through all the drama of the press and then the IPCC inquiry.

'I must admit that I was surprised with the case being referred to the IPCC, that you didn't get suspended,' he said.

How much to tell him? It would have been a massive relief to talk it all through, get another, more objective view on where she found herself. But in the end she couldn't. She was cop to her bones. He had been part of the original CSE investigation and she still didn't know him that well, although that looked as if it might change, soon, she found herself hoping. The arrival of the lasagne gave her the space to think before replying.

'The Chief's rationale is that it was a unique, one-off sort of situation. If he took me off the Cold Case Unit, he would need to disband it. He hasn't got anyone else to lead it at the minute.' She smiled. 'And I managed to persuade him that we were making progress.'

As soon as the words were out, she felt like kicking herself, anticipating his next question, reminding herself that you should never open a door you don't want someone to step through.

'How did you manage to do that?'

She knew she had to censor herself on what she could say. He knew about the tampering with the CSE case papers so she stuck with that.

'He wants me to follow up on the tampering issues we've already talked about. He thinks I can be independent enough as I wasn't here when the original inquiry was made. And you know what the archives are like, so that'll take up half the team's time. And one of the taxi drivers has been nicked in West Yorkshire. I'm following that up.'

'Any joy there?'

'West Yorkshire have got him bang to rights on their case, so he's more or less putting his hands up to ours to get it all over and done with. But he hasn't added much to what we already know, and he claims to know nothing about the murder – claims that it came out of the blue for him and the other drivers. He took advantage of the hiatus it raised to move away, hoping that the CSE would go away if he could keep his head down. Which it did of course.'

'He didn't give you anything that links the two?'

'Not so far. I think we need to find at least one more driver, see if we can get them in a bidding war with information. In fact, I'm still a bit stuck there. The only thing that link the inquiries is the fact that Rana was a main player in one and victim in the other. And that both inquiries ended up being headed by Frank Fowler. You know Fowler, what do you think?'

'I was only a DS and he was chief superintendent so I didn't know him as such. He had a solid reputation for getting the job done. Although his style was closer to *Life on Mars* than *Midsomer Massacres*.'

She laughed.

'Was he into local politics?'

'Or politicians? Not that I heard.' He looked questioningly at her. 'Is he in the frame for the changes to the CSE case papers?'

'If only someone was, it would make my life much easier. No. He's just another common denominator. I need to re-interview him in due course, even if only to eliminate him.'

'Good luck with that,' he said with a smile, 'he'll bite the head off anyone even implying that he might be bent.'

'He might bark, but he's retired. He can't bite me, not any more. Anyway, enough about me, how come you're back here so soon?'

'I pop back and forward a lot, we've just never bumped into each other before. A new target came up and I took the chance to come up and check it out personally.' He smiled. 'I could probably have done it on the phone but then I wouldn't be sitting here having this delightful meal, would I?'

They were interrupted by the waiter taking away their plates which gave her another opportunity to think through the next step with him. She decided that honesty was best.

'Mark, you know I was married to Tony Bradshaw?'

'The talk in the Department was of nothing else when you both came up from the Met – two for the price of one.'

'The thing is, since we broke up, I've made it my rule that I wouldn't get involved with another cop. It makes life all too public, too bloody complicated.'

'Funny,' he said, 'I've got the same rule, for more or less the same reasons. But I'm sure you've already checked that out,' he added with a wry smile. 'But you know what they say about rules, they're for the guidance of wise men and the blind obedience of fools. And neither of us is a fool.'

'I think you need to speak for yourself there. I don't feel all that clever about my decisions – job or personal.'

'You must know that the whole force, service probably, thinks that you made the right decision about the murders.'

'But not about Tony.' This with the hint of a smile.

He laughed. 'Come on, Rachel, you know better than that. Never make judgements about other people's relationships – it's bound to come back and bite you on the arse.'

They did not want coffee. He had already signalled to the waiter for the bill. They agreed with some reluctance on his part to split it. That done, they found themselves standing, close together, outside the restaurant. Before she could speak he said, 'I know, you go that way,' he pointed in the direction of her flat, 'and I go this,' pointing in the opposite direction.

He took her hands in both of his. 'Let's stick to the rules for the minute, Rachel. There's no rush. But next time I think we should have a proper date, you know, where I get to pick you up and pay the bill. Move from being friendly colleagues to being friends at least?'

'OK, wise man, you're on.'

With that, she kissed him briefly on the lips and walked off, feeling his eyes on her back, and enjoying it.

She was at the newsagents so early the next morning that she needed to help untie the bundles to get at the copies. She restrained herself from reading them until she was safely ensconced in her office, coffee in hand.

The *Guardian* piece was pretty much as the draft copy she had seen the day before, but with the added barb that *the case shows that the PCCs may after all have some worth as it is rumoured that it was only by PCC Naeem holding the Chief Constable's feet to the fire that this case got referred in the first place.* Naeem would love that, she thought, a *Guardian* finding that she was the conscience of the police service.

The Sun and *Daily Mail* both took a totally different approach. Megan Freeland had been very clever in that mysteriously, Emma Bolton's family contacted *The Sun*, and Tracey Gibbons' family independently contacted *The Mail*. Each had an exclusive interview which made it worth their while running the story, both with much more prominence than the *Guardian*. *The Sun* had lots of pictures, the family, the tent of the murder scene, a flattering picture of Stone herself, and relatively little text. But what there was was punchy, and on her side, or that of the families.

THE SUN

FAMILY'S FURY AT THREAT TO TOP DETECTIVE

Top cop, DCI Rachel Stone, is now to be investigated by the Independent Police Complaints Commission (IPCC) for being SUCCESSFUL! DCI Stone managed to detect the murderer of Emma Bolton within two days of her being reported missing. She persuaded the alleged killer, Michael Fleming, to show her where he had buried Emma's body. He went on, allegedly, to take her to where the body of another victim, Tracey Gibbons, was buried. For these acts, she will now be investigated by the IPCC with a view to her being sacked. Unbelievable but true! The family of Emma Bolton, in an exclusive interview, gave their astounded reaction to THE SUN. Emma's mother, Pam, said, 'It's just unbelievable. Rachel was fantastic in what she achieved. She found Emma within hours of taking up the case. She gave us early closure. Because of her, we have some chance of putting our life back together. She should get a medal for what she did, instead she is being hounded out of the job.'

The Mail took the same line, this time from Tracey Gibbons' family's perspective.

FURIOUS GIBBONS FAMILY BACK DETECTIVE

In an exclusive interview with The Mail, Tracey's father John said, 'This is worse than ridiculous. Rachel Stone did a fantastic job. Tracey had been missing for three years. In that time, we had been living in hell, not knowing what had happened to her, but always fearing the worst. The fact that that b****** Fleming said nothing after he got access to a lawyer shows that DCI Stone did the right thing – certainly by us, the victims in this. To see her being hounded out of the job she does so well is a travesty. We may not be able to get justice for Tracey's death because of the stupidity of the legal system, but we can and will fight for justice for Rachel Stone.'

There were the usual pictures, plus a picture of Naeem wearing a headscarf with a caption underneath: *Mrs Akila Naeem, England's only Muslim PCC, who wants top detective sacked*. No matter how comforting it was to have this level of national support, it grated with her to find that *The Mail* used her to get in another of its not-so-subliminal racist messages.

The phone ringing put a stop to her thoughts. She checked her watch. Still only 7 a.m. Who knew she was here for God's sake? Reluctantly she picked up.

'Rachel, it's Megan. I assume you've read the papers.'

'Yes, I have. I can't thank you enough for—'

'Nothing, Rachel. I did nothing. It was the families' idea to get in touch with the papers, remember.'

'Well, can you thank them for me – or should I do that myself?'

'No. That's why I'm phoning. Local radio and TV are interested in doing a follow-up but I consulted with the Chief and we are blanking them. Our stand is that this matter is under investigation by the IPCC and it is inappropriate to comment. I'd advise you to do the same. Fleming hasn't been tried yet and it's difficult to say anything without breaching the contempt of court rules. The good thing is that they'll ensure that it all runs out of steam in a day or so. In fact, some of the comments in the papers probably breach the rules but since most are quotes by the families, I don't think anything will come of it. The only danger is if Fleming's counsel complains – unlikely as he's pleading – but that may change if it looks as if the CPS is being pressured into changing their minds about Tracey Gibbons.'

'OK, Megan. I'll keep my head down and see how it pans out. But I'm worried now that Naeem has made this personal by leaking against me.'

'I can understand that but I don't think there's too much to worry about. Peterson isn't very good, certainly not as good as me. And I've got better contacts. We're ahead on points, Rachel, and that's where I intend to keep us.'

They hung up and Stone noticed that while she was talking to Megan, a message had come in. She didn't recognize the number but opened it anyway.

Hi Rachel. Just a quick note of support and a reminder that there is always this bolthole down in Dorset if you need it. Or I could come up. Tom

That's always the way of it, she thought, no men for ages then two come along at the same time.

Chapter 32

Tom Gregson's text prompted her to think how much easier it would be to visit Dorset if she were back in the Met. Although her application had been accepted, no final decision would be made on the transfer back until the IPCC had reported. And they always took forever. Maybe there was something she could do about that. She had no intention of denying anything. The outcome would depend on the merits of her decision that the rights of the victims had equal standing to that of their murderer – or fall on its non-compliance with PACE. It was time to take the fight to the enemy.

The three members of the IPCC team were using an office in the Policing Standards Department. As Stone guessed, they were still in the start-up phase of the day, sharing a wake-up coffee. Their reaction to her entrance was almost comic. First disbelief, followed by a panicky gathering up of papers scattered on the desktops in a vain attempt to ensure that she had no chance of reading them. A waste of time as she knew what was in them. But it did put them on the back foot. She intended to keep them there. The lead investigator, Douglas Banks, was the first to speak.

'Chief Inspector Stone, I think you know you shouldn't be here. I'd like you to leave now.'

'I will – in a moment. First I'd like to make you a one-time offer.'

'I'm not sure what you mean.'

'Well, we can do this the way you always do it – you interview everybody and their aunt to make sure there's nothing you could have missed. Then you arrange to interview me. I come with a lawyer and say as little as possible. You go away and take a couple of months to come to a recommendation.'

'We do the investigation as quickly as we can. You are a detective, you'll know—'

'I am, and I do. That's why I'm making this offer.' She paused for effect. 'I'll come back for an interview with just a Federation rep as a witness in,' she looked at her watch, 'two hours' time. Eleven o'clock. I'll give you my statement and answer any reasonable questions.'

'Or? I think there's an 'or' in there.'

'Or, you take another month or so covering your backs, I come for the interview with a lawyer a few weeks after that and say as little as possible.'

'You can't bring a lawyer. We are only looking at discipline, not crime.'

'You can say that but the fact is that any serious malfeasance by a police officer can constitute a failure to carry out a public duty. For your information, that's a Common Law misdemeanour. You can't cover the discipline without considering the criminal. You can't exclude a lawyer. If you try to, I'll go to court for an injunction. We both know the Federation will support me in that.'

Banks sat back down at his desk, thinking through what she had said.

'I can't make that decision,' he said after a bit.

'Don't try to bullshit a bullshitter, Mr Banks. It's your investigation. You have my offer. Call me in the next half hour with your decision. That'll even give you time to cover your arse with head office.'

With that she left, trying but failing to keep the look of satisfaction off her face. She knew it was an offer no investigator could refuse.

At 11 a.m., Stone walked into the interview room accompanied by Inspector Nick Wainwright, the Federation rep for inspectors. He had done his best to try to persuade her against giving the interview, but failed. Banks and his assistant, James Oxford, were already in the room and had set up the tapes, ready to go. As soon as they had gone through the formalities, Wainwright said, 'I want to put it on record that I have advised Chief Inspector Stone not to go through with this interview at this time, and that she should have legal advice before making a decision. Since she insists on going ahead, I'm here solely as a witness and not as an adviser.'

'That's noted, Inspector,' said Banks. He turned his attention to Stone. 'Chief Inspector Stone, you're aware of your rights and are here voluntarily, indeed, here at your own request?'

'That's correct.'

'I have some—'

'It may save time,' said Stone, 'if I give you this duty statement.' She passed copies of her statement across the table to Banks and Oxford. 'For the record, I'll read it out then I'll answer questions if I can.'

'Go ahead,' said Banks.

She picked up the statement and began to read.

'*I am Detective Chief Inspector Rachel Stone, currently leading the Cold Case Unit attached to Granbyshire police headquarters. On 7 October 2015, I was the SIO investigating the disappearance of Emma Bolton. She had been missing for two days. We had identified a Michael Fleming as a strong suspect both from CCTV and from other inquiries. At the time we did not know if Emma was alive or dead. CCTV had indicated that Fleming had taken Emma to Frankton Park. I had Fleming arrested on his way to work for the offence of suspected abduction of Emma and brought to me to the car park there. I thought that by doing so I would be better able to get him to tell me what he had done with her. She may have still been alive and I believed that her right to life overrode his rights as a suspect. Within a few moments of his arrival at the car park, Fleming admitted to having taken Emma and he volunteered to take us to where he said he had buried her. We found the body of Emma Bolton where he indicated. Shortly after we had begun uncovering Emma's body, Fleming volunteered to take us to where he said he had buried another girl. I arranged for the work to proceed at Emma's grave and followed Fleming's directions to a nearby wood. There we uncovered the body of another girl at the spot that Fleming had indicated. I suspected that the second body was that of Tracey Gibbons and this turned out to be the case. I accept that under PACE I should have rearrested Fleming and taken him to the police station at the point where he told me of the second grave. However, I was unwilling to lose the momentum to the investigation that this would have caused and believed that it was the only certain way of discovering the whereabouts of the second body. In both cases, I believed that Fleming's right as a suspect had to be balanced against those of the missing girls and their families. I believe that my decision was vindicated by the fact that when he was taken back to the station and given access to a lawyer, Fleming then said nothing in the interviews that followed, presumably on advice of counsel. I regret that the CPS have decided, on advice of counsel, not to proceed against Fleming for the murder of Tracey Gibbons. I believe that this should have been a decision for the court and the jury.*

I regret that Tracey's family are being denied justice by this decision.

I wish to add that my assistant, Detective Sergeant Patricia Downing,

disagreed with my decision and did her best to persuade me to follow the
PACE procedures.

    Signed Rachel Stone, Detective Chief Inspector, Granbyshire Police.

She put her copy of the statement on the table and looked across at Banks.

'Do you have any questions?'

'When Fleming arrived at the car park, did he ask for a lawyer?'

'He vaguely mentioned it but he went on to tell me where to find Emma.'

'Do you accept that you should have stopped questioning him at the point where he asked for a lawyer?'

'No. I accept that PACE says that I should, but I still believed that Emma may have been alive and my first responsibility was to her. It was a classic *Dirty Harry* dilemma. It is also the sort of exigency that's impossible to write into law. As a police officer, I was where the law put me, having to decide the balance of one person's rights against another. I thought that Emma's life may still have been in danger, and that this had primacy. If the law isn't flexible enough to allow that, then it is an arse.'

'So you think you're above the law?'

'No, I took an oath of office. I believe in it. Under it, I believe that my primary responsibility is to protect life. Under the law I can even use fatal force to achieve that in the right circumstances. I thought that there was a chance that Emma could be alive. Her right to live was more than marginally greater than his right to a lawyer.'

'That did not apply to the second victim, Tracey Gibbons. You knew she was dead. All you could do was find her body. Yet you didn't rearrest Mr Fleming, didn't caution him and remind him of his rights.'

'I'm a very experienced investigator. I acted on my belief that I had to keep up the momentum that I had achieved. That I needed to exploit the relationship I appeared to have with Mr Fleming. I proved to be correct about that. He said nothing after he had spoken to a lawyer, despite the fact that he taken us to the graves voluntarily.'

'You do think you're above the law. That your instincts as an investigator allow you to ignore Mr Fleming's rights.'

'There are all sorts of circumstances where a police officer needs to balance people's conflicting rights. Some of them are even written into PACE, for instance, keeping a suspect incommunicado in the interests of the investigation. I took the view that Tracey Gibbons' family's right to know what had happened to her overrode Fleming's right to a lawyer. I still believe that. I would make the same decision again in the same circumstances.'

She turned to Wainwright. 'I think I'm done here, Nick.' Then back to Banks. 'I've said all I'm going to say, Mr Banks. You have more than enough there to come to a decision. If you want to re-interview me, it'll be with my lawyer there. But I can tell you now that I will not add anything to my statement.'

Banks nodded and at his cue, Oxford completed the formalities and reminded Stone that she would get a copy of the tape. They all stood to leave.

'I'd appreciate it if this can be wound up soon,' said Stone. 'I'm not denying anything and I want to get on with my life.'

'It will take as long as it takes, Chief Inspector,' said Banks. 'But then you know that already. Thank you for your cooperation thus far.'

Chapter 33

WHEN SHE GOT BACK TO the office, the others were clearly waiting for her to tell them the outcome of the meeting with the IPCC, but were too polite to ask. Before she could say anything, Shepherd spoke.

'We've just had West Mids on the phone, boss. They've located Kevin Howard in a half-way house in Handsworth. They've asked about his father but he says he has no idea who he is. They also got his mother's details and I've checked her out. She's still alive, which is a bonus, and is living in Derby. According to her record, at the time Kevin was born, she was a pretty heavy user and was on and off the game. That supports what Kevin says. I suggest that a couple of us go to see her, see if she can give us any pointers. But looking at her form, I'm not very hopeful.'

'Bollocks,' said Stone. 'I thought that that'd be a banker. Let me think about that. First, I'd like to deal with Fowler. It's shit or bust time with him.'

'Why, boss?' asked Ahmed. 'It doesn't look like enough to me.'

Dyer nodded and Shepherd grunted in agreement.

'OK, let's look at what we've got.' Stone listed the points.

'– We know there was a bent cop involved with Rana and the CSE;

– we know that the CSE case papers were doctored;

– we know that no connection was made by the murder inquiry to the CSE;

– we know that a big white guy was given access to the girls;

– we know that Fowler, a big white guy, headed up both inquiries.

If he wasn't a cop, we would have lifted him long ago.'

'But he is – was, rather,' said Dyer, 'and I don't think arresting him will do any good. He's hardly going to just come out and admit it, is he?'

'No,' said Stone, 'but if we arrest him at his house, we can search it. Cops are just like everyone else, they keep things, even things that are potentially dangerous.'

'Not him,' said Shepherd, 'he is much too shrewd to do anything like that. And if he had, he'd have got rid of it the moment you left his house last time.'

'Maybe,' replied Stone. 'But, and I admit it's a big but, maybe he's too confident, just arrogant enough to think that he's bullet-proof.'

She paused to take another look at the briefing board then turned back to the group.

'The fact is I don't think we're going to get any more. Rana is dead, Kelly can't ID the man and the case papers were too easy to access.' She opened her arms in supplication. 'Unless anyone else has a better idea?'

She paused long enough to allow anyone to come in, and getting nothing but averted eyes, she continued. 'So we go for it, tomorrow morning, a 6 o' clock knock. I've set up the search team but they won't know where we're going until we're about to go out the door. No one is to be told about this.'

'Not even the Chief?' asked Dyer.

'Not even the Chief.' Stone smiled. 'I've always found it easier to seek forgiveness than permission and we need to move on this, get some momentum back, take the fight to him.'

'You're that certain that it's him, boss?' asked Shepherd.

'Absolutely. I just can't prove it,' she laughed, 'but there's nothing new in that, is there, Colin?' She turned to Dyer. 'We need to make sure he's there when we go in. Barbara will house him and watch till midnight. Iftikhar, you'll relieve her. Colin and I will meet here at 4.30 for the briefing, then we go.'

'I'd like to be in on it,' said Dyer.

'You won't get much sleep.'

'No matter, I'd like to be there.'

'OK.'

She looked around the team. Normally they would get a real buzz when a decision to act was taken – cops prefer action to words. But their body language shouted their concerns at her.

'Look, I know you all have reservations about this but I spoke to the IPCC today and I don't think I've got much time left to get a result. This is the best I can do.'

The black mass of the river passing below her window whirled and eddied around unseen underwater obstructions, its threatening presence softened by the reflected light of the surrounding apartments. The gloom of the early evening reminded her of why she both loved and loathed the place. She loved the view over the river where the building, an old riverside warehouse, backed directly onto it. Opposite was a small park, now another black patch lit only by the string of lamps that followed the footpath along the riverside. A view like this in London would be well beyond her means. Loathe was too strong a word on reflection, unloved was better. The enormous living room of the flat ran from back to front, the full width of the building, with ridiculously high ceilings, bright and energizing in the sun, dark and gloomy in the evening light. The cavern effect was exacerbated by the fact that she only used a few standing lights. The low lighting let her look out but left black holes in the room that sucked in what light there was. She was sitting at the end of the dining table, glass of Chablis in hand, over the remains of a meal, seabass in a beurre blanc sauce. The table was big enough for eight people, not that there were ever eight sitting at it, but anything smaller would have looked ludicrously out of proportion to the room – at least so the decorator she had hired had insisted. When she bought the flat, she was in the middle of a double murder and a divorce so she had given the job over to a professional. The result, black, white and brushed steel, was aesthetically pleasing but had all the warmth of a builder's show home.

The meal had been worth the effort and, as always, she found herself wondering why she didn't do it more often. Cooking was so relaxing. In the background she had a Classic FM compilation playing; Beethoven, she guessed. She switched off the table light and her image in the window disappeared, replaced by the black and glitter of the river and the park. She had heard someone on the radio answer the question what would she have liked to have done in her life instead of her current career and she had replied that there were a lot of things she would like to have done as well, but nothing instead. Considering her own life, that was exactly how she felt about the job, lots of things as well, nothing instead. Except marrying Tony, that was a definite instead. So, with this inquiry, she would do the best she could.

That was what she had told the team. And it was, albeit her inadequate best. She knew that Fowler was involved in the Rana murder and in the abuse of the girls, but she had nothing to pin on him. Tomorrow's arrest was an out-and-out fishing expedition. The combination of worrying about how tomorrow would turn out, the relaxed feel of the meal and the wine, made her think how bloody wonderful a cigarette would be, a perfect ending to the meal. Her phone buzzed the arrival of a text. *On a plot. How's the inquiry going? Back in Granby tomorrow. Dinner date? Mark*

She smiled to herself. He was certainly persistent. If nothing came of the arrest tomorrow, she would certainly have the time. She texted back, *V. Early start a.m. bed now. DATE is on. Pick up 7.30. Rachel*

Having hit send, she stared down at the phone. To call the Chief and tell him about the upcoming arrest or not? She would need to do it as soon as she made the arrest anyway. If it leaked out to him from anyone else, she would be so deep in the shit she would need a snorkel. But there was a chance that he would call her off, a chance she would need to take as she must keep at least one chief officer, if not on her side, then at least off her back. She called up his number and hit the button.

'Why are you calling me at home, Stone?' No preamble, just an annoyed voice.

'Sorry, sir, but I thought I should give you a heads up. We're arresting Fowler tomorrow morning.'

'Unless you've got more than you told me, that seems more than a bit premature.'

'I don't think I'm going to get any more than I already have. But if he hadn't been a cop, he'd have been arrested by now.'

'But he was and he'll know you're playing him.'

'I know, but I need to search his place sooner rather than later and this is the easiest way to do it.'

'Have you talked it through with anyone else?'

She knew he meant anyone in the ACPO team. 'No, only my team. I've got a search team lined up but they'll only know who we're doing as we go out the door.'

'Is this because you spoke to the IPCC today?'

The old man obviously had a good intelligence system.

'No. If they take their usual time, I'll be able to retire before they come back with a decision. It just feels right.'

'OK, Stone. Good hunting.'

'I tell you about it officially, along with the ACPO team, as soon as we arrest him.'

'Understood. Goodnight.'

Well, she thought, he didn't say no, that would have to do.

Chapter 34

Stone and Dyer sat opposite Fowler and his solicitor, George Warburton, in the interview room at Granby police station. The search team was still working at Fowler's house but had so far found nothing. Fowler's manner, relaxed and just this side of gloating, told Stone that he didn't expect them to find anything. He looked totally composed. Stone began.

'I'll remind you again, Mr Fowler, that you have been arrested for perverting the course of justice, you are still under caution and if you fail to answer our questions, that can be used in evidence.'

'Let's get on with this so that I can go home.'

'When we arrived at your house this morning, both you and your wife were up and dressed. Did anyone warn you that we were coming?'

'We're both early risers.'

'From your experience, that's really unusual, isn't it, people with no work to go to up and about at that hour?'

'We're both early risers.'

'If it had happened to you in the job, wouldn't you have found it unusual?'

Warburton cut across his client. 'Mr Fowler is here to answer questions to fact, Inspector, not to speculate. He's already answered the question. Shall we move on?'

Fowler maintained eye contact with Stone, the merest hint of a smile touching the edges of his mouth, near enough a sneer to get under her skin.

'At the case conference on the abuse cases concerning Kelly Brooks, Liz Ryder and Brittany Selby, no notes were taken of the discussion, only a final note on the decision. That's not usual, is it?'

'As far as I remember, the case conference was called by the council's child protection people. It was their meeting so they were responsible for the notes. You need to ask them. I was only there as head of CID. I took the case papers I was given and acted on the recommendation that the investigating officer had made.'

'Which was what?'

'You've read them. All of the agencies, police, council, CPS, took the view that the girls were totally unreliable witnesses. But we are not here to revisit that, are we? You went over that already when you came to my house. Can we get on? Get to the point?'

'According to the investigating officers,' she checked her notes, 'DS Dryden and DC MacLean, two of the girls put Bashir Rana, the owner of the taxi firm and the victim of the murder you later investigated, in the frame for abusing and trafficking them. Do you remember that?'

'No, I don't. If I had, then I would have included that line of inquiry in the murder investigation. I know that I didn't.'

'How do you account for the fact that the case papers had been doctored to remove Rana?'

'I think it's your job to do that. At least it was when I was in the Job. You're the detective, God help us, but you are. You've arrested me for doing it, so where's the proof?'

'The investigating officers say that Rana was included in their reports. You were in charge of CID. You took the case to the case conference where Rana was apparently not mentioned. The case papers now have no mention of Rana—'

Warburton interrupted again. 'Are you saying that the detectives personally handed the case papers to Mr Fowler?'

'No, they would have been sent through the system.' As she said this, Stone knew what his next point would be.

'So, any number of people could have access to these papers in the process. Anyone in the HQ CID, in fact?'

'Not anyone.'

'You can guarantee that, Chief Inspector, can you? Swear to a jury that it could only have been my client and no one else? That they were kept in a filing system to which only he had the key?' Stone said nothing and Warburton continued. 'I thought not. This whole arrest has been a fishing expedition, hasn't it?'

Dyer said, 'The girls also mentioned a masked white man, a local. He's not in the case papers, either.'

Stone tried to work out how to deal with this interjection by Dyer. She had wanted to come at the issue with a bit more subtlety, more obliquely. She thought that she and Dyer had agreed on this. Before she could say anything, Fowler said, 'And?'

The look on Dyer's face told Stone that nothing short of physical intervention would work. She was a woman on a mission.

'You know who he was, don't you?' Dyer said.

'What proof do you have that I do?'

'We both know it was you, don't we, Fowler?' said Dyer, pointing a finger across the table at Fowler's chest. 'I've spoken to two of the girls. Rana gave you access and you needed to protect him, didn't you? Come on, Fowler, we both know your style, don't we?'

Stone had difficulty in keeping her face free of expression through this exchange. Where did that accusation come from? It hadn't been part of their pre-interview discussion. But Dyer's voice carried conviction and she had seen Fowler flinch and pale at the accusation.

Warburton must also have noticed his client's reaction and he stepped in. 'Where's the evidence for this outrageous accusation? In fact, where's the evidence for any of this? Did any of the girls identify my client?'

Stone looked at Dyer, giving a small hand signal that she needed to deal with the question.

Dyer leaned across the table, getting her face as close to Fowler she could, her index finger stabbing at him, stopping inches short of his chest.

'We both know it was you, don't we, Frank? That you can only get off by going in up the arse. You probably prefer little boys but don't have the nerve or the access for that.' By now she was on her feet, shouting, spittle flying across the table into Fowler's face. 'How's that for one for his nob, eh, Frank?'

Stone leapt out of the chair and pulled Dyer away from the table and towards the door, telling her to be quiet, that that was enough. Behind her back, she could hear Fowler saying, 'Always knew we shouldn't have women in the Department. Just not up to it …' Then he shouted, 'And you always were more than a bit hysterical, Sergeant Dyer. I'm surprised you've lasted this long without cracking up.'

'You bastard,' shouted Dyer, trying to push past Stone to get at him. The uniform constable who had been waiting outside must have heard the commotion and opened the door, allowing Stone to push Dyer through it.

'Get her away from here,' Stone said to the constable before closing the door and returning to the table.

'For the sake of the tape, DS Dyer has now left the room. We'll take a break and resume the interview in thirty minutes.'

She switched off the tape recorder.

'Don't waste your time and ours, Chief Inspector,' said Warburton. 'On my advice, Mr Fowler will not answer any further questions. Not until you have provided us with some real evidence. His arrest this morning was clearly a pretext for a fishing expedition to search his house. You have no evidence. I demand that he be released forthwith.'

'I hear what you say, Mr Warburton. I need to consult my colleague before we go any further. Mr Fowler is still under arrest. I'll be back directly.'

With that, she opened the door, told the uniform officer waiting outside that she would be back directly, and left in pursuit of Dyer. She needed to find out what the hell was going on.

Chapter 35

THE INTERVIEW ROOMS WERE PART of the custody suite, so Dyer would have to get someone to let her out. Stone had hoped that this would slow her down enough to allow her to catch up, but found from the gatekeeper that Dyer had already left, run off towards the front office and presumably out of the station. The station car park was only big enough to take marked patrol cars; the private cars were parked in a multi-storey ten minutes' walk away. Talking to Dyer would need to come later. As she made her way back to the interview room, Stone called Shepherd on her mobile. She explained what had happened.

'Blew up,' he said, 'swore at him. That's not like Barbara, she's usually such a cool customer.'

'I know. I think I can guess what's behind it but I need you to find her for me, straightaway. Drop everything else.'

'Any idea where to look?'

Stone was now outside the door of the interview room. 'You're a detective, Colin, or so you keep telling me. Just find her by the time I've finished here.'

She ended the call, took the time to get her wits back together and then went back into the room. Fowler and Warburton had been talking but stopped and looked expectantly at her. She sat opposite them at the table, looking Fowler in the eye. She switched the tape on again.

'It's now 9:30 a.m. Present are Mr Fowler, Mr Warburton and DCI Stone. Exactly what did you do to her, Mr Fowler?'

Warburton made to answer but Fowler stopped him with a wave of his hand.

'All I've ever done is my job. I bet you wish you could do it as well, get my clear up rate. I've no idea what happened to that,' he paused, 'woman. She never should have joined the job in the first place.'

'What's the history between you?'

'Nothing I can remember.'

Stone sat back in her seat. She needed to decide now whether to go on with the interview and use up precious PACE time, or cut her losses, find out why Dyer had imploded, regroup and try again. She felt as if she was firing blanks while elsewhere there was some lethal ammunition that could bring Fowler down. A no-brainer really, provided she could manage the flak that Warburton was about to fire her way.

'I'm terminating the interview at this point. It is 9:35 a.m. I need to remind you, Mr Fowler, that you are still a suspect and that you may be rearrested for the offence of perverting the course of justice.'

'And I need to put on record, Chief Inspector,' said Warburton, 'that this whole shambles of an investigation has been nothing but a fishing expedition which has been carried out by an officer clearly not in charge of either her facts or her staff. With the paucity of evidence, I assume that there will be no question of putting my client on police bail.'

'Your client is still a suspect in a serious crime. Police bail will apply and there will be conditions that he does not attend Granbyshire police functions or make any attempt to contact any potential witnesses.'

'That's outrageous. He's a retired police officer. Most of his friends are connected in some way to Granbyshire police.'

'The bail conditions will not prevent him from meeting his friends provided it is not on police premises. Now, if you'll excuse me, I need to find out what your client did to my sergeant.' She stood up and looked down on Fowler. 'And find out I will, Mr Fowler.'

As soon as she had arranged for Fowler to be bailed and he and Warburton to be escorted out of the station, Stone made her way to the car park. Dyer's car had gone. She decided to go back to headquarters but to drive via Dyer's house. When she was a few moments away, Shepherd called her.

'I found out from the staff at Granby nick that Barbara had driven off, so I came here to her house to see if she's here. Her car is in the drive. Do you want me to go in?'

'Great minds and all that, Colin, I'm only a couple of minutes away. Wait till I get there.'

'I'm parked about fifty yards away from the house. After what you said had happened, I didn't want to spook her by sitting outside.'

'Good thinking. I've got you in sight now.'

Stone parked behind Shepherd's car and joined him in the front passenger seat. She tried first Dyer's mobile, then her landline, both went immediately to messaging.

She looked at Shepherd, shrugged and said, 'We've no option.'

They got out and walked to the house, a small bungalow sitting in the middle of a beautiful cottage garden, one created and maintained with love. Stone knocked, gently at first, then getting no reply, more insistently. When that in its turn got no response, she shouted through the letterbox.

'Barbara, we know you're in there. You need to let us in.'

Nothing.

'If you don't, we're coming in anyway. After what happened at the station, you know I need to talk to you – for your own good if nothing else.'

Nothing.

'I need to know that you're all right. You're a police officer, you know that.'

Nothing.

'All right, Barbara, you know what's going to happen next. In ten seconds, Colin is going to put the door in. You know I mean it.'

She stood up and took a step away from the door, indicating that Shepherd should go ahead. He stood back and was about to kick the door at the lock when it opened.

Dyer looked dreadful. She had aged twenty years in the hour that has passed since she had stormed out of the interview room. Her face had no colour other than the black shadows under her eyes, emphasizing their red rims. She stood silently at the half open door.

'We need to come in, Barbara.'

Dyer began to protest then stopped, her arms dropped by her side and she turned and walked back into the house, pulling the door fully open as she did so.

Stone turned to Shepherd. 'You go back to headquarters now. I'll deal with this.'

She followed Dyer into the house, closing the door behind her.

The trouble, thought Stone as she followed Dyer towards the living room, the trouble in handling cops who found themselves in distressing circumstances was the tendency to treat them solely as cops, not as human beings. Measuring their actions against some undeclared professional standard rather than one of common humanity. Understandable, maybe even essential, at a time of crisis, but not necessary or even helpful when time was an ally and not an enemy. Dyer's behaviour in the interview room was professionally unacceptable. But it was clear that talking to Kelly Brooks had disturbed some deep-seated issue and that the cap of her emotional volcano had been blown off by Fowler. Something had clearly happened between them. She was not looking forward to finding out what that something had been.

She found Dyer sitting in an armchair in the gloom of the living room, having drawn the curtains in her pathetic attempt to exclude her pursuers.

'Shall I make us some tea or coffee?' asked Stone softly.

'No. I don't want any tea or coffee. I don't want any fucking pity or under-standing. I do want to be left alone. You've seen me. I'm all right. My resignation will be in the post tomorrow. I've enough leave and time owed to work out the month's notice.'

When speaking, her head had been bowed, making it look as if she was addressing the carpet. She looked up sharply.

'I should have done that ten years ago and saved myself a lot of heartache. Got a proper job for a woman, a teacher, a nurse. Got some distance between me and misogynist bastards like Fowler.'

The little living room was filled by a three-piece, pale leather suite. The chairs and settee made an almost unbroken U-shape around the fire. Stone squeezed between one of the chairs and the settee and sat at the end closer to Dyer, their knees almost touching.

'What did he do to you, Barbara? I think I've already guessed.'

'I told you. I'm done. I really would like you to go away, Rachel.' She was sobbing now, oblivious of the tears streaming down her cheeks, of her nose beginning to run.

Stone got up, went to the kitchen, filled and plugged in the kettle, came back with a kitchen roll and handed it to Dyer, saying, 'Tissues would be a bloody waste of time.'

Dyer took the roll, tore off a couple of sections and wiped her face. It took a couple more before the stream of tears began to dry up and the sobbing began to quiet. In the meantime, Stone made the coffee. She brought two mugs back in and took up a seat on the sofa. They both sat quiet, sipping the still too hot coffee.

'What did he do, Barbara? Rape or some sort of perverted assault is my guess.'

'He raped me.'

'Tell me what happened.'

And she did. And when she was done they both sat in silence, a silence that Stone eventually broke. 'He's won once, Barbara, do you want him to win again? That's what resigning means. He wins. The bastard walks away – again.'

Dyer said nothing, just sipped her coffee.

'Things have changed, Barbara. Attitudes have changed. And we both know you won't be the only one. If we can get him arrested, charged, who knows how many others might come forward. And the CPS and the courts come at it differently now.'

Dyer gave a wry smile. 'Yes, I know, it's all wonderful now, isn't it? You don't need to prove that you resisted, show the bruises. Everyone is so much more open to the victim. That's why the conviction rate has rocketed from four per cent to eight per cent. And I'm a police officer, Rachel, I knew what to do. I've as much chance of getting a result as I have of pulling George Clooney. We both know that.'

'But we've got Kelly's evidence as well. The two were so similar that they'll act as corroboration.'

Dyer's smile turned to bitter laughter. 'The evidence of a space cadet and a hysterical, over-promoted woman versus a long serving, upstanding pillar of the community. You forget, Rachel, I've sat where you're sitting. I've given victims the same line of bullshit so that I could get the case past GO, get the rapist in the dock. Only to see the CPS back off, or the judge give some killing direction to the jury, letting the bastard walk. I'm not going through that. I'm not like you, I've no escape tunnel dug to the Met. I'm stuck here with the looks, the little barbs, the conversations I'm not part of but that are loud enough for me to hear. I don't even get bloody anonymity. Everyone in the force will know who victim X is.' She looked up sharply. 'And by the way, after Kelly, I didn't just sit under it. I went to see Libby Grainger, tried to persuade her to testify.'

'You what? That was bloody stupid. That could have cost …'

'Me my job. I know. But I was certain she knew who the white guy was.'

'And did she?'

'I'm sure she did but she wouldn't admit it. But the thing is I tried. I told her what Fowler did to me. She wasn't willing to come forward so why should I think that anyone else would?'

Stone felt her shoulders droop in resignation. Don't bullshit a bullshitter, she always said. Yet here she was, trying to do exactly that. It would be uphill, for exactly the reasons Dyer had described. But she had to bloody try at least.

'Look, don't decide anything today. Think about it and I'll talk to you again tomorrow, OK?' Dyer gave a little nod of the head to one side, neither agreeing or disagreeing. 'What about tonight? Do you want me to stay? Would you prefer to come and stay at my place? Don't be alone, please.'

Dyer slowly got up from the chair and Stone reluctantly followed her lead, accepting that Barbara wanted her gone.

'Don't worry about me, boss.' She gave a dry laugh. 'I've lived with it for ten years, I think I'll manage another night on my own. Anyway, I wouldn't do anything that would give that bastard any satisfaction. You're right, I'll think about it. I'll call you tomorrow morning. Right now, I'd really, really like to be left alone. I think that I've earned the right to that at least.'

Chapter 36

Stone was briefing the ACPO team in the chief's office. The four were sitting at the end of the conference table, the Chief at the head, Stone to his right, opposite her Peter Unwin, the Deputy Chief Constable and Bob Jackson, the ACC.

'What do you think that Dyer will do in the end, Rachel?' asked Hill.

Stone had been expecting to brief the Chief on his own and had been surprised to find the whole team there. But now that Fowler had been arrested, that cat was out of the bag. The chilly atmosphere when she entered the office was testament to the fact that they had been very unhappy to find that the Chief had kept them out of the loop before the arrest. Throughout her briefing on the arrest, the failed interrogation and Dyer's explosive revelation, they had both sat stony-faced. People used to power have a very unsubtle way of letting you know when they are unhappy.

'I honestly don't know, sir. When she was raped by Fowler, she became clinically depressed.' She thought she saw Jackson wince at the word rape and was glad to have used it rather than some euphemism. It had happened on his watch and she was not going to take any crap from him about keeping him in the dark. 'I'll do my best to ensure she's supported this time. But I don't think it will make any difference in terms of prosecuting Fowler. I think we've lost that one.'

'What do you mean?' Jackson barked across the table. 'If we can successfully prosecute ageing DJs for what they did twenty to thirty years ago, what's to stop us doing the same to Fowler?'

'I've discussed it with the CPS. They say that they'll make a final decision once we have taken Barbara's statement and they can look at it overall. But their first pass is that it won't run.'

'That's fucking ridiculous.' Jackson again.

'I agree,' said Stone, 'the trouble is the timing. If Barbara had made a statement before interviewing Kelly Brooks we'd be quids in. The problem is she didn't. We'd be relying on Fowler's M.O. to use similar fact evidence, that would be key since Kelly can't ID her rapist. Now Fowler can claim a stitch-up by, to use Barbara's own description, a space cadet and a hysterical over-promoted woman. Against this we have Fowler's status as a long-standing pillar of the community. As Roger Cartwright in the CPS says, it's only proof beyond reasonable doubt if there is no other likely explanation. If there is, we're talking possibilities or probabilities, not near certainties. He thinks we need more.'

'Maybe if I'd been consulted—' Jackson began.

'We've been through that, Bob,' said Hill, intervening. 'That decision was mine and we've been through it; we are where we are.' He turned to Stone. 'Is there any chance we can get more?'

'Yes, I think we can. We're a long way forward. We don't *think* he might be involved any more, we know he was. Now we can focus on that. We know who and what we're looking for. I'll try to find the original digital records. That can tell us a lot more about when the changes were made. I've still got to re-inter-view Mrs Naeem. That's not going to be easy for all sorts of reasons, but she was a key player in deciding not to pursue the CSE allegations. There are still three other taxi drivers in the wind. But the key difference is we know where to look and what we're looking for. I'm confident we'll get him.'

'What's happening to him in the meanwhile?'

'He's on police bail with conditions, not allowed on police premises, not to attend any police functions. I can't stop him having a pint with an old mate, but giving him pariah status should help. I've also had the locks on the portacabin changed and organized CCTV to watch over it, with a feed to the control room.'

'That's a bit extreme, isn't it?' said Jackson. 'We're not all bent in this force, no matter what you may choose to think about us.'

'I'm sorry if that offends you, sir, but somebody warned Fowler that we were coming, that much is obvious. I'm coming from this as if I was from an outside force.' She turned to Hill. 'This way you're seen to be doing all you can to protect the integrity of the investigation.'

Hill nodded and spoke directly to Jackson. 'The fact is, Bob, we know this force nurtured a particularly rotten apple. My job is to get him convicted, him and anyone else involved. Rachel has my authority to do whatever is needed.'

Peter Unwin, the DCC, who had been silent till now, spoke. 'The Chief has explained why we were kept out of the loop earlier, Chief Inspector. I can't say I like it, but I do understand it. But Fowler has been arrested now so the need to keep us out of the loop is no longer necessary. I expect to be kept informed of any developments that may involve my remit on Professional Standards.'

Hill came in before Stone could speak. 'Of course, Peter, that's taken as read.' He turned to Stone. 'Isn't it, Rachel?'

'Of course, sir. I'll do my best.'

'I just hope your best is good enough,' said Unwin, 'for your sake at least.'

The only room in the flat that Rachel had taken a serious hand in decorating was the bathroom. Next to the bedroom, it was probably the one that she spent most time in. The space meant that she could have an old-fashioned, high sided, roll-top, cast-iron bath. Beside it there was a small glass topped table for the radio, a book, her wine glass and a tall rose-scented candle. Other candles were scattered around the room wherever a ledge or surface could be used without being a fire hazard. The tiling was white, broken by a border of the red tiles which circled the room; a few tiles depicting poppies were randomly placed among the white tiles for colour. The heat, the light, the bubbles could always be relied on in combination to take the edge off the worst day. The scent of the candle compounded the therapeutic effect. What was left of her worries could be dealt with by a large glass of cold white wine, a New Zealand Pinot tonight. It had already shown that a decent bottle of wine could turn even cheese on toast into a half decent meal. Today had been a high stress day, well deserving of this second glass of wine. The failure to find anything worthwhile at Fowler's house; the catastrophe of the interview; the missed chance of Barbara's rape accusation; the outright hostility of the ACC and the DCC, all reminded her that she needed to get a result and then out of Granbyshire and back to the Met – soonest.

She hadn't known when the Chief's briefing would take place, only that it would be at the end of the day, so she had cancelled the dinner with Mark. Then Shepherd and Ahmed had asked her out for a drink. It was a bit of a breakthrough with them and she knew that she should have taken them up on the offer, taken a chance to talk them through what was happening, especially with Barbara. But she'd had enough talking for the day, especially to bloody men. She needed some comfort too, and this glorious bath would do for the meantime. She could hear her phones ring – first her mobile, then her landline. She let them both go to messaging. Nothing was getting her out of this bath until she was ready.

The combined effect of two bath tops-up and one glass top-up later had her almost staggering out of the bathroom as she dried herself. As she did, she played the answering machine. It was Mark. He has such a soft voice for a northerner, seductive – or was that just the wine? As he spoke, she found herself drying her thighs, stroking between her legs, moving on only when the message stopped, a tired smile later. He was coming to HQ tomorrow and did she fancy lunch. Great, his company without the need to think about where or how far to go afterwards. She texted acceptance and made her smiling way to bed.

Chapter 37

THE BUZZING OF HER PHONE dragged Stone awake. The bedroom was still dark. The clock said 5:10 a.m. She groaned and picked up.

'Yes.'

'Rachel, it's Megan Freeland. Have you been getting any calls?'

'About what?' Then she answered the question. 'No, should I be?'

'You will. More of the proverbial has hit the fan.'

Stone sighed. 'Megan, it's 5 o' clock. My brain's still asleep. What the hell is going on?'

'I've just had a call from a mate in local radio. There's another *Guardian* piece on you. It was in the late editions this time so that they couldn't be upstaged again. It's going to be on local morning news, radio for sure and probably TV.'

'About what for God's sake? Fowler's arrest was really low-key. A non-event.'

'It's not about Fowler. It's about you, a piece by your friend Bates. Another leak. This time he's saying that the IPCC is going to recommend that you be disciplined for gross misconduct and that you should be sacked.'

'Shit. Is that true?'

'I don't know yet. I'm on my way into HQ to try to sort it out from there. I'd advise you to do the same. It's only a matter of time before someone tries to doorstep you.'

Stone was already out of bed and checking the road outside the block. No one there yet.

'Thanks, Megan. I'm on my way. I'll see you there.'

*

By the time she reached the Press Office at HQ, Megan and Hill were already there. As soon as she arrived he said, 'Close the door, Rachel.' That done he continued. 'As far as anyone else is concerned, this meeting has not taken place.' In response to Megan's questioning look, he added, 'I want to make sure that I'm in the loop as far as discipline is concerned. If it ever looks as if I've already come to a judgement, I'll be excluded. The PCC will make bloody sure of that.' Both nodded nervously. 'So, Megan, what's the score on this leak? Have you got anything?'

'I'm pretty sure it's the same as last time, the PCC through Ryan Peterson. The IPCC packed up their tents yesterday and moved back to London. Before they left, they saw Mrs Naeem – she is the complainant. Maybe they told her their preliminary findings. From what I gather, Rachel here hasn't made their job difficult,' she turned to Stone, 'have you?'

'No. I told them what I did and why.' She couldn't refer to another conversation that hadn't taken place so she repeated to the Chief, 'I wanted it done. They can take forever. I thought I'd move things along. It has worked, after a fashion.'

'It's worked only too bloody well. Naeem is going to use this to demand again that I suspend you. You realize that?' He chewed on his lower lip. 'It would have helped if we'd gotten something out of Fowler yesterday. What's happening about that, Rachel?'

'I'm having a team meeting this morning. A lot of my immediate actions rely on Barbara Dyer. If she comes in this morning, then we can act on the rape allegation. If she doesn't, I'll try to talk to her again. Otherwise I've got to hope that we get a break through the three drivers we're still looking for.'

'That looks like a wing and a prayer to me. What's our line on this?' Hill asked Freeland.

'The usual. We don't comment on leaks. End. Anything else just opens up a can of worms.'

'What about the families? They really weighed in behind Rachel last time.'

'It's too late for the papers today but local TV and radio might contact them.' She looked at her watch. 'I didn't want to disturb them too early, but it's nearly 7 a.m. so I'll get started on that.' She turned to Stone. 'We know they'll support you, Rachel. But my advice to you is to follow our "no comment" line and leave it to the families.'

'Right,' said Hill, not waiting for Stone's reply, 'we're agreed. Heads below the parapet time.'

At 7:45 a.m., Hill heard a rap on his door and, as it opened without the rapper waiting for an invitation from him, he rightly guessed that it was Naeem.

Without ado she began, 'You've been listening to the local news, I suppose?'

'Do come in, Akila, sit down. What can I do for you?'

'You know exactly why I'm here, David. Your press office will have told you about the story that is dominating the local TV and radio.'

'About DCI Stone? Of course. The leak. It certainly didn't come from us. Was it you?'

'It's irrelevant where it came from. I know it's true. That's all that matters, surely?'

Hill gave a long sigh. 'No, it's not all that matters. First, there's the matter of trust. Then there's the fact that I need to wait until I have the final recommendation of the IPCC before doing anything. I don't act on leaks, I don't even comment on leaks, never mind acting on them – other than trying to find the source, of course.'

'But they're going to recommend that she is charged with gross misconduct. That means you'll need to sack her, won't you?'

'I need to see the evidence, their recommendation, then, and only then, decide what's in the best interests of the force.'

'So, you're not going to sack her?' Her voice was rising in disbelief.

'I'm not going to do anything until I see the evidence and their recommendations. If I do, I automatically disbar myself from making any decision. I have tried to explain this to you before.'

'But you can tell me in confidence, surely?' The look on his face must have reflected exactly what he thought of that idea as she went on, 'I am the Police and Crime Commissioner. It's your duty to keep me informed.'

'And I am. The current position is that we are awaiting the final report and recommendation of the IPCC and that we don't comment or act on leaks.'

'But you will suspend her now. You've no option. She's in danger of getting the sack. She must be suspended. The public will demand it. I demand it.'

'Given the circumstances, Akila, there was always the possibility that she may face the sack. This leak changes nothing.'

'I know that you think that I'm a lame-duck Commissioner now that I've announced for the mayor's job, David. But these new mayors are the future. With the state of the Labour Party, the Tories are in for the duration. It's one of their central planks for devolution. All local services will come under them. Maybe even the police in time. I may not be such a lame-duck at the end of the day.'

He was still a cop at the end of the day and did not react well to threats.

'The service has seen all sorts of governance come and go, Commissioner, so I need to take my chances on that. I made my professional judgement at the start, based on the circumstances. They haven't changed. I'm not suspending her to give you a little political fillip. What she did to Fleming was a one-off, the circumstances were unique. And she's doing a valuable job for me at the minute.'

'Digging into my past, trying to drag me down.'

'She can only go where the evidence leads, Commissioner. I'm sure you have nothing to worry about there, have you?'

Naeem got up and made her way to the door. 'You're making a big mistake here, David, in more ways than you know.'

With that she left, not quite slamming the door behind her.

Stone had been watching and listening to the story play out on local TV and radio bulletins. As Megan Freeland had predicted, the families began to be brought into play by about 8 a.m. Their support was gratifying as was the Chief's, if only in that he did not appear to be ready to suspend her. But if she was charged for gross misconduct, the Met would decide that it was not in their interest to go ahead with the transfer. She'd be stuck here in the bloody waste-lands of the Midlands forever.

Everything felt out of kilter, unbalanced. Dyer hadn't turned up. Stone had been dithering about grasping the nettle of contacting her for the last hour. Shepherd and Ahmed were working the leads to find the other drivers, her only other hope of salvation. She was standing in front of the briefing board, hoping that something she hadn't seen before would jump out at her. The door to the portacabin opened, bringing in a draft of cold air. Barbara Dyer came in, followed by a pretty, young, blonde woman.

Chapter 38

'UNCLE, THANK YOU FOR TAKING my call. I know how busy you must be.'

'I always have time for my favourite niece, Akila. What can I do for you?'

'You will have seen by now my leak to the press about the IPCC?'

'I did … Are you sure it was the right thing to do? Hill and Stone will know that it had to have come from you.'

'I thought that I had to take that chance, Uncle. You must see that?' There was a silence on the other end of the line so she continued. 'Hill will still not suspend her.'

'Then you have only two choices, take him on or back off.'

'Taking him on would mean acting to get rid of him. I would probably need to suspend him too.'

'And the deputy, how malleable is he?'

'Not at all, I think. The Home Office don't like promoting someone through all three ranks of ACPO in the same force, and he's never even been in the running for a chief's job as far as the Home Office are concerned. So there's nothing in it for him. Anyway, I'm not sure I have the grounds, there's just not enough. And this close to the election, I don't know that I want the sort of publicity it might bring if I get it wrong. And I seem to be getting it wrong these days, don't I?'

There was no reassuring answer, only a pause and then, 'That means there is only the alternative. Back off. Express concern, but be careful. The mayoral election is now our focus. The families of the girls are clearly behind this woman and *The Sun* and *The Mail* address more of your voters than the *Guardian* does.'

'What about Fowler?'

'He's been released, hasn't he? Even if they can get him for the abuse of the girls, he has no evidence against you or me. You acted on the information he brought to the case conference. And it is in his interest to keep you out of it. Anything else is likely to blow up in his face. Don't worry, Akila, I've been here before. All we need to do is keep our nerve.'

'If you say so, Uncle.'

Stone, Dyer and Libby Grainger were in Stone's cramped office at the end of the portacabin.

'Libby saw the local TV bulletin,' said Dyer, 'and the piece on the IPCC that said you should be sacked. She phoned me and decided to come in to talk to you. I explained to Libby that if you go, I didn't think anyone else will be allowed to take the case on. That Fowler will get away with it.'

Stone was still trying to get over the shock of Dyer bringing Libby to the office. She was manna from heaven, the ideal witness; a pretty, educated, successful mother of two. But she knew she had to come at it slowly. She reminded herself of the old adage told to her by an ancient DS when she joined CID. When you have a potentially crucial but difficult witness, he said, you should always treat them as if they were carrying two buckets, one full of gold, the other full of shit. If you reached too quickly for the gold, you inevitably found yourself in the shit. That must not happen here. If getting Fowler would change everything for her, the converse was also true.

'I'm not going to lie to you, Libby,' said Stone. 'There are no certainties. As the case stands, without you we're short of evidence and there are too many obstacles. But your evidence, with Barbara's and Kelly's, puts it in an entirely different light. I'm sure he'll go down. And for a long time.'

Libby took her time to think about it then said, 'I think we both know that I wouldn't have come in unless I was willing to go ahead with it. Barbara says that I'll be anonymous, that no one will know it was me.'

'That's true insofar as it goes.' The gold bucket was close now. 'The press can't name you and you can give your evidence either remotely or behind a screen. But your husband—'

'Brian already knows. I'd been fed lies all my life. I couldn't build a marriage on one.'

'That should do it. With your evidence, Fowler might plead guilty, try for a reduced sentence. He knows the score; knows he would pay a heavy penalty for dragging you all through a trial.' She made sure that Libby was looking at her before she spoke again. 'But I can't guarantee that. You should only come forward if you accept that it may go to trial.'

'I appreciate that,' she said. 'I know I can do it.'

'And we'll give you all the support you need. You'll have an officer dedicated to looking after your interests.'

'Can that be Barbara?'

Stone shook her head. 'No, she's too heavily involved, there's too much danger of her being accused of influencing you. But that doesn't mean that you can't support one another as victims.'

'You know I'll be there for you, Libby, that's the least I can do,' said Dyer, taking Libby's hand in hers.

'So, what happens now?' asked Libby.

'We need a detailed statement from you. I'll get someone from the Family Protection Unit to do that. Would you prefer it to be a woman?'

'Yes, please, if that's possible.'

'That's not a problem. But first can you identify Fowler definitely as one of the men who abused you?'

'Yes.'

'How, if he was always masked? Did he ever take it off with you?'

'No, but after he'd had me a few times, I think he must have become a bit careless, complacent. A couple of times he parked his car outside the flat. I saw him and Bashir go to it, talking together. Then I saw him on TV, making some appeal for witnesses in a murder – an old lady, I think.'

'We can check on that when we've got your statement. But you're sure it was Fowler?'

'Positive.'

'I'll arrange for somebody to come across from the Family Protection Unit to take the statement now. I need to get them briefed first on our case and one of them will be your liaison officer.'

'Can't Barbara do it?'

'No, she has too much of a conflict of interest. If she gets too close it could compromise us when we get to court.'

'I know the people in the unit, they're all good at what they do.' said Dyer, laying her hand on top of Libby's. 'You can trust them.'

'I'll go along with whatever Barbara thinks best,' said Libby.

'Good. Barbara, can you set that up? I want this done today.' She turned back to Libby. 'Take your time, and tell them what you know. I know what it must have taken to come forward like this, Libby. I swear to you I'll make it work.' She turned back to Dyer. 'I need to go and talk this through with the

Chief and the DCC now.' She smiled. 'Then we go get the bastard.'

As she made her way to the Chief's office, she remembered her lunch date with Mark.

Big developments, she texted. *Got to cancel lunch. Talk this evening?*

She arrived at the chief's office at the same time as the DCC and they went in together.

'We're not going to get another crack at Fowler, Rachel. How confident are you that this young woman will come up to proof?'

The three were sitting around the head of the conference table.

'Very. She's intelligent and knows exactly what she's taking on. And of the three, Kelly Brooks, DS Dyer and her, she has an absolutely rock-solid reason for not coming forward before. She knew he was a police officer, and a very senior one at that.'

'Peter?' said Hill, looking to the DCC.

'I agree. She changes the whole picture. Intelligent, has made something of a life and had the perfect reason for staying silent. I think we've got to go for it. Strike while the iron's hot. My only reservation is should Rachel be doing it after the leak from the IPCC this morning?'

'As far as I'm concerned,' said Hill, 'it makes no difference. My reasons for putting Rachel on this case and not suspending her are still the same. I'll decide what to do about the IPCC when they've made an official recommendation. I'm not running this force at the whim of Naeem's fucking press officer.' He looked directly at Rachel. 'Let's do it. But this time I really need his hide pinned to the wall. And so do you.'

Chapter 39

IT WASN'T AS COMPLICATED SECOND time around. There was no need for the search team. They had taken the place apart first time and found nothing. Fowler was on bail, knew another arrest was possible. If he had anything to hide, the one thing that could be guaranteed was that it wouldn't be in the house. Now that Dyer was no longer a usable part of the team they only needed the one car and a uniform patrol car as back-up. As they blocked the drive, Stone could see that they were probably out of luck. Fowler's silver Mercedes was not there. Mrs Fowler opened the door as they walked up the short driveway.

'He's not here. He's gone.'

'We need to check, Mrs Fowler.'

'You need a warrant.'

'No, we don't.' By now they had reached the door and Stone pushed gently past her. 'But we do need to check.'

'I've only just got the place back to looking normal.' She was close to tears, having difficulty holding on to what was left of her dignity.

'It's all right. We're not going to do another search, but we need to check that your husband isn't here. You come with me to the kitchen while these officers check out the house. We won't make a mess, I promise.'

As they entered the kitchen, Mrs Fowler said, 'Don't offer to make me a cup of tea. I want you all out as quickly as possible.' She looked across the kitchen table at Stone. 'He knew you were coming, you know. He did the last time too, got a phone call.'

'Who from?'

'I don't know, do I? He tells me nothing.'

'Then how do you know he was warned?'

'Last time it was late, just before midnight. After the call, he told me we needed to get up early. Get dressed before you lot arrived. When I objected, he told me that it was up to me if I wanted to do it with a police officer watching.'

'What about this time?'

'That was about half an hour ago. He didn't say anything. Got in the car and drove off. He's had a bag packed and in the boot since he came back from the station after you arrested him.' She paused. 'And he's got a gun.'

'Where the hell would he get a gun?'

'After that shooting in the school in Scotland …'

'Dunblane?'

'That's right, Dunblane. People had to surrender their guns, didn't they? He brought one to the house, just in case, he said.'

'In case of what?'

'I don't bloody know – I'm not the bloody detective.'

'Did he take anything else?'

'Only his medicine, for his blood pressure, his prostate and his angina. There doesn't seem to be much of him that doesn't need medication these days.'

'What about money?'

'Look, Chief Inspector, isn't it? I don't know. We've hardly spoken for the last five years. Didn't do it that much before then, either. He lives his life and I live mine. We sleep separately and usually we eat separately.'

'Why do you stay?'

'Because I'm a coward and I'm comfortable, and I know that if I tried for a divorce, I wouldn't be. He can be a nasty bit of work when he puts his mind to it. And I wasn't going to do anything that would set him off.'

'You think he's gone for good, don't you?'

She gave a little smile. 'I bloody hope so. If you do find him, then don't bring him back here. I've got someone coming round later to change the locks.'

Ahmed and Shepherd came into the room, both shaking their heads.

'Let's get back to headquarters,' said Stone, 'get an All Ports Warning out and the car number circulated, see if these number recognition cameras are as good as they're made out to be.' She turned back to Mrs Fowler. 'If he comes back and you don't tell us, you'll be in trouble, you'll be an accessory.'

'He won't be back, if only because he knows I'll give him up – in a moment.'

As soon as they were back in the portacabin, Stone confronted Shepherd and Ahmed.

'How the hell did he know we were coming? Did either of you say anything to anyone?'

They both vehemently denied that it could have been either of them.

'Maybe somebody saw us leaving headquarters as a group and jumped to the right conclusion,' volunteered Shepherd.

She examined their faces. Shepherd's was professionally blank but Ahmed had difficulty in holding eye contact.

'No,' said Stone, 'he knew before we left headquarters. Somebody must have told him. Are you sure neither of you told anyone here? Iftikhar?'

'I didn't tell anyone who didn't know what was going on already,' said Ahmed quietly, a worried look on his face.

'But you did tell someone?'

'When you were across briefing the Chief and the Deputy, Chief Inspector Dryden phoned to find out if there was any chance you might make your lunch date after all, that he'd had a text from you cancelling it. I told him that I knew you were going to be really busy for the rest of the day because we were going to make an arrest. I didn't say who.' He added quickly, opening his arms in supplication, 'I thought he already knew, that you and he would have discussed it. It's pretty common knowledge that you've been seeing each other recently.'

Stone was furious, more with herself than Ahmed. Why shouldn't he have come to that conclusion, two senior detectives starting to become an item? She had deluded herself that Dryden wanted to get close to her for her own sake. Because he knew about the first arrest too. And she had been the one who had told him. This time the warning call to Fowler was too close to her text and his conversation with Iftikhar to allow any other conclusion.

'That's OK,' she managed to say. 'You both get on with circulating him and following up on the drivers. I'm popping across to Personnel.'

The walk across to Personnel took forever, her humiliation growing with every step. The bastard had played her beautifully. Mr Open and Honest, butter wouldn't bloody melt. The thing about having rules is that they are there for a reason. But he had found a way of getting her to break hers. As far as relationships were concerned, all coppers were indeed bastards. On and on went the loop of recriminations until, thank God, she reached the Personnel offices.

The clerk in charge of personal records was initially resistant to giving her a copy of Dryden's file, a resistance that melted in the heat of Stone's eyes and the threat of invoking the Chief Constable and the Deputy Chief Constable. The compromise that Stone read the record in the personnel office was acceptable. She immediately homed in on the two decisions to promote Dryden, first to detective inspector, then to detective chief inspector. Both were made on the basis of Fowler's very strong recommendations and in both cases, Fowler chaired the promotion board. And Dryden said he hardly knew him. Somehow, during the CSE inquiry, he must have got the black on Fowler and had made sure of his own career before Fowler retired. A clever boy. She'd need to be very good if she was going to get him.

The rest of the day was spent organizing the manhunt. Fowler would know what they were going to do. He didn't need to ditch the car, only the number plates. And if he'd organized a grab-bag and a gun, this seemed more than likely. The number recognition cameras were probably now just so much technical roadside junk. Stone had to work on the basis that he had access to money; the safest place to keep a gun would be a safe deposit box, an excellent place to keep money. An alternative identity was also possible, but much more difficult. He was an old man. His poor health made him older than his years. He had been corrupt but, as far as she knew, only as far as it satisfied his sexual perversions. There hadn't been even a whisper about him being on the take. But she couldn't rule it out. Money didn't last long when you were on the run and she had taken steps to freeze the accounts that she knew about.

When she came to check out friends and acquaintances, she found out what a narrow life he had led. They all seemed to be cops, or retired cops. Little chance of succour there. The thought that her life was panning out to be the same jolted her. Something else she would need to address when this was done.

At 6 o' clock she called it a day, for her and the team. They had done as much as they could and, like her, they were knackered, the anti-climax of the almost-arrest draining their energies. On her way back, she picked up a takeaway curry. That, a glass or two of wine and a hot bath would set her up for the grind of the chase tomorrow.

As she entered the flat, she caught the whiff of tobacco. Her sense of smell must be getting better, she thought, if she could catch the remnants of her old habit above the smell of the curry. In the living room, it was stronger. Switching on the lights showed her the source. Fowler was sitting in her armchair, a glass of her whisky in one hand and a menacing black pistol fitted with a silencer in the other.

'Put the bag down and walk into the middle of the room,' he said, waving the gun in the desired direction. 'And don't do anything stupid. I can take out your thigh first and you can bleed to death, or you can cooperate. It's up to you.'

Chapter 40

'How did you get in here?'

'A warrant card and a locksmith who owes me, not that difficult.'

He held up the glass of whisky. 'This is good stuff. I've always gone for quantity rather than quality, but this is really good.' He downed it, put the glass down on the arm of the chair and reached for the bottle that was by its side. He checked the label. 'The Balvenie, classy.' He poured three fingers worth into the glass and put the bottle back. All the while, the gun was steady, aimed at the centre of her chest. The bottle had been nearly full and now it was half empty. But he was clearly a drinker, it didn't have any effect on him at all.

'Why didn't you make a run for it while you had the chance?'

The one thing she did know was that she had to keep him talking, drag this out, buy time. The trouble was so did he. Her mouth was incredibly dry and the tensions of the long day and her fear were getting to the muscles in her back and her legs. She could feel her calves quiver and hoped that he couldn't see it. She could not afford to give him any more power over her.

'Can I sit?' She pointed to the sofa that faced him.

'No. I like you where you are. You know, you're not a bad looking woman when you take the time, good figure, too. I suppose you go to the gym.'

'No, just a bit of running and the occasional squash game.'

'Maybe I should have done that. Only PT I ever did was Egyptian,' he gave a laugh, 'but I was good at that, lots of practice.'

'You still haven't said why you didn't run.'

'I thought about it, started to, but you know that. Then I realized I'd left it too late, should have done it as soon as you reopened the case. Sell the house, give the bitch a share, go somewhere far away with no extradition treaty.

Thailand seems to be the place for retired cops and old villains these days, so I'd be in good company whatever happened.'

'But?'

'Enough. Where's your mobile?'

'In my bag.' She half-turned and pointed to it lying by the wall.

'Get it and come back to the middle of the room.'

The exchange was an opportunity. Could she get a foot under it and kick it up at his face? If only she had played football and not netball. She realized she was more likely to end up flat on her arse if she tried. Once she had recovered the bag he said, 'Put the bag on the floor and kick it over to me. Make sure it reaches me.'

The floor was highly polished wood so the bag slipped easily across.

'How did you know we were coming?'

As she spoke he reached down, picked up the bag, rifled through it and brought out the phone.

'You're the detective, you work it out. I'd been in the job a long time. Lots of people owed me.'

'It was Mark Dryden, wasn't it?'

'There,' he said, switching off the phone. 'Can't be too careful these days. There doesn't seem to be anything these little buggers can't do.'

'It was Dryden, wasn't it? I've seen his file. Two promotions in three years, both pushed through by you, the last one just before you retired.'

'He's a good detective is Mark. Knows what he wants and what to do to get it. Only got what he deserved. A man after my own heart, but without the same weaknesses. Now – strip.'

'What?'

'You heard – strip. I'm sorry there's no music,' he said with a leer.

'I will not—'

The shot came as a surprise. No threats, no warning. It was louder than she thought it would be with a silencer, but not loud enough to bring anyone. She felt the pressure wave of the round as it passed by her ear before splatting into the wall behind her. The air stank of cordite and plaster. She could feel her legs trembling. He'd done it so casually.

'Strip. Now. Or I'll do it on one leg.' He aimed the gun at her thigh.

'All right, all right.' Her fear made unbuttoning her jacket a nightmare. He was going to do it, rape and then kill her. Time, she needed time, really needed him to drink much more of the whisky.

'Was it you who had Bashir Rana killed?' she asked. Her jacket was off and lay on the floor.

'He wouldn't stop, that was old Bashir's trouble. He liked it too much and thought he was in control.'

She began unbuttoning her blouse, her trembling fingers having difficulty with the tiny buttons.

He waved the gun at her. 'Rip it off. Stop messing about with the buttons. You're not going to wear it again anyway.' When she didn't react he shouted, 'Now!'

She gripped the edges of the material and pulled. The buttons popped, scattering on the polished surface. The blouse joined her jacket on the floor.

'How did he have control?'

'He didn't, that was his mistake. He thought he did after Naeem and I covered up his involvement with the girls. Thought he had us both in his pocket.'

'Naeem?'

'He went to her when Dryden started his inquiry, that had taken control out of the hands of the local council. Then she came to me, told me that she knew I was involved too, and we agreed on how to cover it up. She's ambitious, so is her uncle, the peer. Couldn't have the family associated with paedophiles and traffickers. The deal was we covered it up, Bashir got rid of the drivers, and it all stopped, leaving nothing for Dryden to work on.'

With her blouse off she felt very vulnerable, wanted to delay the inevitable next stage. He noticed the pause and waved the gun again. Her bra came off, leaving her stupidly conscious of the slight asymmetry of her breasts.

'Now the rest.'

She unzipped her skirt. 'But he didn't stop, did he?' she said, stepping out of it.

'No, he thought he was safe.'

'And when he wouldn't, Naeem or her uncle organized the hit, didn't they?'

'Does the Pope go to Mass? They're both probably shitting themselves now that I'm on the run.'

Another wave of the gun. 'We both know that you're doing this to drag it all out, look for a bit of time, a weakness. But I don't mind, makes the pleasure last longer, and you won't be able to do anything with what I'm telling you. Tights and knickers now, come on, get on with it.'

Once they were off she stood erect. She wouldn't give him the pleasure of seeing her cringe or try to cover up with her hands or arms.

'No Brazilian for you. You're really crap at picking men, aren't you? No reason to get dressed up, have you, not even down there.'

She knew that it was all about power but that didn't help her. She could see what was coming and couldn't think of any way to stop it. Not at this distance, not with him with the gun. He took another big hit of the whisky, refilled the glass then reached behind the bottle and brought out a pair of high heels, black and silver, her high heels. He'd been through her wardrobe as well as her drinks cupboard. Still, they had some possibilities as a weapon.

He kicked them across the floor to her. 'Put these on. They're the nearest thing I could find in your wardrobe to a pair of 'fuck me' shoes. And that's what I'm going to do, Stone, fuck you before you fuck me.'

She stepped into the shoes. They'd gone from being weapons to being liabilities, no chance of moving quickly in them.

'If you put that thing of yours in my mouth, I'll bite it off. You know that, don't you?'

He laughed. 'I've been doing this for a while, girl, I know what I can do and what I can't. I'm not going to put this in danger,' he patted his flies, 'but I might put this in.' He waved the gun. 'Get you to do a cowgirl on my silencer – that would be something to see.' Another laugh. 'Anyway, you've read the statements, you know how I like it, so turn around.' She did. 'Now bend over, put your hands on your knees and keep looking at the wall.'

Her mind was a melee of conflicting thoughts. Positioned like this, presenting her sex to him so openly, she felt all the vulnerability and helplessness that Barbara and every other victim she had dealt with had described. At the same time, this was going to be her only chance. He had to come close. He'd left himself a lot to do for an old, sick bastard. She had been very compliant, hadn't given him any reason to tie her up or restrain her. She had to hope that his arrogance would get the better of him. As soon as she felt him close behind her, she would act. She found herself perversely hoping he could get it up. He needed control, needed to humiliate his nemesis. If he couldn't get it up, he would do as he promised and put the silencer into her, that would freeze her up, she knew it would. She managed to get herself past that thought and mentally rehearsed what she would do. He would come up behind her, close, thinking that the weapon gave him control. Actions are always quicker than reactions. As soon as she felt anything touching her skin, she would rotate and come up, her right elbow aimed at his head, pushing the aim of the gun away from her body. The position he had put her in actually gave her extra leverage, the heels valued extra height. She would drive the sharp point of her elbow through the side of his head, then stamp on him with the heels. Aerate the bastard! She was surprised when she heard him speak, still from the chair.

'You know, you've got a really nice arse, Stone, really nice. But you should exercise more, a bit of the dreaded cellulite's beginning to show there. But a really nice arse, nonetheless. I should have got to know you sooner.'

Then the shot. She flinched, waiting for the impact. Stupid really at that range, both would happen at once. Was he just playing with her? Dragging it out? That would be his style. Hoping she'd wet herself or worse? The splat of the shot was still resonating and the stink of cordite filled her nose. But nothing from him. No taunts. Nothing. She risked bending forward further and looking back through her legs. The upside-down imagery looked weird at first and she couldn't quite take it in.

He'd shot himself. His head had been thrown back by the impact and she could see the entry wound under his chin. The gun lay in his lap where it had fallen, his hand still loosely gripping it. The bullet didn't seem to have exited. Old ammunition and the silencer must have reduced the muzzle velocity. No mess at all. Her legs gave and she slowly crumpled to the floor, nothing left in her. She lay for a while, trembling, on the edge of sobbing, not daring to believe it was over. For a long while she couldn't move. There was no strength in her arms or legs. Eventually she managed to kick off the shoes and crawl across the floor. She picked up the Balvenie, took a swig, coughed, then took another, longer one, the alcohol buzzing through her system, accelerated by the adrenaline that was there already.

Restored after a fashion, she stood up, still clutching the neck of the bottle. With the heel of her free hand, she wiped the tears from her eyes, made her way to her bedroom and dressed between slugs. Satisfied that she looked the part of a DCI again, she returned to the living room via the kitchen where she deposited the bottle and collected a black plastic bag. All the clothes she had been wearing went into it. And it went into the rubbish chute. Back in the flat, she picked up the phone and dialled, then asked for police, just police.

Chapter 41

'Akila, did I not tell you it would be all right?'

'Only as far as we know, Uncle. He spoke to her for some time before he shot himself. We don't know what he said, what he told her, especially about me.'

'It does not matter what he told her. Anything he said is hearsay. Trust me, she has no evidence, no proof.'

'But she knows!'

'She's known for some time, but just knowing can do her no good, Akila. She has nothing that proves anything.'

'I don't think you fully understand, Uncle. I had to do a lot to become involved in the case conference. The decision was normally one that would be made by the head of Children's Services.'

'You did it because of your passion to look after children. A passion reflected in what you have done as the Police Commissioner.'

'I made myself a key part of the decision making process.'

'But only one part. And the decision was based on the evidence that Fowler presented in order to cover up for himself. He had to write himself and that idiot Rana out to protect himself. You have told me that none of the council records show that Rana was involved. Don't worry.'

'I do worry about that bloody woman, Uncle. She is so determined to harm me.'

'I know. And I know how you worry. But do not. I have already taken steps to remove her from the picture.'

'Not by …'

'Of course not. The best way to get someone to do what you want is to offer them something that they really desire. In that way, the only logical choice is the one that they want to make. Trust me, all will be well.'

'It's easy for you to say that, Uncle, you have never been directly involved. I'm feeling very vulnerable. She may think that she has enough to arrest me, interrogate me. I don't know that I could stand being locked up, even for a little while.'

'Akila, listen to me. I have been around politics in England for a long time. The English are very fair, they only act on evidence, not rumour. Once you are in the mayor's office, you will be surprised at the power and influence that you will have. Just hold your nerve, act normally, be glad, if asked, that it has all turned out well and that no-one else was killed.'

'I'll do my best.'

'I know you will.'

Chapter 42

'So, how are you, Rachel? It's only been three days, you know, you could have taken longer off. In fact, I'm told that the medics wanted you to take much longer.'

Stone and Hill were in his office, he behind his desk and she in a chair by the side, her chair the same height and style as his. He'd read all the right books about communication and signals.

'I wasn't hurt. Terrified, but not hurt.'

She had told no one about her humiliation by Fowler. And she wasn't going to tell anyone about it now. But he had taken away any opportunity for her to balance it out in her mind, take the fight to him, find out if she would have had the nerve in the end to carry out her mad plan of attack, rather than suffer the humiliation she had expected. That bit of self-doubt would always be with her now. The old git had had the last word, there was no getting away from that.

'No nightmares, flashbacks?'

'No – or I should say not yet, according to the counsellor I was made to talk to about it. She still thinks that post-traumatic stress is a probability and I should keep it in mind. Thank you for asking but I really am OK. I really want to get on with the rest of my life – if the bloody IPCC will let me, that is.'

She leaned forward to pick up her cup from the coffee table between them. She had been given the choice of tea or coffee, a sign that everyone was still handling her with kid gloves. She had chosen tea, her tooth enamel wasn't up to another of the Chief's coffees.

'That was the other reason I wanted to see you,' he said, 'to put your mind at rest about that.'

'How so, sir? I thought that once they took over the investigation, it was out of your hands.'

'You're right. The investigation is. But not the final decision. They can recommend. I'm the one who decides.' He took a sip from his coffee and put the cup back in its saucer. 'You've made no bones about what you did and why. They will come back with the recommendation you be disciplined, probably in the circumstances for gross misconduct. Being sacked is a possibility but it's not mandatory. We in the ACPO team agree that it was a unique situation and we don't think the service can afford to lose you.'

'Thank you for that, sir.' She had difficulty in keeping the emotion out of her voice, maintaining a stoic face to disguise the depth of her relief. 'But you said the service, not the force, not Granbyshire. Or am I reading too much into that?'

'No, you're only proving how right our view of you is. That's the other reason I wanted to speak to you. The Deputy Commissioner of the Met has been in touch regarding your application for a transfer.'

She bristled. 'I suppose they want to withdraw their offer?'

He took another sip of coffee and then smiled across at her. 'No, the opposite, in fact. He'd like you to go as soon as possible.'

Stone sat back in her chair, rocking it on its spring. 'Why would he want that?'

'He says it's because they have a chronic and growing dearth of good SIOs. You've proved that you are good – and of course you know and understand the Met and policing London.'

'They've got over 35,000 officers. One more isn't going to make that much of a difference.'

'I did put that to him. But he was insistent. The only thing he wanted from me was the reassurance that we will not require you to resign. And that was easy to give. As I said, the IPCC will almost certainly recommend a charge of gross misconduct. We'll agree to that and give you a written warning. There will be a bit of a backlash from Liberty and the other bleeding hearts, but you've got the families on your side, and they bring with them *The Sun* and *The Mail*. Job done.'

'That's fantastic. You have no idea what a relief that is to me.' She could feel her face relaxing for the first time in what felt like months. She couldn't stop herself grinning inanely.

'There is a small potential catch.'

The grin disappeared, tension flooding back. 'And what would that be, sir?'

'They want you there yesterday.'

'But I've still got quite a lot of leave outstanding.'

'I know. They'll let you carry it over.'

'And there's still the Rana murder. We now know that Naeem acted with Fowler on the CSE and that she and her uncle organized the hit.'

'I agree, but you've no proof of either. We've both been cops a long time, knowing it and proving it are very different. Fowler doctored the CSE case papers. We know that, but he had his own reasons for doing it. And he's dead. He was the only link between the papers and Naeem. It's just not a runner, Rachel.'

'But there's still the murder. We know that they organized it.'

'But you can't prove it, can you?'

'There still a lot that we can investigate, that might take this forward, the other taxi drivers we haven't yet arrested for instance. And of course, there's the driver from the getaway car, he must have been local. Now that we know that Naeem and her uncle were definitely involved, we can work backwards from them to find him.'

'And what do you want me to do about the Met?' he asked. 'What do I tell them? That you don't want to go?'

She puffed her cheeks and exhaled in one long breath.

'Doesn't this strike you as being more than a little bit peculiar, sir? Taking me with the discipline still hanging over me? Insisting that it happens so quickly?'

He shrugged. 'I can only go by what the Deputy Commissioner says. I'm sure it's just a coincidence that Lord Malik is one of the most senior advisers to the Home Office on all things Muslim and has the ear of the Home Secretary.'

'But how would he explain it?'

'In the current political climate, that would be surprisingly easy. The Prevent initiative is the Home Office's major thrust for getting the Muslim community onside. It would be an understatement to say that it's floundering at the moment. If you go, I haven't got anyone else to lead the unit so there will be no chance of stirring up the local Muslim community, no upsetting the Prevent programme. And the Met get back a very able investigator whom the Tory press think is wonderful – double whammy. How can it fail?'

'I don't like being played like this, sir.'

'That's good, because neither do I. But there's a limit to what we both can do. You've got a week, Rachel. After that you either go back or stay here. Your choice. I'm more than happy to keep you, I've not got so many good SIOs that I can afford to lose you. But in the end it's up to you.'

She thought about it, but only for a few seconds. The choice was easy. She would not be played having got this far.

'I'll take the week. If I'm not getting anywhere by then, I don't think I ever will.'

Chapter 43

'WHAT CAN WE DO IN a week that we haven't been able to do up till now?' Shepherd was doing his usual dour analysis. 'Fowler's dead, the local Pakistani community isn't talking to us, and now we know the Commissioner will make bloody sure of that.'

'It's not that bad, Colin. We still have two open lines of inquiry; the driver of the getaway car and the other three taxi drivers. Until we get them we don't know what they can tell us,' said Dyer.

Her whole manner had changed. She stood straighter, walked taller, was more confident about taking the lead. She had been the first to talk to Stone after Fowler's suicide. Had come in and insisted on it, guarded Stone like a Rottweiler bitch would an imperilled puppy. She had made it clear to Stone that she knew that Fowler would not have gone as quietly into the night as Stone had described; that he would not have passed up the chance the situation presented. But Stone didn't give an inch on her description of what had happened. To have done so would have brought the whole rickety edifice down about her ears. She would not give the bastard the posthumous victory he had failed to get in life.

'Now that Fowler is out of the way, we may get more from the taxi drivers,' she said. 'Chaudhry's lawyer has already left a message reminding me that his client had told us that there was a senior officer involved, hinting that there may be more on a quid pro quo basis. That may move up a gear if we can arrest at least one more. How is that coming on, Colin?'

'I'm pretty certain that one of them, Lak, is still in the country. I thought I was getting close, had an address in Birmingham, but when we arrested Fowler the second time, he disappeared off the map completely. There are just too many ways they can do that with our border controls – get the ferry to the continent and go back from there. I've got a live inquiry going in Southall in London. But the difficulty is the names,' he said with a wry smile directed at Ahmed, 'all these bloody Pakistanis seem to have the same names, so we need a positive ID, prints, photo, before we can arrest.'

'If he's in Southall, it'll be hard,' said Stone. 'That's been an Asian heartland since the seventies. Still, keep going. What about the getaway driver? He had to be a local or British-based so as to recce the scene and arrange the theft of the car.'

Ahmed came back in. 'I've got nowhere with it, boss. The CCTV was useless, the car was burnt out and now the few people in the local Pakistani community who had been willing to talk to me have clammed up completely. Word is that we are harassing Naeem and the barriers are up.'

'We know that she was involved in the cover-up,' replied Stone, 'and that she and the uncle must have organized the hit. There has to be a weak link in there that we can exploit. We need to try harder, look harder.'

'That's difficult at the minute, boss, with the threat level so high. We're already getting feedback from the Prevent team that we are causing them to be shut out, too. And they don't like it. Everyone is on edge after the shootings in Paris. And we haven't got the gendarmerie's firepower if it happened here. Prevent is about it.'

Two telephones began to ring simultaneously, one on Ahmed's desk, the other in Stone's office. They both moved to answer them. Stone sat at her desk then picked up the handset.

'Is that Detective Chief Inspector Stone?' A male voice, London with a touch of something else.

'Yes, who's speaking?'

'You're the one who arrested that corrupt cop?'

'I'm the one who isn't saying another word until she knows who she's speaking to.'

There was a pause.

'My name is Khurran Rana, I'm the son of Bashir Rana. I think you're investigating his murder?'

'Word travels fast around the world if it's even reached you in Pakistan.'

'It didn't travel that far, I'm in London.'

'We were told that the family had moved back to Pakistan shortly after your father was killed.'

'We did. I'm back in London, at university, UCL, studying law.'

'You were, what, nine or ten when your father was killed, weren't you? What can I do for you? How can I help?'

'It's more how can I help you, Chief Inspector.'

'What do you mean? You were only a kid when it happened.'

'But a kid with big ears. Look, I'm not going to talk over the phone. Can you come here? There's no way I can come up to you. It wouldn't be safe for me – or my family.'

'All right. Tomorrow. I'll come to Gower Street.'

'Not the college. I'll meet you outside Waterstones, do you know it?'

'Yes, only too well. Let's make it around 10 o'clock. That'll give me time to get there.'

'OK – tomorrow, 10 o' clock.' He cut the connection.

She went back into the main office.

'That was Rana's son. He's back in London as a law student at UCL. Wants to meet. I set it up for 10 o' clock tomorrow morning.'

'That's a coincidence, boss,' said Ahmed. 'That was Southall. They've located Lak, housed him and know where he works.'

'Momentum, folks, that's what Fowler topping himself has given us. Now we've got to exploit it. Iftikhar, get back to Southall, ask them to do a 6 o' clock knock tomorrow morning. Barbara, Iftikhar, we'll take one of your cars to go to Acton, that's the custody suite for that division. I'll leave you both there to start on Lak and take the tube into town to meet Rana. Colin, you hold the fort, who knows what stirring the pot like this will bring to the surface.' She punched the air. 'We've got momentum, folks, we've got to keep it going.'

Chapter 44

'Where do all the bloody people come from?' said Ahmed. 'Are we ever going to get there?'

Stone smiled in wry amusement at his frustration. It always amused her how the occasional visitor to London, especially those coming in by car, was surprised, then annoyed, by its size and its teeming streets. Even for those from the metropolitan cities of Birmingham and Manchester. London seemed to go on and on, its traffic slowing through the gradual bottlenecks of the M1, the North Circular and now here on The Westway. They had left Granby at 5 a.m. and were now a part of the daily crawl into central London, which seemed to have started at Luton.

'Not far now,' she said, 'turn right there at Horn Lane and the nick is down on the right at the junction with the High Street.'

A call en route had confirmed that the Met had arrested Lak at his home. Their search of the house had produced nothing but they had seized the family computer and his mobile. They would be checked out back in Granby. As they pulled into Acton police station yard, she went over the plan for the day, again.

'I'll leave you to it here and catch the tube to Russell Square. That's only a short walk from Waterstones. You can both do the necessary here. Remember, no questioning him about the CSE. In fact, other than to confirm his identity, no questioning at all on it. I want to maximize the time we've got with him back in Granby.'

'That doesn't stop us having a conversation with each other about the shit he's in, does it, boss?' asked Dyer.

'Not if it's a conversation about Rana and Fowler. I don't know how much

Lak knows about them but it would be good if he sweated on what we know for the length of the trip back.'

She got out of the car and spoke through the open door. 'I'll get the train back and see you at the nick.'

As she strolled to the tube station, she thought over her approach to Lak and Rana again. The PACE clock was the straitjacket the investigator needed to work with. Effectively, it gives twenty-four hours to question the prisoner, with a superintendent able to extend it by twelve hours. But when the prisoner was transferred between forces, the clock only started ticking either when he arrived in the second force or if he was questioned about the offence in the first force. The safest method would have been to send an escort to the Met who had nothing to do with the CSE investigation. But her main focus was on the Rana murder. The trip back should give Dyer and Ahmed more than enough time to warm Lak up for anything he knew about that. If it gave her some problems with the CSE case, so be it.

As she emerged from the Piccadilly line station into Russell Square, she was reminded of why she had wanted to come back to the Met. The sheer buzz of the place made her smile. The diversity almost overwhelmed her – the voices, hardly any speaking English in this tourist hub, the elegant buildings, the red double-decker buses circulating around the classic London square of fenced-off greenery. She knew what Rana looked like. Like most his age, he couldn't resist having a profile on Facebook. About six feet tall, good-looking with a slightly pouty lower lip which she had to admit some women might have described as sexy. She recognized him straight away, pacing up and down the pavement outside Waterstones. She watched him from a distance, then timed her approach to arrive at exactly 10 o' clock. As she closed in on him, she held out her hand.

'Mr Rana, DCI Stone. Pleased to meet you.'

His surprise was echoed in what he said. 'You don't look anything like a policeman.'

'That's because I'm a policewoman.' The pathetic attempt at humour at least getting a smile.

She looked round. 'Is there somewhere here we can get a decent cup of coffee? Not a Starbucks, something independent.'

The blocks to the north were solidly filled by the university in its various guises; University College itself; a couple of museums and University College Hospital. They walked west to the clattering commerce of Tottenham Court

Road, to an Italian place close to Goodge Street tube station. The noise of the traffic made the exchange of anything other than banalities difficult. Once in the café, they ordered at the counter and Stone found them a table tucked away in a corner.

'Thanks again for getting in touch, Mr Rana.'

'You make me feel very old with the 'Mr Rana', I am Khurran.'

'Thank you, Khurran. Do you want me to bring you up to speed with where my inquiry is?'

'Please.'

'I'm afraid there is only bad news and even more bad news.'

'What do you mean?'

'The bad news is that I have some idea who was behind your father's murder. I suspect that it was a domestic matter, something concerning the family.' As she spoke, Khurran nodded his head from side to side, neither apparently agreeing nor disagreeing. 'The even worse news is that I have found out that back in 2006, when he was murdered, your father was involved in the abuse of three young white girls, the youngest was thirteen, and that he was a main player in trafficking them to be abused by other men. I now know that the two are connected.'

'You're sure about that?'

'Certain. But there's no point in following up the trafficking and abuse as far as your father was concerned. We are pursuing the others who were involved and have already arrested two of them. It's your father's murder that I'm interested in. What can you tell me about it?'

He was silent for a few moments, probably still taking in what she had said about his father. He didn't question it or make any protest about it so it clearly hadn't come as news to him. But it is one thing for something to be known within the family, quite another for it to be known by the police, officialdom.

'My mother packed us off back to Lahore when my father was killed. She always hated it here in England – too cold, no proper food. We moved in with her parents, they are quite well off and have a big house there. So, everything I have heard has come from her family. We didn't have much contact with my father's family. It was an arranged marriage and her family only agreed to it because of Lord Malik's connection. He may be a peer here in England but his family in Pakistan are not of as high a class as my mother's, he's got some very shady connections. After the murder of my father, there was a lot of bad feeling between the families.'

'They talked about it a lot?'

'All the time when we came back, then less and less as time went on.'

'And what did they say?'

'That it had all been organized by Lord Malik. That my father was doing something that was putting his reputation at risk and that he wouldn't stop.'

'That would be the trafficking in the girls.'

'So it seems.'

'Was anyone else mentioned?'

'No – only Malik.'

'Have you heard the name Naeem, Akila Naeem?'

'I know she's the Commissioner of police up in Granby. She's related to my father.'

'But you heard nothing about her in relation to your father's murder?'

'No, as I said, only Lord Malik.'

'So far, Khurran, you've only told me what I already know. Do you have any proof? You're studying law, you know what I need. Proof, not gossip, not hearsay, that he was behind it.'

'Anyone who has that will be in Pakistan.'

'That's no use to me. I can't go there and anyway, they wouldn't talk to me. I need a connection, here, in England.'

'I don't think I can help you there.'

'Maybe you can.' She paused to drink her coffee. 'You know the facts of your father's murder?'

'Two men, believed to be from Pakistan, turned up at the minicab office, shot him, then disappeared.'

'That's a fair summary. They were driven to the office and away from it after the shooting by a third man. The car they used was stolen and was found later, burned out. That meant no forensics. I'm sure that the third man would have been local, based in England at least, so as to set up the theft, drive them about and get them away from the scene quickly. He's the link I need. I need a name.' She looked him in the eye. 'Can you get that for me?'

He shrugged. 'I can try. I can ask around the family, here and in Lahore. Use the excuse that you have reopened the inquiry. I don't think I will get anywhere, but I can try.'

'Don't do it quietly. Make a bit of noise if you can. Stir things up. Maybe it will make someone we've been looking at run. Shake the tree and see what falls.'

They both stood to leave and shook hands.

'I'll try my very best, Chief Inspector.'

'I'm getting very worried about that woman, Uncle. You said you would take care of her. But she's still here. And now she is looking into my past in detail, and my husband's, and his businesses. You can't let her arrest me!'

'Don't worry about her, Akila. Fowler obviously told her something. But we knew that he would. I'm not worried and you shouldn't be, either. She has accepted the Met's offer. She will be gone by the end of the week. She may think she knows something but she can actually prove nothing.'

'And Khurran, Bashir's son. He is here asking questions too, trying to find out who drove the men who murdered his father.'

'And like Stone, he will find nothing. He has lived in Pakistan for the last ten years, he has no connections here. He presents us with no threat, trust me. I have taken steps to take out the last link between us and the shooting. It's already underway. So be patient. Stop worrying. Start canvassing for that mayor's job. It will all be over by the end of the week.'

'If you're sure, Uncle.'

'I am. But there is one more thing I need you to do.'

'What is that?'

'There is still a chance that Stone's team may come after both of us before she transfers to the Met. We need to get rid of these phones.'

'They're encrypted, that will be expensive. Why do we need to do that?'

'We have had too many conversations on them at key times and I will feel better if they are gone. I already have the replacements to hand and will send you one tomorrow. Take yours to the exchange.'

'Yes, Uncle.'

'And stop worrying, Akila. I have taken care of everything so far, have I not? Concentrate on getting elected mayor, that's the best thing for the family.'

'I will do that but I will only feel really safe when that woman has gone and I know that the driver has been dealt with.'

Chapter 45

EVEN THOUGH THE UNIT HAD been running for a very short time, Stone felt like a traitor every time there was a reminder to them that she was going and she could not say what would happen to them. Catching Fowler was a major feather in the unit's cap but it was not enough, in itself, to guarantee its future. Hill refused to commit to it and it seemed fairly likely that it would be absorbed by the next major murder inquiry that needed a large team. After that, the three would likely be returned to divisional work. The uncertainty was undermining everything. With two days to go before her transfer to the Met, she was having a final case conference with the team.

'What about Lak?' she asked Dyer.

'Nothing there at all. He was in tears most of the way up from London. How it would affect his family, how he would be cut off from everyone. I'm certain he knows nothing about the murder. He didn't even seem to know much about Fowler, despite the coverage it got in the nationals.'

She turned to Shepherd and Ahmed. 'Background checks, is there anything at all that we can work on?'

'There's nothing anywhere about Naeem,' said Ahmed. 'She seems to be squeaky clean. Got a good reputation for getting things done for the local community. Malik is a different kettle of fish. He has his fingers in lots of pies here. He began with a taxi business, then some cash and carries, then he got into property development and "import/export". But they all appear to be above board. His family in Pakistan are a lot shadier with some on the edge of the drugs business that goes with the Taliban. He's got the connections there to organize the hit but there's nothing we can ever prove.'

'Then we're back to the driver as our last hope?' said Stone. 'And I can't see how we can find him. Not even phone records after all this time, nothing we can get a handle on.'

'What about Khurran – the son?' asked Dyer.

'I think he'll try his best but I doubt that he'll get anywhere.'

The office phone rang and Shepherd picked up.

'You're sure?' he said into the mouthpiece. 'OK we'll send someone over to speak to her.'

He put the phone down. 'That was GMP, they've located Linda Howard, Kevin's mother. She's been arrested for shoplifting. They asked her about Kevin's father but she's been drinking and is…' He paused. '… less than coop-erative – something about where they could put their custody suite.' He looked at Stone. 'We know they won't have tried all that hard. I suggest that Barbara and I go there and talk to her. She should have sobered up a bit by the time we get there.'

'I agree, it would be good to get another result before I go.'

They began to collect their gear when the phone rang again. Ahmed was nearest and picked up. He listened for a few minutes then covered the mouth-piece. 'It's Chief Inspector Dryden, boss. For you. Says it's an urgent operational issue.'

The surprise registered on all their faces. She had shared her suspicions of Dryden with them, and her frustrations at not being able to do anything about them.

'Tell him I'm not available, to give the information to you.'

He did this then covered the mouthpiece again. 'He insists on speaking to you. Says it's about the murder. Vital is the word he's using.'

Stone reluctantly stood and walked into her office. 'I'll take it in here,' she said over her shoulder. She sat at her desk for a few moments before picking up the handset, thinking over their last conversation. It had been very one-sided. That he was a devious, lying, bent bastard; that she had spoken again to MacLean and knew that he had done some obbos on the girls in his own time and must have seen Fowler; that Fowler had paid for his silence with quick promotions before he retired; and that she was going to get him. He had hung up without saying a word.

'What do you want?'

'Good morning to you too, Rachel.'

'Let's cut the crap. What do you want?'

'I know what you think of me, Rachel, you've made that very clear. But I am where I am because I'm good at what I do.'

'And?'

'And I'm about to show you how good that is.'

'Go on.'

'Two days ago, a French undercover agent came back to Paris from Pakistan where he had been at a Taliban training camp in the Punjab, near the Afghan border. On the same plane, he recognized two men, he didn't know their names but knew that they were involved in drug smuggling, working with the Taliban. By the time he had made contact with his handler, they were long gone but the French know that they made a connection with the Eurostar to London. I've checked our end. After they got off the train at St Pancras, they disappeared.'

'I still don't know why you think it is "vital" to my inquiry.'

'Not your inquiry, Rachel, to you.'

'What do you mean?'

'We've got photographs and have put names to them. Mohammed Gondal and Habib Mahar. I've run them through Interpol. The Pakistani end is not very secure or reliable but they came back with information that they are known killers working for the Guijar group. We know that Malik's family have strong connections with that group. You need to take steps for your own safety, Rachel, at least until we confirm that these guys are back in Pakistan.'

'Malik wouldn't come after a cop. It's a waste of time. I'd be replaced and the hunt would be intensified. It's not me they're coming for but I think I can guess who. Send me everything you've got.' She was damned if she would thank him, it would stick in her craw.

She hung up and strode back into the main office where she briefed the three on what Dryden had told her.

'The target's got to be Khurran. And it's my fault. I told him to make what he was doing so obvious that it would stir things up within the family. Shake the tree to see what would fall out. I didn't think this would happen or this quickly. It looks like he's got closer to finding out who the driver is than I thought he would. It can't be a bloody coincidence that a few days after he starts stirring it up, a couple of hitmen connected to Malik come to England. And he's in London, we're limited to what we can do for him.'

She dialled the mobile number that Khurran had given her but it went straight to messages. She dictated to the machine, 'Khurran, it's Chief Inspector Stone. Get in touch with me as soon as you get this message. It's urgent.'.

She hung up. 'Colin, get back to GMP, tell them to release Howard. She'll need to wait. Barbara, get in touch with the Met. Tell them what we've got and get an armed response vehicle to go to his address and to the university. They need to locate him as a matter of urgency and sit on him until I can set up something more discreet. Something that'll give us a chance to lift these two guys. If we can do that, we might be able to prove the link with Malik.'

An hour later, Stone was still trying to navigate the labyrinthine depths of the Met's Special Ops Division to find someone who could agree to the sort of armed watch she needed to put on Khurran Rana. Once that was done, she would need to get the ACC Ops to make the official request. She thought she had hit pay dirt when Ahmed knocked at her open door.

'The Met have come back on Khurran, boss. He's not in London. According to his flatmate, he came up to Granby two days ago, staying with a relative. The problem is the flatmate doesn't know who or where.'

'Shit,' she said, 'what about his phone? Can his network supplier help?'

'No, I thought of that, but it's switched off. They can't get any response.'

Her first thought was that she was already too late. That they had got to Khurran. That they had baited a trap to bring him up to the Midlands where they could operate more freely. Destroying his mobile would be a logical way of making it harder to find the body.

'Look through the murder case papers. There must be some people in there who are related to Khurran. Phone around them. Everybody on the phones. Someone must have seen him, must know where he is.'

There followed a frustrating hour of disconnected numbers; reallocated numbers; people who couldn't or wouldn't speak English and had to be passed to Ahmed. He suddenly held up his hand and having got her attention, signalled her to come over.

'Fifteen minutes, then, Mr Bhutto – at the park.'

He hung up. 'That was a Ra'id Bhutto, the guy Khurran is staying with. He won't talk to me on the phone but says he'll meet me at Northend Park in fifteen minutes.'

He was already on his feet and collecting his coat from the rack.

'Hang on,' said Stone, collecting her jacket, 'I'm coming with you.'

'He may not agree to talk to you.'

'He will when he feels my hand round his balls. Let's go.'

Northend Park had been named appropriately in the thirties, when it was at the north end of the city limits. It was now a green lung in the middle of the expansion that had taken place in the forties and fifties. The main car park lay at its centre, giving access to a large open grassed area, a small L-shaped lake and a nine hole public golf course. The car park was half empty. They quickly spotted Bhutto's car and parked alongside it, on the passenger side. Before Bhutto could react to her presence, Stone and Ahmed slipped into his car, Ahmed in the front passenger seat, Stone in the rear.

'What the ...' Bhutto blustered. 'Who's she?'

'She's my boss, Mr Bhutto. DCI Stone. That shows you how important this is.'

'I agreed to talk to you, not this *goree*.'

Stone leaned forward so that her mouth was inches from Bhutto's ear.

'You're right, Mr Bhutto, I am a white woman. I'm also a senior police officer and you'll talk to me either here or back at the police station.'

'You can't—'

'If you don't talk to me, you will be obstructing me in my inquiries.' She sat back in the seat. 'Make up your mind, Mr Bhutto, Khurran's life may depend on what you say next.'

Bhutto punched the padded centre of the steering wheel.

'I knew I should never have got involved in any of this.' He turned to Ahmed. 'You understand, it's a matter of family honour. If her family find out, God knows how they'll react.'

'Whose family?' asked Ahmed.

'You see, already I am saying more than I want—' Bhutto looked close to tears.

'Whose family, Mr Bhutto?' interjected Stone from the rear. 'Tell us. I swear I'll only use the information to help Khurran. But his life really is in danger if you don't tell us where he is.'

'It's in danger if I do, don't you understand that – his and hers.'

Ahmed placed a reassuring hand on Bhutto's arm. 'Just tell us, from the beginning. We only want to protect them both. We will do nothing that will endanger them. Tell us. You know you must or you wouldn't have agreed to meet me.'

Bhutto sighed. 'Their families introduced them last year when Khurran began his studies here. Both families thought that they were well suited for each other. Unfortunately, they were right. They liked each other but neither wanted to get married.' He looked around at Ahmed. 'They both wanted to play around a little.'

'Play the field?' Stone added.

'That's it! Play the field. They've been meeting on and off since then. Khurran is an old friend, he knew I had bought a little cottage in the back of beyond. Persuaded me to let him use it.' He punched the wheel again. 'And like a fool I agreed.' He grabbed Ahmed's arm. 'If her family find out – they're very traditional – they'll kill them both. And maybe me for helping them.'

'That's only a maybe, Mr Bhutto,' said Stone. 'We're certain that the same people who killed Khurran's father are out to kill him. Today if they can find him. You must tell us where this cottage is.'

Before he could answer, Stone's phone rang. It was Shepherd so she took it.

'I got a phone call about fifteen minutes ago,' he said without preliminaries, 'I wanted to do some background on it before I called you. Akila Naeem was found at the bottom of the multi-storey in the town centre.'

'By found you mean…?'

'Dead. Looks like she jumped from the top storey. That's where her car was.'

'Looks like?'

'No signs of struggle, no suspicious circumstances.'

'When did this happen?'

'About three hours ago. She had no ID on her so she wasn't identified straightaway. Her face is in a bit of a mess apparently from the fall. It was only a dispatcher matching the body with a call from her election office reporting her missing that identified her this quickly.'

'What's the whole story, Colin?'

'She got a call soon after her campaign office opened this morning. She told her assistant that she was popping out to collect something and would be back in half an hour. They gave her a bit longer than that, we all know she's not a woman to cross by checking up on her. Then they reported her missing, trying to find out if she had maybe been involved in an accident.'

'What's happening at the scene?'

'As soon as I found out, I got onto the Duty Officer and told him to treat it like a crime scene. But you know what it's like once one mind-set is there. They thought it was a suicide. The body had already gone. They've taped off the scene and the roof but I doubt that they'll get anything. We really need an eyewitness. And even at that, we both know that they're probably already on their way out of the country.'

'Thanks, Colin. We've got a lead on Khurran. I think they'll try for him before they go. Keep me up to speed on any developments.' She broke off the call. 'Shit, shit, shit.'

Ahmed twisted in the seat to look back at her, clearly alarmed.

'They've killed Naeem,' she said. 'Made it look like suicide but I'm sure it's not. I've never known anyone less suicidal. Malik is obviously cleaning up.' She leaned forward so as to look Bhutto in the eye. 'If they know where he is, they'll now be after Khurran, that's for sure. Where is this bloody cottage, Mr Bhutto?'

'It's on the edge of the national park, about thirty minutes from here. Near a village called Longacre. I'll show you.'

'That would be too dangerous. Just give us the postcode. The satnav will do the rest.'

Having got it, Ahmed jumped out of the car and into theirs to set it up. Stone got back on the phone.

'Colin, we think he's in a cottage near a village called Longacre, on the edge of the national park. Get the armed response cars to rendezvous in the village. I'll decide what to do when we get there.' She hung up. 'I just hope we're on time,' she said to no one in particular.

Chapter 46

THEY WERE TEN MINUTES OUT from the park when Shepherd came back on the phone. Stone answered using the hands-free.

'Yes, Colin?'

'Sorry to have taken so long, boss. It took a bit of time to get anyone to tell me what was going on.'

'I don't understand what you're talking about. When are the ASUs going to get to me?'

'That's the bad news, boss. The reason for all the secret squirrel stuff is that both of them are assisting Notts in a big raid. Even if I can get them released, it will be well over an hour before they can get to you.'

She turned to Ahmed. 'What do you think?'

He shrugged. 'Let's get there and decide. I don't see that we've got any other option.'

'You're right – did you get that, Colin? We'll make our way there and then decide. In the meanwhile, get some sort of armed response support from headquarters. From South Yorks if they're nearer, although I'd prefer to work with people I know. Get onto the ACC and get his weight behind it if necessary. We'll be in the village soon. I'll decide what to do when we get there.'

The countryside around Longacre was mainly low rolling hills, covered with fields broken by the occasional hedgerow. Longacre itself proved to be less a village than a collection of industrial buildings grouped around a minor cross-road. The grim redbrick buildings with corrugated roofs were a real eyesore in the middle of such lovely countryside. Most of them appeared to be the offices of companies that worked the local quarries, although Stone could not see any sign of the quarries themselves from the car.

'Not even a greasy spoon,' said Ahmed as they pulled onto the apron of an anonymous white garage in order to get out of the way of the steady trundle of lorries. 'What a bloody dump, not exactly a model Peak District village, is it?'

Stone dialled Shepherd's number.

'What's happening about the armed backup, Colin?'

'They're putting a team together and think they can get to you in about thirty minutes. That's the best I can do.'

'What about Naeem, any developments there?'

'No, nothing. Megan is trying to get the local early evening news to make an appeal for witnesses, but that won't get us anything until tomorrow or even later.'

'What about CCTV?'

'They've done a quick check for around the time that she arrived and after her fall. No cars were seen leaving with anyone that looks anything like our pair, so we don't think that they drove there. Maybe they haven't got access to a car, or don't want to drive over here. That would mean they couldn't get out to the cottage.'

'Maybe so. But in Pakistan they drive on the left like us so they'd be reasonably comfortable driving here. What about the regional counterterrorist unit? Can they give us anything?'

'I've tried them. I contacted them and told them what we've got. But they haven't had any further sightings of the pair. At least, not that they're telling me.'

'They're not terrorists as such. I think if they had anything, they would tell us. They did alert us in the first place. But you may be right about them not having access to a car. We'll make our way up to the cottage and have a look. It's not that hilly around here so we may be able to suss them out from a distance, not get too close.'

She turned to Ahmed. 'Good job I brought my own car here, the four-wheel drive and raised suspension will definitely be a bonus if we have to drive on a track.'

She checked the satnav. 'According to Bhutto, the entrance to the cottage is about a mile and a half up that road,' she said, pointing to the minor road that branched off to the right of the crossroads. 'Shall we go?'

'You're the boss.'

'Yes, I am,' she said, engaging the drive.

Chapter 47

THE DIRECTIONS PROVED TO BE right. Just over a mile along the Roman-straight road, they saw the start of a long, paved track which ran for about a quarter of a mile then disappeared around a bend behind a low hill. At the beginning of the track was a gate with the sign *Tithe Cottage* fixed to the middle of its upper rail. The gate was the first of three that they had to open and close en route. She would have preferred to have left the gates open for the armed response units or for a quick retreat, but there were sheep in all the fields and the threat seemed low. After a mile or so they reached a point where they had a clear view of the cottage. It was one of a group of buildings lying in a slight hollow, below the ridge of the hill. On the ridge itself was a small copse, further sheltering the buildings from the prevailing wind. It had obviously been a working farm at some time. There was the farmhouse itself, a small two-storey building made of local stone. Behind it they could see the roof of what must be a barn and on one side was a large shed. A small blue saloon car was parked by the front door.

'Just the one car,' said Ahmed, 'it should be safe enough to go in.'

Stone just nodded, then drove forward and parked alongside the blue car. Once out of the car, she went to the front door and Ahmed checked out the interior through the window. He indicated that he could see nothing and Stone tried the door. It wasn't locked so she went in, calling Khurran's name.

'It's DCI Stone, Khurran, are you there?'

She heard hurried movements upstairs and a few minutes later, Khurran emerged at the top of the stairs, still trying to tuck his shirt into his trousers. As he descended, he was followed by a very beautiful young woman who had been more successful in dressing quickly. When they reached the bottom of the stairs, Khurran started to speak but Stone held up a hand to stop him and turned to Ahmed.

'Wait out there where you can see the track. When the armed backup arrives, tell them we're OK. I don't want them storming the bloody place by accident.'

She turned back to Khurran and the woman. 'Why don't we all sit down?' she said, pointing to the kitchen table. 'I need to tell you why I'm here.'

'Chief Inspector, I ...' began Khurran.

'You both need to listen to what I have to say before you say anything, Khurran.' She templed her fingers. 'We've received reliable intelligence that a pair of hitmen have arrived in England from Pakistan. They've come via Paris. We strongly believe that they're connected to Lord Malik, the man we believe to be behind your father's murder.'

This elicited a quick intake of breath and an 'oh my god' from the woman.

'The timing of their arrival makes me believe that you may be their target. We couldn't contact you by phone.'

'The battery's flat. I forgot to bring my charger.'

'And you'd disappeared off the radar.' She looked at the woman. 'But I can see the reason for your disappearance now.' She turned back to Khurran. 'The combination of the three – the hit team, your disappearance and your phone being turned off led us to think that they had already got to you.'

Khurran had become paler and sat stock still as she spoke. The woman on the other hand became much more agitated, picking up and putting down her handbag, wringing her hands in between and squirming on the edge of her chair. Finally, she exploded, 'You stupid bastard, Khurran. How could you expose me to this? My father – my family—'

In the face of this, Khurran sat, staring at the threadbare carpet at his feet. Time to make the peace and move on, thought Stone.

'He didn't do any of this, Miss...?'

'Bhullar, Daneen Bhullar.'

'We need to get you both back to Granby and Khurran back to London.' She looked at Daneen. 'Why don't you go upstairs and get your things together? I need to talk to Khurran.'

After Daneen disappeared up the stairs Stone said, 'Now, Khurran, we need to decide what to do next.'

'What do you mean?'

'You do want these guys caught, don't you?'

He took a deep breath. 'Of course. What do you want me to do?'

'This pair will almost definitely have planned to be here for only forty-eight to seventy-two hours. They probably have their preferred method of exit already laid out. That means that we've only got one more day if we're going to catch them.'

'But you've got their names, their descriptions, their photographs...'

'We've got the names and descriptions of two men we think are here up to no good. So far we haven't got any evidence on them.'

He nodded grimly, ahead of her already. 'You want me to be the bait, don't you?' he said softly, almost to himself.

'Only for a day or so.'

'I'll do it for as long as you like if it will help get the people who killed my father.'

'We'll keep you safe, I promise. But we do need you to move around in public, look natural.' He said nothing so she ploughed on. 'I'd prefer it to be back in London. That's probably where they're still looking for you.' She continued as if he had agreed. 'The Met has lots of experience with this, and they've got the manpower to do it well. And I'll be there. If we don't get them now, Khurran, we may not spot them next time.'

He sat nodding, having a quiet conversation with himself then said, 'All right, let's do it.'

Just then her phone rang.

Chapter 48

'What is it, Iftikhar?'

'There's a black Jeep Cherokee coming up the track. It's got tinted windows so I can't see who's in it. Wait, they've stopped at the gate. Someone is getting out to open it. I can't make out his face from this distance but he's definitely Asian. It must be them.'

'Shit,' said Stone. 'Malik's informant network is bloody good.' She thought for a brief moment then turned to Khurran. 'Get upstairs with Daneen. Keep away from the windows.'

She was already walking towards the door.

'What are you going to do?'

'We'll draw them off. When they see Iftikhar, my guess is that they'll think it's you. I'll go cross-country from here. As soon as we're out of sight, you drive back to the village. I've got an armed backup team coming here. When you see them, tell them what's happened.'

With that, she went out of the door to the car and signalled Ahmed to join her.

'Wait by the passenger door until you're sure they've seen you, then get in. It's important that they think you're Khurran,' she said when he reached the car. 'I'm going to find a way through that copse up there and back onto the road.'

'What road?'

'Any fucking road. Just make sure that they see you.'

As the jeep rolled over the brow of the hill, Ahmed waited by the door, looking directly at it then got in. He was still closing the door when Stone floored the accelerator and the Honda CRV took off, the four-wheel drive

215

reducing the fishtailing on the loose surface. The Jeep did not react at first and continued towards the farmhouse. Just as she was thinking the ruse had failed, it turned after them and she could hear the big three litre engine roar into life. She prayed she'd get to a road soon as the Jeep was massively superior in cross-country running compared to the citified CRV.

The copse was little more than a line of trees and undergrowth. She aimed at the least wooded area that gave enough room to get the car through between trees. She'd done a half day cross-country course when she first came to Granby. There wasn't much call for cross-country driving in Chelsea, despite all the tractors. The main lesson was to go as slowly as you could while maintaining momentum. A complete waste of time now. She burst through the bushes and found out exactly what Bhutto had meant by the edge of the park. The ground dropped away from the copse down a steep rutted slope. The CRV seemed to be airborne forever. The engine roared as the wheels lost traction. She screamed and heard Iftikhar yelling beside her. She managed to slam the automatic drive into low before the rear end hit the ground with a bone shaking and suspension jarring thump. She stopped herself touching the brakes but concentrated on keeping the car going straight down the slope. Any turn would end up with them rolling. She thanked God she had remembered the other lesson, to keep her thumbs on top of the wheel or the jolting would make the spokes dislocate them. As they neared the bottom of the slope, she could hear Ahmed trying to call HQ to hurry up the armed support. The noise of the engine, the crunch of the transmission and the jolting were not making his job any easier.

At the bottom of the slope, she floored the accelerator again, heading out into the field, scattering the flock of sheep it held, praying that she wouldn't hit one and get it trapped under the front wheels. She had no idea where the bloody Jeep was now. All she could see were sheep and stone walls.

'I need a way out, Iftikhar. Look for a bloody gate!'

'There!' he yelled.

'Where the fuck is "there" – give me a clock direction.'

'Eight o' clock.'

'I see it,' she said, turning towards the gate.

She could see the Jeep again in her mirrors. It was gaining. A bigger engine, better tyres and of course, crossing a field would be a piece of piss compared with most of the roads in Pakistan. The nice green field which looked level and even was full of dips and hollows. The wheel bucked and juddered in her hands. Every time they hit one of the bigger dips, she expected to hear the suspension collapsing. Only the seat belt kept her in her seat, keeping her steady enough to control the car. Another quick glimpse in the mirror told her she would reach the gate before it could be blocked by the Jeep. As she drew nearer, she could see a track on the other side of the gate.

'Left or right?' she shouted at Ahmed.

'Left is towards the village.'

She aimed the car at the latch end of the gate. It exploded away from the Honda and she swung the car to the left, she felt the rear end swing violently right then left as the tyres tried to gain traction on the smooth chalky surface before she could straighten it up. They gained a few seconds when the gate swung back, catching the front nearside of the Jeep and pulling it momentarily to the side.

'They can't get past us on this track and we are as fast as they are now. Where's the bloody armed support?'

'I've told HQ and they're trying to get them, but the signal out here keeps coming and going. We really need to outrun them, boss.'

'I know! I know!'

The road ahead ran straight for about half a mile then disappeared to the right around the small hill. She reckoned that the village would be about half a mile beyond that. They were going to make it.

Chapter 49

THE HILL TURNED OUT TO be a quarry. As she turned the corner, the desperation of their position hit her. The sides of the quarry went straight up from the track, making it impossible to do anything but keep going straight ahead. The Jeep was now only fifty metres or so behind. Ahead of her the track turned again, to the left this time, back, she hoped, towards the village. It may have been so but to get there, the car would need to be amphibious. The track sloped away for fifty metres and ended in a green lake. She braked hard, screaming, 'Brace!' just as the jeep rammed into their rear end, pushing them down the slope.

She rammed the drive into reverse and tried to push back on the Jeep. The noise of the engine and the grinding of metal on metal made thinking impossible. She was now in survival mode. The Jeep was pushing them relentlessly towards the pool, its superior weight and power aided by the slope. The Honda would grip for a few seconds, then the tyres would polish the surface and the grip would go, inching them towards the edge of the water. The sides of the quarry going steeply up from the track made it impossible to even think about running for it.

They were soon only a few feet from the water's edge. For all she knew, the track only went a few yards into the water then fell off the quarry edge. She opened all the windows.

'Open the doors before the water gets to them. If we go in, we might be able to swim for it,' she shouted above the din of the engines and the scream of metal.

She tried swinging the car from left to right across the track, trying to jam it against one of the sides. The driver of the Jeep easily countered her every move, pushing on the opposite back wing of the Honda, straightening it up easily every time. The noise of the roaring engines blotted out all other sound. The Honda's front tyres were soon in the water and she could feel the purchase lessening as the car slid forward more and more quickly. She opened her door and Ahmed did the same. As soon as she did, the passenger in the Jeep jumped out and aimed his pistol at Ahmed.

Instead of firing, he looked up and called something to the driver. Suddenly, ripples appeared on the surface of the pool. Seconds later, their blue and yellow saviour appeared. The door of the police helicopter on their side was open and a police marksman was aiming his H&K carbine directly at them. She saw a flash from the muzzle and the gunman spun away, hit on the right shoulder. The marksman then aimed the carbine directly at her and she saw another two flashes from the muzzle. She instinctively ducked. When she looked up again and into her rear mirror, she could see two starred holes in the driver's side of the Jeep's windscreen. The pressure on the Honda immediately eased, then it began to push the Jeep slowly backwards.

Seconds later, two armed policemen appeared from around the corner, turned the gunman on his face, searched and then cuffed him. As she looked back at the helicopter, the marksman moved the carbine away from his face, revealing a grinning, jubilant Mark Dryden.

The quarry was now just another scene of crime. Both vehicles had been left in situ, the entrance had been taped off and now had an officer to log movement in and out. The Pakistani driver was clearly dead and was left in place until the scene was cleared by the forensics team. The wounded gunman had been taken away under armed guard by ambulance after being stabilized by the paramedic. Ahmed had gone with them in the unlikely event that he was willing to say anything. If he did, it would be evidentially useless but could have some intelligence value.

Stone and Dryden were standing by the helicopter, now landed in the field adjoining the quarry, enjoying the last few minutes of being the senior officers at the scene. Tony Bradshaw was on his way as the SIO and the Chief was sure to refer the case to the IPCC who would take over the investigation. But for the moment, no one could tell them what to do. Someone had managed to provide Stone with a plastic cup of coffee and a cigarette.

'How do you feel?' asked Dryden.

'Pretty shaky. It's not every day that someone tries to drown me and I get shot at.'

'I wasn't shooting at you.'

'That's not what it felt like. Why didn't you just take out the tyres?'

'I couldn't see them. You were in the way. And I had no idea where the track ended and where you might disappear over the edge.'

'That was my thinking, too.'

She took a long drag on the cigarette then slowly exhaled, enjoying the kick of the nicotine and the feeling of calm that it was slowly restoring. 'How did you know to come?'

He smiled. 'I told you. I'm good at what I do.' Seeing her arched eyebrows, he went on. 'We're told about every request for armed support. We are the counterterrorist unit. When I was told it was you and why you needed it, I just had a gut feeling about it. We've got priority on the use of the helicopter and I called it in. Forty minutes in a car is ten in a helicopter. When we got to the farm we saw the chase. I was still trying to work out how to take the Jeep out when you drove into the quarry.'

'I owe you my life. I'm grateful for that.'

'I was only doing my job, Rachel.'

'I know, but nonetheless, thank you.' She drained the coffee cup, put it on the floor of the helicopter then turned back to look him in the eye. 'But it doesn't change anything, Mark. It doesn't change the fact that you knew about Fowler and did nothing about it ten years ago. It doesn't change the fact that you warned him, letting him terrorize me and put my life in danger.'

As she spoke, Dryden shamelessly returned her eye contact. When she had finished, he gave a wry smile.

'I don't know what you're talking about, Rachel. You've absolutely no evidence to back any of that up.'

'I've no evidence, Mark, but I do have something else. My gut instinct,' she paused, 'and you're not the only one who is good at what they do.'

Before he could say anything, a caravan of vehicles appeared on the quarry road led by a Range Rover. She took a final long drag at the cigarette, threw it on the ground and ground it out.

'Flash git Tony is finally here. I'd better go and hand over to him.' She started to walk towards the quarry then turned to face him. 'Thanks again for saving my life, Mark, but watch how you go in future. I certainly will.'

Chapter 50

'I CAN'T SAY I'M HAPPY with any of the decisions, sir.'

'I don't remember that making you happy was part of my job description, Rachel. And it's not only my view. I've discussed it with the Chief HMI and he agrees. There simply isn't enough to take it any further. And we both know there's no chance of there ever being enough.'

'But everything Fowler told me fits. They had the motive and the means. Both pairs of gunmen were part of the clan.'

'Fowler's dead. Nothing he said was recorded. And even if it had been, everything he told you is hearsay. Inadmissible, not worth the paper it isn't written on.'

'What about Dryden? I'm certain he was the one who warned Fowler.'

'And I'm sure you're right. But where's the proof? You checked Fowler's phone calls, didn't you? The calls that were most likely to have been the warnings came from a burner. You've no idea whose it is and right now it's probably in bits in a rubbish tip or at the bottom of a canal somewhere.'

'But the promotions? Both were on Fowler's say-so.'

'Fowler was head of CID. He got a lot of people promoted in his time. Dryden has proved to be highly effective in both promoted posts. All it says is that Fowler was a good judge of potential.'

'But Dryden's a sly, amoral, devious son of a bitch.'

'That should make him very effective with the spooks and mandarins he needs to work with in his current job. Anyway, he works for central government now and not for me. He's only on our payroll because of the bureaucracy. You need to let it go, Rachel. You'll only drive yourself mad.'

'It's all right for you to say that, sir, it wasn't your bed he was trying to get into.'

'You're right, Rachel, I can't top that. But I've marked his cards and what goes around usually comes around. You need to be satisfied with that.'

'But we know that Malik has organized two murders and there was the attempt on me. Surely we can't let that go?'

'The gunman we arrested hasn't said a word, only his name. We've nothing to connect him with Malik or Naeem's death. He'll do a few years in prison for the attack on you and then we'll deport him, he'll probably be more comfortable in goal than he would in Pakistan. Malik's a senior adviser to the Home Secretary on all things Islam. We do not have an iota of evidence. You're going back to London now, that's where he is based, maybe you'll get another crack at him there. Although I would advise against it – let it go would be my advice.'

'At least you've got rid of me now.'

'Yes, and that was peculiar, I must admit. Someone who can pull strings obviously wants you back in the Met.'

'Or as far away from Granbyshire as possible, no chance of keeping the inquiry going on the back burner. That's all down to Malik, isn't it?'

'You may think that, Rachel,' he laughed, 'but, as they say, I couldn't possibly comment. Look to the future, Rachel, we know the discipline is effectively over and done with, all a paper exercise. Unless you tell me you're going to do it again?' When she began to speak he cut across her. 'That was a rhetorical question, Rachel. I don't want a bloody answer.'

He took a final swig of his coffee. 'On your future, Rachel, have you thought of coming out of CID? You've got a good brain but you need to widen your experience if you want to go beyond superintendent, do some work in planning or policy development. Get away from the Maliks and Fowlers of this world for a while. Lots of room for that in the Met.'

'I hadn't thought beyond getting back, to be honest.'

'Well, you should. You've already shown an awareness of how the politics of today's policing work. The service needs people like you in more of a leadership role.'

'I'll need to think about that, sir. It would be a big change.'

'Do that.' As he spoke, he pushed back his chair and she took his cue to do the same. The interview was over. He walked her over to the door and shook her hand.

'Any plans for your leave before you take up post back in the Met?' he said as he opened the door.

'A couple of weeks at my parents' holiday home down in Dorset.'

'Sounds good, fresh air and exercise.'

'Lots of exercise,' she said with a smile.

'Good luck in the Met, I'm genuinely sorry to lose you.'

She hadn't argued with the Chief in their little talk. His intentions were good but he had never been a detective or he would have known why she couldn't follow his advice. Not for a while anyway. She hadn't given up on Malik. Young Khurran hadn't given up, either. He was desperate to work with her to get either justice or revenge for the death of his father. That gave her a toe-hold into the Pakistani community in London. Someone like Malik had to have made some enemies there. With Khurran as a recruiting officer, she knew that she would be able to build up her own network. She had also been working on Iftikhar Ahmed, trying to persuade him to transfer to the Met. With both on board, she would have a lever to get into SO15. The intelligence community was a small world, there would be lots of opportunities to poison Dryden's well; if she couldn't get him directly she could do her best to ensure the bastard didn't prosper.

She broke into a smile as she thought of what she was going to do back in her natural hunting ground, and of the next couple of zipless weeks in Dorset.

Glossary

ACC	Assistant Chief Constable
ACPO	Association of Chief Officers, shorthand for the chief officer team.
CC	Chief Constable
CTU	Counter Terrorist Unit
DCC	Deputy Chief Constable
DCI	Detective Chief Inspector
DCS	Detective Chief Superintendent
DI	Detective Inspector
DS	Detective Sergeant
D/Super	Detective Superintendent
ID	Identity/Identify
NCS	National Crime Squad
PCC	Police and Crime Commissioner
SOCA	Serious and Organized Crime Agency (NCS predecessor)
Skip/Skipper	Met. Police uniform sergeant
Baradari na bandah	a brother, a clan member
Goree	a white woman